I0685799

Defining DESTINY

Books by Deanna Chase

Jade Calhoun Novels
Haunted on Bourbon Street
Witches of Bourbon Street
Demons of Bourbon Street
Angels of Bourbon Street
Shadows of Bourbon Street (March 2014)

Coven Pointe—A Bourbon Street spin-off
Marked by Temptation (May 2014)

The Crescent City Fae Novels
Irresistible Magic
Influential Magic
Book Three in the *Crescent City Fae* series (June 2014)

The Destiny Novels
Defining Destiny
Book Two in the *Destiny* series (Fall 2014)

Defining
DESTINY

A Destiny Novel

Deanna Chase

Bayou Moon Publishing

Bayou Moon Publishing
dkchase12@gmail.com
www.deannachase.com

DEDICATION

For Trisha, Sarah, and Megan.
He's not gone, only waiting.

Acknowledgments

A huge thank you to Susan Sheehan, Lisa Liddy, Chauntelle Baughman, and Anne Victory. You four keep me out of trouble. And a special thanks to my MAD girls for making this year special. You know who you are.

CHAPTER 1
Lucy

Exhilaration. It's the only word to describe the post-concert high. At least for me. The cheering audience is in another state altogether. Peaceful. Joyous. Enlightened. It still amazes me that this is our gift to the world.

"Amazing show!" Les calls over the roaring crowd and gestures to Cadan and me. "I swear, that connection you two have gets stronger every day."

Cadan gives me a self-satisfied smile. "See, Lucy? I told you they'd love the new songs."

Irritation sours my good mood and I snap, "They would've been just as happy with the old ones."

His smile turns patient as he puts an arm around me. "Oh, come on, babe. They're great songs. We had to debut them at some point."

I slip from his grip. "No. We didn't. Besides, they're mine. It was my call, not yours." We have a bunch of songs we've written together that are fan favorites, but in the last twenty minutes of our set, Cadan had started singing the new ones I'd written. He'd managed to get the band to practice the music without me even knowing.

"It was a surprise. For you."

When I don't respond, he frowns. "What's wrong, Luce?"

Jesus. He never listens. "I wasn't ready yet, Cadan. I told you that." Those songs are important to me. They're the ones I wrote a few months ago after my father died, and while I'm proud of them, they're deeply personal. They're for me. I'm not even sure I want to release them.

"Oh, babe," he says softly and pulls me to him. "I didn't realize this would be so hard for you. But look at what happened out there. Everyone was deeply moved. Think about what you gave them."

It's the only thing that got me through the three songs he'd sprung on me. Twenty seconds into "You're Always Here," the crowd hushed as the bittersweet lyrics and melody wound their way into their hearts. The connection with the audience had touched me to my core. But that was beside the point. I was tired of Cadan steamrolling me. "I admit—"

"Encore," Les yells over the noise and pushes us back onto the stage.

Cadan's amber-flecked eyes flash with triumph, then he leans in close to my ear. "I knew you'd come around."

It's too loud for me to correct him. I'd been about to say I was pleased with the reception, but I hadn't been ready and I was still pissed as hell he'd forced the situation. Not to mention how utterly violated I feel by the way he'd exploited something so personal to me.

We take our positions center stage. The deafening volume of the crowd ratchets up a few decibels. I beam at them. This is what makes being on the road three out of every four weeks bearable. The soul-mate connection Cadan and I share is meant for them. Not me. And not Cadan. Though I'm pretty sure he thinks it's all about him. He's twenty-four and full of rock-star ego. Reining him in is impossible most days. It's only during the rare, quiet moments we get together that he's anything like the guy I fell in love with two years ago, before our records hit any charts and before our lives were turned upside down by success and fame.

Cadan gives the cue, and I mentally prepare for "After the Fall," our most popular song. It's how we close every show. But instead of the strum of the guitar, the keyboard player starts a slow, haunting melody. My heart stops, and I gape at Cadan.

He pretends to not notice my reaction, but his knuckles are turning white from his death grip on the mic. He's worried. And he should be. Because I'm frozen. The words are clogged in my throat.

Tears are already burning my eyes as emotion chokes me. Cadan cuts his gaze to me, waiting for me to sing the first lines of the song. I shake my head violently. How could he do this to me? I can't do this. I'll never make it through the lyrics. My heart will burst wide open on the stage.

But then I glance at the rapt audience. Their faces are turned up expectantly, already drawn into the sad music filling the club.

And when Cadan takes over, singing the part that I can't, he hits every note perfectly with his clear tone. Haunted by memories and the melody, I want to bolt. To be home, hiding under the covers the way I had for almost three weeks straight after Dad passed. But I won't leave the stage with the audience expecting more from me… and Cadan knows that. The bastard.

He holds out his hand to me, and I have no choice but to take it. The media frenzy if I dismiss him during a concert would be a shit-storm resulting in official statements to the press where no one wins.

The moment our fingers touch, something inside me calms. Cadan is my soul mate. And I don't just mean he's someone I have a deep connection with. He's my destiny in a magical sense. The one supposed to understand me better than anyone. And together, we make music that is beloved by millions of people around the world. Everybody has one true soul mate. I've been told we're lucky. We found each other three years ago.

The first notes of the chorus start, and with Cadan's emotional support, the words come out as a whisper. It's enough for the magic to take over, and the effect is instant. A collective sigh reverberates through the crowd, followed by a few gasps. Tears are streaming from one of the fans in the front row, and I have no doubt she's not the only one. It's a stronger reaction than usual, but it's because of me. My emotions for this song in particular are too raw. I'm giving too much. How can I not?

I'm counting the days until I see you again.
Until then, keep an eye on me.
There are no good-byes. Not today.
For now I'll say
Until we meet in heaven, until I see you again.

My voice catches on the last line, and Cadan gives the signal to wrap up the song. It's too much for me. I'm not ready for this. Not this song. He knows and pushed it anyway. Why?

The crowd is on their feet, though instead of the roar, they are silent, waving their arms back and forth to the painfully gorgeous melody our keyboardist is still pounding out.

Cadan takes the lead and pulls me into a bow for the audience. It's the signal the show has ended. I'm barely conscious of what's going on as Cadan gently tugs me backstage. His arms come around me, and he pulls me close, cradling my head with one of his hands. "Shh," he says through my sobs. "I'm sorry, babe. I messed up. Don't cry."

I sob harder, memories of Dad flashing through my mind like a slideshow. Christmas morning as Dad dishes up pecan pie for breakfast. Dad laughing as we race personal water crafts across Lake Shasta. The way his eyes crinkle when he makes up stories of his childhood. And a million other memories of him coming to every singing recital and competition within a two-hundred-mile radius. Then the days when he lay in the hospital while I waited for him to recover.

Only he hadn't. And I'd been left alone.

I still have family. My mom isn't too far away. Then there's Cadan and my best friend, Jax. But none of those relationships come close to the one I shared with Dad. He was my rock. The one I long to talk to when I have news, good or bad. He was my anchor.

Now all that is left is his house on the side of the cliff.

Cadan walks me backward until we get to the couch. Then he sits and tugs me into his lap, whispering how much he loves me and how sorry he is.

He's always sorry. But that never stops him from hurting me.

A knock sounds on the door. Cadan ignores it, all his intensity focused on me as he rubs my back and kneads the base of my neck. This is what he's good at. Keeping me from losing it in front of millions of fans. Lord knows there's been plenty of opportunity lately. I'm not exactly handling things well.

"You need some rest. I think a break is in order." His arms are so comforting wrapped around me, and the light scent of his cologne is so familiar that I almost forget it's his fault I'm barely holding it together. That song. He had no right.

Reluctantly, I extract myself from his embrace and nod my agreement. I need my bed. Need to crawl under the covers and block out the world. "You're right. I do."

He pulls his phone from his back pocket and taps out a message. A second later it buzzes with an incoming text. "Phil will meet you around back and take you to the hotel." He kisses me on the forehead and guides me toward the back exit.

I pause at the door, suspicion nagging at the back of my mind. "You're not coming with me?"

He flashes me his practiced, apologetic smile. Anger pushes aside some of the anguish crushing me.

"Never mind," I say before he can give me one of his fucked-up excuses. You'd think he could abandon the band and label execs for one night to make sure I get back okay. Especially considering this latest breakdown is his fault. Not that I even want him around. But this is an emerging pattern. Put Lucy in the car with Phil while he stays out all night doing God knows what. I'm so sick of his shit. I don't even want to look at him. "I want to be alone anyway. Just… give me space."

He jerks back at my clipped tone and grimaces as if finally realizing just how pissed I am. "Do you want me to stay with one of the guys tonight?" he says carefully.

"Fine." I stalk off before he can say anything else, the crack in my heart forming a small crater.

I wake to the shrill of the hotel phone. My gritty eyes won't focus in the bright morning light, and I fumble around until my hand closes over the cool plastic of the receiver. "Hello?" My voice is gravelly and full of sleep.

"Ms. Moore?"

"Yeah?"

"I have Cassie Patricks on the line for you."

I fall back on my pillow. Why in the world is our label rep calling me at seven in the morning? "Okay."

"Lucy, good morning," she says, her voice full of excitement.

"Good morning."

"My apologies for calling so early. But I've got great news. We're fast-tracking the new song. We need you and Cadan in the studio this afternoon to start recording. Two p.m. Don't be late."

I sit straight up and clutch the phone with a death grip. "Which new song?"

"'Meet You in Heaven.' A bootleg video has gone viral over the Internet."

Oh my God. No. Not that one. My stomach clenches with a wave of nausea. I take a deep breath, trying not to vomit right in the bed. "But that song isn't ready. I'm not sure I even want to record it."

"You're just getting cold feet. I told Cadan it's perfect just the way it is when he was here to sign the publishing contract on Friday. Now take a deep breath. It's going to be huge. Especially if we capitalize on this PR ASAP. See you this afternoon."

The line goes dead, and I stare with horror at the phone. *Publishing contract?* I didn't sign over any of my new songs. What did Cadan do?

My feet hit the floor before my brain processes what I'm doing. Wearing only pajama pants and a tank top, I tear out of the room and head down the hall. When I reach Phil's room, I bang both fists on his door. "Cadan," I yell. "Open up."

There's no answer.

I bang again, this time continuously, making it impossible for anyone in this wing to sleep. The door to the right opens, and a woman snaps at me to keep it down. I don't even acknowledge her. Right now, all I need is to talk to Cadan. If he isn't inside, Phil will know where he is.

The door finally opens and a tall, slender blonde with bleary, mascara-smudged eyes stares at me. "Where's the fire?"

"Is Cadan in there?" I don't wait for her to answer. I just push past her and stalk into the suite. "Cadan?"

The bedroom door opens and Cadan stumbles into the sitting room, his sandy-blond hair still mussed from sleep. "What's wrong?"

He's still buttoning his jeans, and the first thing I notice is a hickey on his chest. "What the fuck is that?"

"What?" He glances over his shoulder at the closed door.

"This." I stalk up to him and poke the hickey with my finger. Then I turn to the blonde. "Is this your parting gift? A way to make sure I know he's unfaithful?" My tone is cool and controlled as if the scene isn't making bile rise in my throat.

"Me?" she ekes out. "No, that was Natasha."

Without speaking, I push past Cadan and open the bedroom door. Inside, a honey blonde with perfect, smooth skin is sprawled naked over the bed. A condom wrapper is lying on the floor.

"Oops," the skank who answered the door says and disappears into the bathroom.

My entire body goes numb. I'd suspected Cadan wasn't always faithful, but I'd never been sure. Now the truth is battering me over the head. Stunned into silence, I turn and leave the room, closing the door behind me.

"Luce," Cadan says.

"Don't Luce me, you fucking two-timing piece of shit." I keep heading toward the door but stop when I remember why I came in the first place. I spin. "Why does Cassie think we have a publishing deal for the new songs?"

"Babe." He walks slowly toward me with his hand stretched out. "I made a mistake. We were drinking. Just a few beers. I think mine was spiked. Acid. Or Ecstasy. I don't remember anything."

My fists clench, and I have to fight to not punch him in the nose. "Gee, you don't look like you've been drugged. Not like the band does after a rough night. Try again."

"I swear, I didn't—"

"Fucking shut up!" I yell. "You're a real piece of work, you know that? Do you think I'm stupid? I know you knew what you were doing. I can see you calculating the best way to get out of this. You're not even sorry. Not at all. The only thing you're sorry about is that you have to deal with me now. Well, guess what? I'm about to make it real easy on you." I lash out and push him away from me with both hands. "I'm done. This soul-mate thing? It's over. Go ahead and fuck whoever you want. Sing whatever you want, just as long as it's not one of my songs, because no matter what you told Cassie, those songs aren't for sale."

Fear flickers in his copper eyes. "Lucy, now wait."

"I'm not waiting for a goddamned thing. You've hurt me for the last time, Cadan. I can't live like this."

I've got my hand on the door handle when Cadan says, "The contracts are already signed. The songs will be recorded no matter what you do. Are you prepared for someone else to sing them?"

My heart races and my vision clouds with darkness. Dizzy, I turn slowly and look him in the eye. "What do you mean the contracts are signed?"

His shoulders hunch forward. "I signed for you. I thought you just needed a push to get you through this grief about your dad. You love spending time in the studio, and with these songs, I knew the label would make us a priority for the next record."

"You signed? *For* me?" The urge to kill him is so strong, I take a step back toward the door.

He shrugs. "I have before. The signature matches."

Son of a… shitballs! He had signed for me. There was a time when I was taking care of Dad when I'd been too overwhelmed to deal with business and had left Cadan in charge. He mastered my signature just to make it easy on me. He's got it down to perfection. Shaking, I take three steps forward and say in a careful tone, "You will tell Cassie what you did and you'll tell her I'm no longer part of the deal. Forget the rest of the tour. I'm not doing it! If she wants to sue me for breach of contract, so be it, but I'm out and I'm taking my songs with me."

"It won't be that easy," Cadan says, his face white.

I'd just put a major wrench in his plans. He's a great performer, but the reason most of our fans come to see us is for the magic our combined harmony produces. Without me, he's just another lead singer of a garage band.

"Cassie isn't going to let you walk. And if she sues you, it will be for a hell of a lot more than what they've paid us so far. You can't go. Not now. Do this one last album, then you can cut ties with me. But give me a chance to apologize. To make it up to you. I promise no more booze and no more opportunity for"—he waves a hand toward the bedroom—"this sort of thing. If I don't go out with the band, the temptation is removed."

I can't believe he's standing here negotiating with me. It's as if he has no clue how much he's hurt me. I pull the door open, cast him an uncaring glance, and step into the hall. Then I turn back to level him with a steely glare. "No. Not now. Not ever again. Stay the hell away from me, Cadan. My lawyer will be in touch about the songs."

"Lucy!" He follows me out into the hall. "Wait."

I stop in front of the room that's supposed to belong to the pair of us. "Go back to your guests. I'm sure within ten minutes this fight will be the furthest thing from your mind."

As soon as I get into our suite, I flip the security lock and then sink to the floor, my entire body shaking with adrenaline.

"Lucy," Cadan calls through the door.

It makes me physically ill to know he's standing out in the hall barely dressed. I have to get away. As far away as possible.

I do two things. First, I call my lawyer about the songs and breaking my contract. He's dubious, but says he'll do his best. Then I call Jax, my best friend.

"Lucy! I miss you," she says by way of greeting. "I saw that video. Your song is amazing. I can't wait to listen to a live version."

I grumble. "We're not recording it." My voice wobbles, and being Jax, she notices it right away.

"What happened?"

I suck in a breath. It gets caught in my throat, and I swallow hard. "Cadan sold it without my permission. Then I walked in on him with two girls this morning."

"Jesus," she says quietly. Then she screams into the phone, "That asshole! I'm going to kill him."

"Get in line."

"I will." She's seething enough for both of us. Then she takes a deep breath. "What can I do?"

"Pick me up at the airport?" I move to the closet and yank my suitcase out. "I'm coming home. Today."

CHAPTER 2

Lucy

The four-inch heels on my thigh-high boots wobble with each step through the gravel parking lot. Dammit. I'm going to sprain an ankle before we even get inside. Maybe that wouldn't be so bad. Then I wouldn't have to go through with Jax's birthday present. I'm probably the only twenty-one-year-old in the state of California who would rather sacrifice a limb than spend the evening drinking with the beloved local band.

Jax runs ahead and stops in the club's doorway. "Hurry up, Lucy. It's freezing out here."

I make a face and wrap my wool coat tighter, blocking out the sea-scented wind blowing off the ocean. "I'm coming. Keep your skirt on."

She tugs at her micromini and laughs. "For the next few hours at least."

I manage to make my way to the door without falling on my ass. "Don't be slutty just because it's your twenty-first birthday."

She tucks her arm through mine and presses close to me. "Since when did I ever need an excuse to be slutty?"

"Right. I forgot. Jax the man-eater. They'll never know what hit them." My tone is dry with sarcasm. Jax is hardly a virgin, but she's only been with one guy—her high school boyfriend. And she hadn't given it up until after graduation. They broke up nine months ago after Brad met his soul mate. That's the way it works. One minute you're happy, in love, and then bam. Your boyfriend meets his mate and everything changes.

"Exactly." Jax tugs me into the club. "Tonight's the night. Mission Boy Toy commences."

I give her an indulgent smile and slip off my jacket. The coat-check girl scans the length of my body and makes a tsking noise as if I'm wearing Julia Robert's hooker outfit from *Pretty Woman*. Give me a break. My dress isn't *that* bad.

"Damn, girl." Jax whistles appreciatively, her silky blond hair slipping over her shoulder. "Tonight's supposed to be about me finding a man, not having them fall to their knees after taking one look at you."

She's teasing, and I know she doesn't care what I wear, just as long as I'm here. She's been begging me to go out with her for over three months now. I finally caved, but only because tonight is her birthday celebration. I couldn't let this milestone go by without me. Besides, I made a promise, and I intend to keep it.

"You're lookin' pretty hot yourself," I tell Jax. She's wearing a black miniskirt paired with a whore-red halter top that's open in the back and red fuck-me pumps. Her exercise of choice is swimming, so her traps and delts are cut, but not too bulky. She looks sexy as hell, and with her outgoing personality, I'm betting she'll have more than half a dozen guys begging to take her home by the end of the night. Not that she'll go. She talks a good game, but when it comes down to it, she always keeps them at arm's length.

I smooth my hand over the silver-sequined minidress and point myself toward the bar. I won't last another two minutes without some liquid courage. "I need a shot of Patrón."

"Now you're talking!" Jax bounces up to the bar, her boobs practically spilling out of her low-cut top, and leans over, waving at the bartender. At least someone's excited.

I *should* be excited. I should be euphoric. Six months ago, I would've been so amped up I wouldn't have been able to sit still. But tonight all I feel is dread. I force myself to glance up at the empty stage. My second home. The only other place I ever feel truly myself. Tonight the lonely microphone taunts me. Cadan won't be beside me. I'll be singing with a band

I've only practiced with once and everything will be different. Including my voice.

"Bottoms up," Jax says and hands me the shot glass.

We each go through the ritual of licking salt off the fleshy part of our palms and then down the amber liquid.

I grimace and bite into a lime, washing away the sting of alcohol. "One more."

She lifts an eyebrow in question. "You sure?"

"If you want me up on that stage in ten minutes, then I'm going to need another."

"Okaaaay. Give me a minute." Jax waves at a tall, vaguely familiar blonde across the room and says, "I'll be right back." She disappears into the growing crowd while I wait for the tequila to start working its magic.

The coat-check girl eyes me again as she walks by, and she huffs something close to disapproval. Someone has a serious case of bitchitis. I snap my head to the side. "What's your—"

Oh, holy hell.

The words fly out of my head, and I gape at the tall, dark-haired specimen lounging two stools down. He leans against the bar, a beer bottle dangling from two fingertips as his eyes travel to the hem of my dress. At home, the fact that it only fell about five inches past my butt hadn't bothered me. Now I feel naked.

Heat rushes to my cheeks, but I don't look away. I can't. His brilliant green eyes are undressing me right here in the bar. And God help me if I'm not doing the same to him. Both of his arms are covered in brightly colored tattoos. A dragon is snaking its way under the sleeve of his black T-shirt. My fingers ache to reach out and trace the vibrant green scales.

He clears his throat.

I snap my gaze back to his.

"You're new," he says.

"Um. Sort of." I mentally shake myself to keep from jumping him right there. *Whoa, Lucy. What the hell?* I don't even know this guy's name, and here I am, dreaming of ripping his shirt off. "I've been away for a while, but I grew up here."

"In Mendo?" he asks, using the local's slang for Mendocino. "How come we've never met?"

I shrug. "I haven't been home often in the last three years." Also, prior to that I'd lived with my mom and her husband for a while. But I'm not going to bring that up. "You didn't grow up here. I'd remember." No female with a pulse could forget eyes like those.

His lips curl into a slow, knowing smile. The one that says he knows exactly what his proximity is doing to my hormones. "No. We moved here right before my senior year in high school."

"Ouch. That's rough." I'd been a sophomore when I'd been carted off to Mom's house. My life had been a walking nightmare right up until the day I'd left to tour with Cadan.

His smile fades, and he glances at the floor as shadows darken his eyes. "It wasn't so bad."

The change makes me want to place a hand on his arm, ask him what memories are haunting him. Find out what secrets are buried beneath his gorgeous shell. But I don't even know his name, and Lord knows I'm not willing to spill my guts to some stranger, no matter how sexy he is.

"Hey, hooker." Jax slides up beside me, handing me a second shot of Patrón. "I see you found an interesting way to keep yourself occupied while I was gone." She smiles and waves. "Hi, Seth. You're looking especially hot tonight."

My mouth forms a shocked *O*. Seth? Seth Keenan? *This* is the guy Jax keeps talking about? The guy she'd befriended her senior year in high school? The one whose soul mate was killed in a car accident a year and a half ago? The one I'd told her she should date to get over Brad? *That* Seth?

His gaze travels to her ample cleavage, and he gives her an appreciative nod. "You're not so hard on the eyes either, Jax."

She laughs. "Stop checking out my boobage. You have zero chance with me. Not the way you operate."

I narrow my eyes at the exchange, hating the way my gut clenches with jealousy. But not from his overtly sexual glances.

No, it's the easy banter and playful exchange they have going on. When's the last time I was like that with anyone from the opposite sex? Months.

Leaning into me, she whispers, "Total manwhore. I don't think I've ever seen him with the same girl twice."

He grins and shrugs unapologetically. "My loss."

"You know it!" She holds up her shot glass. "Let's make a toast."

I follow suit, trying to avoid Seth's gaze. The last thing I need is to be interested in a self-aware manwhore. "To Jax and the best twenty-first birthday celebration to ever roll through Mendo."

"To Jax," Seth says. "May some lucky jerk finally get to take you home."

She giggles and presses her glass to mine and Seth's. "To the best friends a girl ever had."

The tequila burns going down and my eyes water. I'm not a big drinker. In fact, I hardly ever drink. But tonight's different. I can't do what Jax wants without a little help. I want to do it. It's just hard to face the memories.

I slam the shot glass down on the bar and stumble forward. "I'll be right back."

"Whoa," Seth says, grabbing my arm to steady me. "Maybe you should sit down for a minute." His words are said with kindness, but his green eyes turn stormy with a mix of worry and judgment.

"I'm fine." I tug out of his grip, irritated at his reaction. How dare he judge me? We're in a bar for gawd's sake. "I've only had two drinks. It's these boots. I'm not used to standing on stilts."

"Uh-huh." He wraps his arm around my waist, steadying me.

Heat sears its way through my skin. His rock-hard body sends electric shocks deep into my center, making me shift uncomfortably. All I want to do is clasp my hands around his neck and press into him as we sway to the Maroon 5 song blaring over the club's loudspeakers.

"Aren't you supposed to sing in a few minutes?" he asks.

His question snaps me out of my drunken lust haze. "Um, yeah."

He clutches me tighter and chuckles. "This should be entertaining."

"What's that supposed to mean?"

"Nothing. Just looking forward to the show, no matter how it turns out."

I glare and step away from him, steadier now. "*No matter how it turns out?* Seriously? Don't be a jerk. It's not easy to get up in front of a room full of drunken assholes and sing your heart out."

His eyes widen in surprise and he opens his mouth to speak, but I don't give him a chance. "Forget it, dude. I don't need this. I've got a show to put on." I stalk off, praying my ankles hold. Crap. I should've worn the platforms. At least then I'd have something to balance on.

"Lucy!" Jax calls. "Wait."

Her eyes are twinkling with laughter, and I force myself not to scowl. "What's so funny?"

"You."

"What did I do?"

"Nothing. Except you totally put Seth in his place." Her tone is light, but I can tell she's feeling out my mood and wants to say more.

"What?"

Her smile falters, but she pastes it back on and leans in to whisper, "Don't you think you might've been a little defensive back there?"

I push through the door leading to the dressing room. "Maybe, but I'm tired of that shit. You know how I feel about people who bag on performers." Why is it that people who don't sing or act think it's okay to trash those who do? It's like a damned sport for some people to see who can be the meanest.

She stops in front of the door marked Band and crosses her arms over her chest. "Yes, I do. But I think he was making fun of your inability to hold your alcohol, not the fact that you're finally going to sing. Jeez, Luce, he's only been listening to me brag about you for two years now. I think he expects tears of joy to rain down from heaven when you put those pipes to work."

"Jax!"

"Well, it was almost true when…" She bites her lip. "Sorry. It's just that when you were with Cadan, you two made people weep. How could I not talk about it?"

"I'm never singing with Cadan again." The words make me cringe. There was a time when I thought I'd always be singing with him. When our voices melded, it was almost as if the universe stopped. A light would fill my soul and a deep-seated peace settled over everyone within earshot. People said it was a miracle. And it was for those who'd endured life's hardest challenges. To be able to take away a moment of suffering had been a gift. One I cherished. Cadan had taken that from me, too.

"I know," Jax says, patting my arm.

She's sympathetic and tries to be understanding, but she doesn't know what I'm going through. She hasn't met her soul mate yet. And until she does, she'll never understand the devastation of losing that connection. I lean against the wall, staring at a guitar case. Someone had covered every square inch with a violent ocean scene, the waves crashing over the sides of the case.

I'm lost in the beautiful destruction and it hits me. That's exactly what I'd had with Cadan. Beautiful destruction. Everyone else saw the beauty of our harmony, while I was stuck with the shit he created with his selfishness.

I'm done letting him treat me as if I'm nothing but a meal ticket on his way to fame and fortune just because I happen to be unlucky enough to be his soul mate. No. I'd watched my mom be that person for the last eight years. I'll be damned if I make the same mistake she did.

The door to the dressing room swings open and three guys dressed in all black, with various facial piercings and tattoos, file into the room.

Jax pastes a huge smile on her face. "Ahh, you're here!"

The tallest one, Mike, leans down and picks up the guitar case I'd been eyeing and nods in her direction. "We've been here. Just waiting on your girl." He glances at me and gives an appreciative nod.

"Oh, well, she's here now and I can't wait." Jax rushes to my side and leans in to whisper, "I'm sorry about that Cadan stuff."

I grit my teeth, wishing she'd drop it already.

"Really I am. Honestly, it's been so long since you've performed without him, I can barely remember what it's like to hear just you."

Perfect. It's what I'm afraid of most—having my performance compared to what I sound like when I'm with Cadan.

Jax pulls the door open. "Break a leg." Then she eyes my boots. "I didn't mean that literally."

I shake my head, feeling my lips twitch into a small smile. "I hope I don't disappoint."

"Not a chance of that," Teo, the lead guitarist, says. "Fuck, we'll be lucky if they let us off the stage at all after they hear your pipes."

I blush. These guys hadn't known me during the period I like to refer to as my "Cadan days." They'd heard of me, of course, but had promised Jax they wouldn't bring him up or the fact I'd left him. And they hadn't. Thank God. Our practice session had been the most fun I'd had onstage in years. But there hadn't been anyone staring at me expectantly from the audience. There would be tonight if anyone recognized me.

It happens everywhere I go these days. Lucy Moore, the famous singing soul soother. It seems everyone wants a piece of me, and all I want to do is sing.

CHAPTER 3

Seth

Across the bar, Lucy and Jax reappear from backstage. Lucy sweeps her dark bangs to the side as she frowns at Jax, but her plump lips make it look more like a pout. Despite the tongue-lashing I just received, or maybe because of it, I can't help but be intrigued. What I wouldn't give to tame her for one night. Not that Jax would approve. Oh, no. Lucy was off-limits, or so she'd said about ten times already.

Lucy disappears into the back again and Jax returns, giving me an apologetic smile. "Sorry about that. Lucy's a little touchy lately."

I shrug. "Whatever. I'm here for you, not your high-maintenance friend." My gaze slips to the V of her smokin' red top, and even though I'm not interested, I linger there, trying to erase the image of Lucy's short skirt riding up her bare thighs as she walked away. And the way her full red lips seduced the rim of that shot glass. Dammit if I couldn't already taste her lips on me. I harden, feeling myself strain against my zipper.

"Stop, you pig." She slaps me playfully on the arm. "And don't call Lucy high maintenance. She really isn't. Tonight is a big deal for her, that's all. She hasn't performed for an audience in over three months, and she's only doing it now because I begged her."

I raise an eyebrow. "Begged?"

She shakes her head, laughing. "Is that all you ever think about?"

That's not what I meant. I work with Mike, one of the guitarists in the band, and overheard him talking about Lucy's amazing voice. Why did Jax have to beg her best friend to sing for her on her birthday? But I play along, letting her think whatever she wants. "What do you expect from a manwhore?"

"True. Anyway, you're going to either die or want to take her to bed after you hear her sing."

"Half the guys in this bar already want to fuck her," I say. "It's those damned boots."

She eyes me slyly, seeing right through me. "Ah. You included, I see."

I say nothing and watch as Jax takes a sip of her margarita. Her lips attack the straw with a vengeance, eliciting a purely physical response south of my belt buckle. "Jesus, Jax. Stop that before you hurt someone."

"I'm trying to get noticed."

"Trust me. The other half of the bar is already undressing you." Hell, if she were a stranger, I'd be right there with them, angling to get her alone for an hour or two to find out what those lips could really do. Then Lucy's face clouds my vision, and all I can think about is wrapping her booted legs around my waist as I slip into her, hard and fast.

"Stop looking at me like that." Jax makes a face. "You're freaking me out."

"Like what?"

"Like you're wondering what exactly is underneath this sexified outfit."

I laugh. "Not even close, Russo. Your clothes hadn't even crossed my mind."

"That's because you probably were imagining me without any."

"Naked is always better." I nudge her shoulder to make sure she knows I'm joking. I own my player reputation, deserve it many times over. But I'd never go there with Jax. She's the relationship type. And I'm not. Not anymore, anyway. The last thing I want to do is hurt her by treating her as a one-night stand.

I wave down the bartender, holding up my beer. "Another." I point to Jax's drink. "And a refill for her too. Put it on my tab."

Jax eyes me and then the beer.

Irritation starts to build before she even says anything.

"Who's—"

"Derek's the DD tonight." I shift to stare her in the eye. "Don't start. Not tonight."

She holds her hands up in surrender. "Just asking."

"And what about you? How are you getting home after your shots and margaritas?"

"Marty's coming after work. It's his present to me."

"His present?" I grimace with irritation. "To drive you home? What a dick."

"No, you idiot. To take care of me and Lucy. You know, make sure we don't end up with total losers or drugged, and then he's going to take us out for breakfast before we go home and suffer the worst hangovers of our lives. It's what big brothers are for."

"If you say so."

"If you had a little sister, you'd understand." She smiles patiently and takes another sip of her margarita.

I make a noncommittal sound. I still think he's a dick. But that might have something to do with his comment the day of E's funeral. *Don't blame yourself, man. It was her choice to come pick your sorry ass up.* A familiar rush of anger and helplessness fills me, and I slam the door on the memory. Not here. I won't think about that now.

Cold air whips across the bar as the front door opens and a line of people file in. The show is about to start, and apparently everyone between the age of eighteen and thirty within a fifty-mile radius has come out of the woodwork.

"Dude." Derek leans over the bar and grabs a bottle of water from a bucket of ice. "Of all the nights to ask me to be the designated driver, you had to choose this one?" He twists the top and takes a long slug. He's just come from work and is still wearing his blue firefighter T-shirt. He'll have five girls begging him to take them home within forty-five minutes. Or less, if he starts buying them drinks. "How am I going to get through this without something to take the edge off?"

"Get through what?" I purposely ignore the way he's looking at Jax. He's had a slight obsession with her for as long as I can remember, yet he's never made a move. And as far as I know, he never plans to.

He lifts his water bottle to the crowd. "A night of barely dressed hot chicks. Are you fucking blind?"

I might as well be, because right now, I don't see anything except the girl strutting out onstage in her sex-bot boots, swaying her hips and seducing the crowd with her eyes before she even opens her mouth.

Jesus. She's going to kill me. I'm going to combust right here in the bar just staring at her pouty lips. She picks up the microphone and smiles tentatively at Mike, waiting for his cue.

"Omigod!" Jax squeals and grabs my arm. "She's actually going to go through with it."

I glance down at her and smile at her huge grin. Jax hasn't looked this happy in months. Not since before the big breakup. "You were worried she wouldn't?"

She lets out an ironic huff of exasperation. "Are you kidding? I wasn't even sure I'd get her to the bar, let alone near the stage." Her pretty blue eyes meet mine and her smile fades. "Whatever happens, promise me you'll be nice to her."

"What the hell, Jax?" I pull away slightly and frown at her, offended she has such a low opinion of me. "What do you think I'm going to do? Mock her and throw beer bottles?"

She clutches my arm and pulls me back. "No. Sorry, I didn't mean to imply anything. It's just that this is a huge deal for her and I want it to go smoothly. She belongs up there. She's not herself when she's not singing."

Onstage, the band starts to play, and the girl who'd wobbled her way backstage has transformed into a dazzling, confident crowd-pleaser. She's standing with her feet shoulder-width apart, her head held high, a seductive smile on her face as she scans the room. Her eyes land on me and she grips the mic with both hands. Then she starts singing. I instantly recognize the song as a popular Mandy Taylor number my sister is always playing. But instead of Mandy's pop sound, Lucy's voice is huskier, and she sings it slower. Seductively. She's fucking mesmerizing.

"Holy shit, dude." Derek leans forward, eyeing Lucy as if he's mentally calculating how fast he can rip her clothes off. "Who the hell is that?"

"Don't even think about it, asshole," I growl. Where did that come from?

"Awww." Jax laughs. "You're such a softy. Look at you, all protective of my friend." She slips her arm around me and gives me a sideways hug.

"Yeah, *softy*," Derek mimics and gives me that guy look that says he knows exactly what's going on with me and it has nothing to do with being protective.

I glare at him, making sure he knows it doesn't matter my motives. She's off-limits to the likes of him.

"God," Jax whispers. "Look at her."

My gaze automatically shifts to the fiery pixie onstage.

"I didn't think it was possible, but whoa. She's even better than I remember."

The entire club is riveted, watching her strut around the stage. Then the band pauses and Lucy freezes, the mic held close to her lips. Her eyes scan the crowd, and my breath gets caught in my throat when her gaze lands on me. Something foreign in my gut flips over as her lips turn up into a secret smile I swear is meant just for me.

Jesus, this girl knows what the hell she's doing. She's holding me in the palm of her hand, leaving me salivating for more. And though I'm sure I'm not the only one, I can't tear my eyes away from her to confirm the effect she has on the room.

Her gaze never shifts and she starts singing in the sexiest voice possible, "*When it's just you and me in the dead of the night, I get reckless... reckless... reckless.*"

I hear and see nothing except this girl in this very moment. Her brilliant blue eyes are sparkling with mischief and desire. It takes all my willpower not to stride up to the stage and whisk her away to the back where we can—

"Here." Derek shoves an ice-cold beer bottle into my hand. "You look like you need it."

I take the bottle but don't drink. Lucy is still imploring me with those eyes, seducing me into a puddle of lust and something more I can't quite explain. Something deeper that seems to come dangerously close to touching my soul. "Shit," I mutter and lift the bottle to my lips, downing half the beer in one pull.

Derek laughs. "It's about damn time, man."

I turn around, deliberately tearing my gaze from the stage. "About time for what?"

Jax is dancing in place, her margarita empty. I signal to the bartender to get her another.

"That you took an interest in someone of the female persuasion." He's leaning against the bar, his gaze still locked on the stage.

My body stiffens involuntarily, and I force myself to relax. "There has never been a time when I haven't been interested in a hot chick."

He snorts. "Point taken. But I haven't seen you look at one like that since…" Grimacing, he doesn't finish the thought.

Anger flares to life and shoots through my veins just as it always does when someone brings up E. I don't want to talk about her, and I especially don't want to talk about her after I've been thinking of all the dirty things I want to do with Jax's friend.

Jax's margarita materializes at the same time the band switches to a slower Lady Antebellum song. I hand her the drink, and she smiles up at me, her eyes already glassy from her buzz.

"Thanks!" She takes a long sip and frowns as she watches me.

"Stop." I run a finger over the bridge of her nose, smoothing her worry lines. "I'm fine."

"Of course you are," she says quietly and slips her hand into mine. "But right now I need a dance partner and you're it."

"What?" I'm already pulling my hand from hers when she tightens her grip and yanks.

"It's my birthday. You can't turn down a dance from the birthday girl, that's just bad karma you don't need." Her teasing tone is back, but I see right through her.

She's worried about me.

Shit. I don't dance. Not anymore. But Jax wraps her arms around my shoulders and starts to sway back and forth. I can't just leave her on the dance floor.

"Come on. One dance isn't going to kill you." She scowls at me.

With no way to escape without being a first-class douche, I circle my arms around her waist and pull her close.

"There. This isn't so bad, is it?"

I glance down into her blue, tequila-hazed eyes and force a smile. Yes. It is that bad. The phantom aroma of citrus mixed with oil paints assaults me. E's image swims in my mind, a paintbrush in her hand as she turns the sound up on her old-fashioned radio. Then she dances toward me, that perpetual lust-inducing spark glinting in her espresso-colored eyes. My fists clench and I want nothing more than to stalk back over to the bar and down shot after shot of throat-burning whiskey until the memories exploding around me are buried in the fog of mind-numbing alcohol. "No."

She grins and presses her face to my chest.

Across the room, Derek raises a glass in my direction, saluting my misfortune. I glare back. Dick. I concentrate on the rasp in Lucy's voice and let Jax lead in the body-hugging dance for the rest of the song.

As the last notes fade away, I kiss the top of her head. "Happy birthday, my friend." Then I step out of her embrace and head directly to the bar, where Derek already has two shots of the sweet amber liquid waiting for me. Maybe he isn't such a dick after all.

"Thanks," I say and down the first shot, wincing from the bitter aftertaste.

"Cheers." Derek raises his water in my direction, and I mimic the movement with the second shot.

This one goes down smoother, and although the buzz hasn't started yet, I feel the tension easing from my shoulders. I spend the next forty minutes leaning against the bar, focused on Lucy and those fucking boots.

E never wore boots.

"Seth!" A petite blonde who looks vaguely familiar bounces over, waving vigorously. "I didn't know you were going to be here tonight." Her eyelids flutter as she smiles up at me coyly. "I would've worn that sexy red miniskirt you seem to like so much."

Aw, shit. Carrie. Or was it Carly?

"Where've you been?" Her lower lip juts out in a pout as she turns into me, pressing her modest breasts into my ribs.

I actively work to keep myself from recoiling. She's not unattractive. Not physically anyway. But the two dozen phone calls after the unfortunate one-night stand we'd had a few months ago was enough to make any man go into hibernation. "Hi."

She laughs. "Is that all you have to say after everything we shared?"

"Uh…"

Lucy seems to materialize out of nowhere and places her hand on my arm. I hadn't even noticed the band announce they were taking a break. But Mike is already a few feet away, talking to the bartender.

"Hey. Who's your friend?" Lucy asks, lifting her dark hair off her neck to cool down after her performance.

I glance from her to Carrie… Carly.

The blonde stares at Lucy's hand, which is still on my arm, and scowls. "I'm a close friend of Seth's."

Jesus. Close friend. More like stalker. I stiffen and shift closer to Lucy. Carly's arm slips away, and before I know what's happening, Lucy replaces her on my other side. I'm all too happy to drape my arm over her shoulders and pull her to my side. And damn if she doesn't fit against me perfectly.

"Friend? My goodness, I don't think my Seth has ever mentioned you." Lucy's tone is upbeat, nothing like the Lucy I met an hour ago. "Old friend?"

My Seth? Sweet Lord, she's posing as my girlfriend. Now I really want to take her home and do all kinds of indecent things to her.

"We go way back," Carly says in a flat voice. Her face is scrunched up, her nose twitching in agitation. She has the look of one of those nervous dogs that gets antsy around strangers. "But he's never mentioned you."

Lucy laughs as if she thinks Carly's charming. "Well, you know Seth. He's got the strong, silent type thing going on."

Carly says nothing as she narrows her eyes at me, clearly trying to cut me down with that female death glare.

Lucy holds out her hand. "I'm sorry. I didn't catch your name. I'm Lucy."

"Oh, sorry," I say, snapping out of my trance. "Lucy, this is Carly. We met—"

"It's Cami, you ass." My one-night stand is now seething and leaning forward on the balls of her feet with her hands fisted. I slept with this? I make a mental note to never drink again. Or at least limit my intake to something a few levels below plastered.

I take a step back, pulling Lucy with me. Cami might scratch my eyes out if she sees an opening. "Right. I meant Cami." I smile at Lucy, trying to downplay the fact that I'm a complete idiot. No one's buying it, though. Lucy tries to hide a snicker by twisting into me. She's soft and smells of lime. My gaze travels to her lips, and we both freeze, caught in the moment.

Cami clears her throat, breaking our connection. She practically sneers at us and then turns and stomps across the bar, taking short, ridiculously slow steps on her impossibly high heels.

Laughing, Lucy pulls away, leaving an aching void beside me. I want to reach out and pull her back but clamp down on the impulse. "Jeez, Seth. You should've seen the look you had on your face."

I pick up my beer and take a long drink. "Was I that obvious?"

"Only if you were wishing to disappear or contemplating the fastest getaway route."

"Yep. Obvious." I smile down at her, enjoying our exchange more than I care to admit. For the last year and a half, with the exception of my friendship with Jax, I've kept my female relationships on a purely physical level. Life is easier that way. "Thanks for the help."

"You owe me." She winks and lets Mike drag her back toward the stage.

I'm still staring at her ass when Jax reappears.

"Stop that." She's clutching the bar and her eyes are bloodshot.

"Stop what?" I ask.

"Devouring Lucy with your eyes." She slurs the words and adds, "She's off-limits."

"Why? Her mate?" There's an ache of disappointment in my chest that takes me completely off guard. Physical. That's all it is. Lucy's hot. And cool. And talented. And completely alluring. I could watch her perform for hours and be perfectly content.

Jax shakes her head and seems to sober a little. "She's done with him. But she's my best friend and you're my other best friend. I can't have her hating you when you don't call the next day."

I nod reluctantly and take another drink. She's right. I won't call, and we both know this as fact.

"Good." Jax climbs up on the stool and pats the one next to her. "Sit. I'm going to save you from Cami. She's over in the corner plotting fifty ways to remove your man bits."

I choke, spraying my beer on the people standing in front of me. "What?"

The beer-covered couple turns and gives me a disgusted look.

"Sorry," I mumble.

"You heard me," Jax says. "I'm sure it's all talk, but I'll be your buffer just in case she goes into stalker mode again."

The music starts, so I give her a half-hug and say into her ear, "You're the best."

"I know."

Lucy starts singing a Colbie Caillat song. The entire bar goes quiet, captivated by her singer-songwriter persona. Is there anything this girl can't sing? Her voice is winding through me when Jax gasps and clutches my arm, her fingernails cutting into my skin. "Omigod!"

"What?" I follow her gaze to find her staring at a guy roughly our age standing just inside the front door. He's staring at Lucy, a stormy expression on his face.

"Who the hell is that?" I growl from pure protectiveness. I can't stand the way he's eyeing her, as if he's ready to drag her off the stage and stuff her in the trunk of his car.

Jax sucks in a breath. "Her ex, Cadan."

CHAPTER 4

Lucy

As I'm strutting across the stage, microphone clutched in my hand, the allure of the stage grabs hold of me, filling my soul with joy. I imagine myself lit up, my eyes sparkling with happiness. It's a state of being I haven't experienced while singing for at least the past two years. Not since before Cadan and I started performing together, anyway. What we'd had was intense. Emotional. Draining in the best possible way. But that had been for the audience, not for me. Then Cadan had turned into a world-class bastard, tainting everything that was good about singing.

This feeling I have right now? It's heady and intoxicating. Maybe even selfish. And I take it all in, loving every moment of it. The music winds through me, and as I scan the crowd, I settle my gaze on Seth. He's tracking me with those smoldering eyes. It only takes one look to know what he's thinking. I feed off his hunger, giving it right back to him through my throaty rendition of "Body and Soul" by Tori Amos.

I can see he's talking to Jax, but his gaze never wavers from mine. My worldview narrows, and though the bar is full of people, I'm singing to just him. I'm taken to another dimension, completely lost in the music. Lost in Seth—the sexy stranger I'm uncharacteristically drawn to.

My body vibrates with excitement and my heart hammers against my ribs. I'm painfully aware I'm moments from being pulled completely under his spell, lost once again to the attraction of a man.

No. Not this time. I tear my gaze away and focus on the crowd closest to the stage. The joy comes flooding back with the pulse of the music and I give them everything I have.

But as the last notes of the song fade away, my attention is pulled back to Seth. Jax is clutching his arm, smiling in my direction. Good, she's enjoying herself. This is supposed to be for her after all.

I'm halfway through an acoustic number when Jax tears away from Seth, heading directly for the door. She pushes through the crowd, and I lose sight of her for a moment. What is she doing? I glance back at Seth. He's scowling, staring after her. Then the crowd parts, and I finally see what everyone else does.

Cadan.

My entire body goes numb and the mic slips from my hand. I barely notice the loud screech when it tumbles to the stage.

"Lucy?" Mike touches my elbow. "You okay?"

I give him a tiny shake of my head, my eyes wide in shock. What the hell is Cadan doing here? He's supposed to be on tour in Colorado. And how did he know where to find me? Jax wouldn't have said anything to him. And I hadn't told anyone else he knows I'm singing tonight. No one except my mother.

Shit. Dammit. Son of... Why can't she leave well enough alone?

"No," I say to Mike. "I'm sorry, but I have to leave. Now." Without waiting for a response, I stalk across the stage and into the back, rubbing my suddenly goose-pimpled arms.

"Lucy!" Mike follows me. "What's wrong?"

I spin and nearly fall over. Jesus. I'm perfectly fine strutting around stage in these suicide boots, but once I'm just regular Lucy, all my coordination flies out the window. "It's Cadan. My ex. I can't see him. Not tonight. I have to go."

"Cadan Kinx?" His eyes go wide with wonder the way every other wannabe rocker's do when they finally meet the famous Cadan.

"Shit," I say again. "Yes. Go out there and stall him. You can even say I sent you. That will get him talking." Anything to give me a few minutes to escape.

He glances at the door and then back to me, clearly unsure of what to do.

"Go!" I push him toward the door leading back into the bar.

"What's going on?" Teo asks as he bounds into the dressing room, still holding his guitar. Justin, our drummer, follows him, his hands stuffed in his jeans pockets.

"You're going out there to stall Cadan," I say, pushing Teo after Mike. "Tell him I'll be out in a few minutes."

"Will you?" Justin asks, eyeing me with a quiet intelligence.

"Hell, no." The tears start to burn my eyes. Why did he have to show up and ruin everything? I'd been happy. Normal even, for the first time since I left him at that hotel three months ago. I steel myself. I will not cry over Cadan. Not tonight. I'm done with that. Done letting him prey on my emotions. Mate or not, I cut him out of my life and no way am I letting him back in.

Teo runs a hand over the spikes of his stiff, gelled hair and nods. "You got it." He's already striding out the door when Mike and Justin turn and follow him.

I don't hesitate. I don't even go into the bar to get my coat. I'd rather freeze in the December air than have to talk to Cadan. One of two things will happen. Either we'll have a huge fight that will end in me screaming at him again, or he'll give me a sob story and try to convince me to do one more show. Neither is on my agenda. I wrap my arms around my torso and use my hip to push open the back door.

The chilly wind assaults me and my teeth instantly start chattering. Oh my God. In my haste, I forgot my keys. Jax has them. Not that I should be driving anyway. I've had way too many tequila shots and margaritas.

Marty. Is he even here yet? I glance at the thin wristwatch on my right arm. Crap. No, he isn't due for another hour. I press against the side of the building and glance up and down the street. The small town is pretty much boarded up for the night. Only the bar is open. I start walking. Jax's house is in town, but it's a good three miles up the main highway. Not exactly a prime walking path.

I glance across the street at the dark Pacific Ocean, nostalgic for the time before I'd ever met Cadan. Then I tuck my head down and run toward the nearest cross street, praying I don't break an ankle.

"Lucy!" a deep voice calls over the noise of the ocean churning against the rocks.

I stop mid-run and turn to stare at Seth. "What are you doing out here?" I stammer, my lips already frozen.

He runs to catch up with me and holds out my coat.

"Oh!" I grasp it and hug it to my body and then quickly slide my arms into the heavenly wool. "Did Jax send you?"

He nods and wraps an arm around my shoulders. "Let's go."

"Where?" I take two steps for every one of his, trying to keep up.

"There's a place a few blocks from here where we can get out of the cold until Marty comes for you." He turns and pulls me down a side street and out of the wind.

"Thank you," I say with a relieved sigh.

He quirks an eyebrow and his lips turn up in a sexy half smile. "I owe you one, remember?"

The sound of his quiet, self-assured tone makes my insides go all tingly. I have a thing for confident men with rough voices. Cadan, while oozing more confidence than is warranted, has a smooth, clear-as-a-bell voice that's perfect for hitting all the right notes but lacks something in the gritty-and-sexy department.

"Right," I say. "I wasn't expecting to collect so soon."

We make a left on the next street and head down closer to the shoreline. Finally we stop at a white, plank-sided house. I glance up and gasp. On what I assume is the third floor is a glass studio with a bird's-eye view of the ocean. "You live here?"

"It's my sister's place. She's out of town." He doesn't say any more, just unlocks the door and shuffles me inside. Warmth envelops me, and I stand there in the cheery yellow kitchen, waiting for my nose to defrost.

Seth shrugs out of his coat and reaches for mine, but I wrap it closer around my body. "Not yet," I say. "Give me a few more minutes."

"I'll turn the heat up." He disappears into the next room, leaving me standing next to a fully stocked bar area. The granite counter and dark wood cabinet don't match the white cupboards and seem out of place in the country-style kitchen. Total bachelor move. But didn't he say this is his sister's place?

"Hey!" I call. "Does she have any coffee?"

"The beans are in the fridge. Help yourself."

Now that I'm slowly regaining feeling in my limbs, I move toward the refrigerator and note my buzz has all but worn off. Between my performance, the panic of seeing Cadan, and my foray into the arctic December winds of Mendocino, my metabolism has done a stellar job of working its way through all that tequila. Fortunately, when I open the door and find the Colombian roast beans, a bottle of Kahlúa stares back at me. "The hell with it."

I grab the bottle then make short work of grinding the beans and starting the coffee. While I wait for Seth to return, I fill my mug with the Colombian blend and top it off with the Kahlúa. Then I sit at a round breakfast-nook table, sipping away as I stare at the full moon shining over the Pacific. Finally I'm warm enough that I shrug out of my jacket.

Seth comes in holding a pair of thick wool socks. He eyes the rum liqueur on the table and chuckles.

"I'll replace it," I say, biting my lip. "I just needed something to take the edge off."

His amused smile fades, replaced by that smoldering look he's been giving me the entire night. My cheeks burn and I know I'm turning multiple shades of red.

"Understandable," he says.

I scramble up from my chair and hurry over to the coffeepot. Without asking, I grab another cup for him and fill it with the Colombian roast. I refill mine halfway, leaving room for more alcohol. I'm not going to get through this night sober. At least, not easily. I hold his mug up to him. "Do you take anything in it?"

He gestures to the bottle on the table. "That's fine."

I smile as I join him, and he doctors his drink before eyeing mine. "Half and half?" he asks.

"Yes." I don't even blink. "It's been a rough night."

"No doubt."

I sit with my hands wrapped around the cup and try to look at anything except him. Not that it matters. His image is burned into my brain after spending the last hour or so staring at him from the stage. He's tall. Six feet, maybe. Broad shoulders. Narrow waist. Angular jaw. Slightly wavy, multi-streaked, bronze-colored hair. Those vibrant tattoos climbing up both arms. And eyes so vibrant green they almost glow. Yeah. No need to look at him. I do anyway.

"You're thinking about something," he says. He's contemplative, trying to figure me out, but he doesn't ask me to share.

I eye the gray socks now lying next to his cup. They're about twice as big as mine would be. "Are you going to put those on?"

He laughs. "They're for you."

"Really? Do they belong to your sister's boyfriend or something?" No girl I know wears socks that big. My toes curl in longing, but I can't wear the socks of some dude I don't even know. Drinking his sister's booze is one thing. Stealing her boyfriend's clothes is entirely another.

Seth shakes his head. "They're mine. I've been known to keep a few things here just in case."

"Ahh." So they are smelly man socks. Except they look really warm and cozy. And my feet are starting to ache.

"They're new."

"Really?"

"No. But I thought that would make them sound more appealing." He gets up, grabs the coffeepot, and refills our mugs. "They are clean, though."

My lips twitch and I reach for the socks but don't move to put them on. I'm too busy watching Seth's back muscles ripple through his black T-shirt as he returns the coffeepot to the counter.

"This is a great place," I say. "I'd kill to see the view from the top floor."

Seth stiffens. He turns slowly, his face set in a stormy expression.

I jerk, taken aback by his sudden change in demeanor. "Sorry. I just love cool spaces. I didn't mean to imply you should traipse me around your sister's house. Forget I said anything."

He closes his eyes and sucks in a breath. "No. I'm sorry. It's… that space is private. No one goes up there."

"Yeah, sure. No need to explain." I glance at the clock. "When is Marty coming again?"

He moves to the bar and pulls out a full bottle of Crown Royal. "We have about forty minutes. Want something a little stronger?"

I shouldn't, but I nod anyway. Anything to numb the barrage of emotions I'm keeping buried so deep it physically hurts to breathe. I don't want to see Cadan. Or talk to him. But I can't deny the connection we have. It will never go away. He has a piece of me, even though I desperately wish he didn't. Then there's this strong attraction I have for Seth. I've just barely met him, and yet I don't want to leave this place. Don't want to leave without finding out what's under that T-shirt.

Oh my God. What am I thinking? I nod to the Crown Royal. "Got anything to mix with that?"

Seth scans the contents of the fridge. "Whiskey Sour?"

"Works for me." I slip out of my chair, meaning to move to Seth's side, but the pocket of my coat starts to buzz, making me jump. I fumble for the phone, drop it, and scramble to scoop it up. It's Jax. "Hello?" I say, breathless.

"Where are you?" she demands. Beyoncé is singing in the background.

"Seth's. Didn't you send him after me?"

She's quiet, and I listen to Beyoncé singing about putting a ring on it.

"Jax? Did I lose you?"

She clears her throat. "How did you get there? Derek is his DD and he's still here." Her tone is serious. Accusing.

"Oh sorry. We're at his sister's house. We walked."

More silence. This time I wait her out.

"Lucy?"

"Yeah."

"Do you mean the white house a few blocks away? The one with the incredible views of the ocean?"

I glance at Seth, who's casting me a quizzical look. "How many sisters do you have?"

"Two. Why?"

"No reason." I turn my attention back to Jax. "Sounds right." I want to mention the third floor, but don't because of Seth's earlier reaction. "We're hanging out in the kitchen, waiting for Marty."

"He's not coming." She's super pissed. I can tell by the way she's clipping her words.

I refrain from rolling my eyes. Her brother is such an ass sometimes. "How does he expect us to get home?"

"That's what I asked. But no. He's going out with some skank from his job instead."

"Asshole."

"Marty?" Seth asks.

"Who else?" I roll my eyes. The guy's reputation precedes him.

"And there's no one coming to give you a ride home?" Seth asks me.

"Right."

He holds his hand out for the phone. When I don't respond right away, he waves his fingers in a give-it-here motion. "Lucy... please."

I reluctantly hand over my phone.

"Put Derek on," Seth says as he walks into the other room.

"Hey!" I stride after him and grimace. My limbs are stiff from bouncing around onstage in my boots.

"Is he gone?" I hear Seth ask. "Just hang out until he leaves. Then you two can come by to pick up Lucy." Another pause. "No. I'm fine here. ... Yes, I'm sure."

He turns around and doesn't seem surprised to see me eavesdropping. He hands the phone back to me.

"Jax?"

"I'm here."

"I'm sorry about your birthday." My voice quavers and I wonder if I'm more drunk than I think I am.

"Are you kidding? It's the best birthday. I got to see you back up on that stage. And you rocked it, girl. But we'll talk about that later."

"Okay." I tug at the hem of my skirt nervously. When I'm onstage, something happens to me. A confidence I don't normally possess overtakes me. But the minute I step off, I transform into Lucy, the bundle of nerves.

"I'll see you soon. Right after Cadan leaves, we'll come get you."

A pit forms in my stomach. "He's still there?"

"Yeah. Soaking up all the attention. Plus, I think he's hoping you'll come back."

I snort. "I think you were right with the first guess."

She laughs. "Probably. See you soon."

The line goes dead and I'm saved from listening to the Madonna song that replaced Beyoncé. She's probably right. Cadan does expect me to come back. I always have before. It's that soul-mate connection. The pull of the two souls born for each other. But he's battered my heart one too many times. He can stay there all damn night for all I care.

Something cold is pressed into my hand. I grab the whiskey sour and down half of it before I meet Seth's eyes. There's something painful and moving in his expression.

He raises his glass to mine. "To right now."

The heavy weight on my heart doesn't lessen, but it shifts enough that I smile and clink my glass against his. "To right now."

We both sip, eyes still locked, then drain our glasses together. I slowly lower my glass to the table, mesmerized by his intense understanding. He knows what it's like to live without a mate. And right now, I need someone who gets that.

Before my brain tells me otherwise, I step forward and grab him by that deliciously tight T-shirt. His gaze shifts to my lips as he waits for me to finish what I started.

My breathing turns shallow with undeniable lust.

"Lucy." His tone is low, almost a growl.

In answer, I wrap one hand around his neck, reach up, and press my lips to his.

CHAPTER 5
Lucy

Oh God, oh God, oh God. I'm kissing Seth. The guy who is not Cadan. Seth's arms come around me and he pulls me close, molding me against his body. He's warm and solid, and all I want to do is wrap myself around him. Tingling with pleasure, I let out a contented sigh.

Seth sucks in a breath and moans as I slip my tongue against his. He ducks down a bit, buries his fingers in my short hair, and deepens the kiss as our tongues tangle in frenzy. He tastes faintly of coffee and cream. I can't get enough. And neither can he. His hands shift to my waist, and he lifts me up, spinning me until my back is against the closed kitchen door. My legs instinctively curl around his hips.

He pulls back just a bit and smiles against my lips.

"What?" I ask through the fuzzy haze of alcohol, running my hands over the slope of his shoulders.

"I've been imagining this since you first walked away from me at the bar."

"This?" I wrap a hand around his neck and press my lips to his once more, kissing him as if our joining is as important to my survival as breathing. He matches the kiss with a fervor of his own, nipping and biting at my lower lip.

This scene had been flashing in my mind while I'd been singing to him, but I hadn't thought I'd actually go through with it. I'm not the type of girl to randomly make out with a perfect stranger. But I can't help myself. Hunger and longing consume me from the inside out. Rational thought flees and all I want is to touch and to be touched in every possible way. I lose myself in the physical act of our connection. My mind shuts down and all I do is feel. Feel his hand slipping lower on my hip. Feel his hot lips trail kisses down my neck, his teeth scraping over my pulse, and the heat pooling between my thighs.

Seth is holding me up with one arm while running his fingers over my bare leg. I close my eyes and press closer, my limbs quivering with anticipation.

"Jesus, Lucy," Seth says in a rough voice as his hand cups my ass. "You're killing me here."

I pull back and gaze into his hooded eyes, so full of desire I wonder how he's holding himself back. "Killing you?"

He nods and steps back, slowly extracting me from his body. My feet land lightly on the tiled floor. A chill washes over me, and I wrap my arms around myself, trying to keep his heat from fading away.

"Something wrong?" I ask.

He glances to the wall and nods at the clock. "Derek will be here before we know it. We probably don't want to be… uh… in a compromising position when he gets here."

Heat burns my cheeks and I bite down on my lower lip. He's still staring at me, his gaze traveling from my mouth to the hem of my skirt. Good God, I've never been so hot in my entire life. The way the muscles in his forearms flex with tension as his hands ball into tight fists and the fact that he appears to be straining to keep from touching me gives me all the courage I need.

I smile and pull out my phone. I tap in a message and then raise an eyebrow at him. "If I hit Send, I'll have to stay over. What do you say?" I can't believe I'm actually standing here, propositioning Seth for a sleepover.

He frowns and takes another step away from me. The heavy weight of rejection settles over my chest. Shit! Had I totally misread the situation? Maybe he's not that into me. More likely, he's used to a few hours of pleasure and then a quick send-off. No muss, no fuss. Ugh. What had I been thinking? Of course he doesn't want a random person inviting herself to stay over. Idiot.

I set my phone on the counter, disappointment eating away at the delicious ache he'd ignited in me. "I see," I say. "Okay then." Sidestepping, I move to grab my empty coffee cup and the whiskey. The Kahlúa isn't going to cut it if I'm going to make it through the rest of the night.

The clatter of my boots against the tile fills the silence as I move, trying to get as far away from Seth as possible. I'm halfway to the coffeepot when Seth's hand wraps around my wrist. I spin, ready to give him a piece of my mind, but he's got my phone in the other hand, holding it up. My message to Jax is highlighted in green, marking it as sent.

"What...?" I don't even know what I'm asking him. Why did he send the message? Does this mean he's expecting me to sleep with him? Because after that awkward exchange, I'm no longer interested in falling into bed with him. The moment has passed.

My phone buzzes with a response from Jax. *L, whaat teh hell? R U being stoopid?*

I laugh at her drunk typing. Clearly her autocorrect is turned off. Before I can type in a message, another comes through.

Jusst ass weel. Tooo drunk to remmemeber anthying. C U timmorow.

I stare at the phone. She's way too far gone to be coherent if I call. Now I don't know what to do. If she manages to tell Derek I'm staying, he won't be coming for me. She probably will. She's chatty when she's drunk. Chances are slim to none that I'll have a ride to anywhere before morning.

"So that's settled?" Seth, still holding my wrist, gently pulls me toward him until our lips are inches apart.

I lick mine and immediately regret it when he grips my hips possessively and yanks me the rest of the way to him.

"Whoa." I put a hand against his chest and gently push him away.

His brow creases as he frowns. "What's wrong?"

"Nothing," I say automatically. Liar. Everything's wrong. Ten minutes ago, I was ready to give myself to this guy. And yet the expression on his face when I suggested sleeping over was one of pure panic. He didn't want me to stay. That was obvious, but clearly his desire for easy sex had won out. Now I have to deal with the mess I just made.

He laughs and stuffs his hands in the front pockets of his jeans. "If you say so."

"I say so." My voice is low, unsure.

Seth studies me. After a moment, he holds out his hand. "I'd like to show you something."

I stare at his outstretched hand, then look up, finding desire still lurking in his eyes, but it's shadowed by something calmer, something closer to curiosity. "Can I take my coffee with me?"

His lips twitch with humor. "It's almost a requirement."

"Good." I sweep back to the coffeepot, refill both our mugs, and before I can ask, Seth has the Kahlúa in one hand and the whiskey in the other.

He shifts his gaze between the two. "Got a preference?"

My gaze lingers on the hand holding the Kahlúa, the hand that had been sneaking its way under my skirt, then moves to the whiskey. I could definitely use a shot, but if I'm going to be shut up in this house with Seth and all the sexual tension still sparking between us, I need to keep the hard stuff to a minimum. "Kahlúa, please."

The whiskey slips to the counter with a soft thump. "Ready?"

"For what?"

He grins. "You'll see." His free hand lands lightly on the small of my back as he guides me through the kitchen and toward the adjoining room. We walk through the door into a poppy-colored room, rich in red accents. It's a color explosion and totally unexpected. Bright yellow pillows line the red couch. Silk fuchsia scarves hang from rods over the picture window in a messy, casual style, and everything about the room screams vibrant and full of life. I could happily stay here for the rest of the night. But Seth continues, and we enter another door into a room lined with natural wood. A large, widescreen TV fills one wall. Directly across from it sits a black leather couch. If it weren't for the kitchen and the living room, I'd swear the house was inhabited by a bachelor. Because this is a man cave if I've ever seen one.

"Have a seat," Seth says and sets the Kahlúa on the table.

I tuck my feet under me, curling into the corner while Seth opens one of the doors on a large cherrywood entertainment cabinet. Blu-ray movies stacked tightly together fill all three rows. He turns and eyes the cabinet. "What are you in the mood for?"

You. But I don't say that. Not two minutes ago, I decided nothing would happen between us. I push it aside. If I can just get through the next eight or so hours until Jax is sober enough to rescue me, I'll be fine. The alcohol will have left my system, along with all the inappropriate thoughts I'm having right now. Like what it would feel like to have his weight pressing down on me as my hands explore the planes of his back muscles flexing under my fingertips.

"Lucy?" Seth asks. His eyes crinkle with worry. Or is that suspicion?

"Sorry. Um, anything really. Except slasher flicks. I'm not really in the right frame of mind for cheesy B-movie gore."

His lips turn up in a half smile. "Do you normally watch slasher films?"

I shrug. "Sometimes. They're funny when I'm in the mood."

"Good to know." He scans the movies for a few seconds. Then he pulls one from each shelf. "Pick one."

I'm not all that caught up on current movies. While on tour with Cadan, we'd spent most of our spare time writing lyrics and rewatching long-running TV series. Stuff that didn't take too much brainpower or require a lot of attention, so I don't recognize any of the choices he offers. One of them stars my favorite actor, Wes Chadwick, so I just point to that one. "*Once Again.*"

Seth puts the other two down, glances at the back of the movie case, and frowns. "Really?"

I laugh. "Dude, you're the one who gave me the choice. Suck it up and put the movie on." At this point, I'd rather do anything other than stare at him. My body is growing warm again and it has nothing to do with the temperature in the room.

He glances down at me. "Have you seen this before?"

"No. I'm painfully out of date on current movies, but I like Wes Chadwick. He was absolute perfection in the remake of *Casablanca*. So I figure even if I don't like the movie, at least the acting will be good."

He stares blankly at me for a moment and then shakes his head as if to pull himself out of a trance. "Fair enough. *Once Again* it is."

I eye him suspiciously. "Have you?"

"No. I pulled it out because it didn't look familiar. Now I know why."

"Romantic comedy?" There's laughter in my voice.

He smiles, but it doesn't quite reach his eyes. "Looks like I'm doomed by my own stupidity."

"I'm sure you'll live through it. If not, there's always more alcohol." What is it with men and romantic comedies? Do they think watching two fictional people work out their issues for an hour and a half means some sort of commitment?

The movie starts and Seth sits a few feet from me on the couch, his mug in one hand and the Kahlúa in the other.

"Do you think you might need the whiskey?" I say, teasing him.

"Probably. But I'll stick with this for now."

A soulful, gut-wrenching melody fills the room with the opening credits. The scene flashes to a graveside service. Yikes. I thought he'd said this was a romantic comedy.

My phone vibrates on the side table where I'd dropped it. This should be good. Drunk Jax. She doesn't drink often, but when she does, the entertainment is priceless. I know because since I've been away, every time she gets even a little tipsy she blows up my phone.

I'm about to hit Accept when I notice the caller. Cadan.

CHAPTER 6
Seth

Lucy stiffens as she stares at her phone. She seems paralyzed and worry lines crease her brow. It can't be anything other than bad news with that look on her face.

I can't help myself. I reach for the phone, intending to intercept whatever it is that's waiting for her on the other end, but she grabs it at the last second and punches the Decline button, abruptly making the vibration stop.

"Sorry," she says. "It was Cadan. I changed my number a month ago. He probably managed to steal Jax's phone long enough to get it. No one else has it. Not even my mother."

"Why not?" I can't imagine a scenario in which I wouldn't hand over my number to my own mother. Even in the horrific days after the accident, when I'd pushed everyone else away, I'd always taken Mom's calls, if for no other reason than to keep her from worrying so much. She'd been hurting too, everyone had been, but I couldn't stand to be the one to cause her more pain. The familiar ache throbs just below my breastbone and it takes me a moment to push past it. The therapist had said this would get easier. He'd lied.

Lucy lowers her gaze to the phone in her hand. "She'd just give it to Cadan the first time he called her."

"Really?" I say incredulously. "Even if you ask her not to?"

"Yeah." Her brilliant blue eyes are ablaze with anger when she looks up. "Mom is a firm believer in sticking with your fated one no matter what happens. Never mind if he's a cheater and a thief. We're *soul mates*. Therefore I should forgive anything, 'cause we're meant to be."

"Shit." I run a hand through my hair and glance at the television, not sure what to say to that. Immense relief washes over me as I realize the funeral scene has ended. The movie has progressed to a year later, and the main character has stopped grieving. She's out with her girlfriends for a Sunday brunch, drinking mimosas while her friends try to talk her into signing up for an Internet-dating site.

"Exactly," Lucy says. She places her phone on the table and it immediately starts vibrating again. This time she doesn't hesitate. With one quick glance, she declines the call and closes her eyes.

"Will he keep trying?" Because if he does, I'm going to have to go back to that bar and beat the shit out of her ex. Maybe break his dialing finger. That would be satisfying. Not only would he maybe get the message, but he'd also be unable to play that slick guitar of his for a few months.

"Probably." She gets up and heads for the kitchen. "Does your sister have any food? I'm feeling a little nauseated."

I'm surprised it's taken this long, considering she's had a variety of different kinds of booze. But she doesn't really even appear to be tipsy anymore. Maybe it's just her ex that's upsetting her. That and the mom talk. I jump up. "I'm sure we can find something."

Her phone buzzes again, but she doesn't even look back. I glare at it and contemplate throwing it against the wall. But then Lucy would likely take out all that barely suppressed anger on me. And right now, I want to be the one who comforts her. Panic trickles into my brain. *Careful, Seth. That sounds a lot like giving a shit.*

"Coming?" Lucy asks from the other room.

"Yeah," I choke out and follow her. Once in the kitchen, I pull open the fridge and scan the contents. "We've got leftover pizza, Chinese, an enchilada, or I can make pasta." I open the cupboard and gesture to a row of ramen noodles.

"Pasta?" She shakes her head, her eyes full of mock pity. "Top Ramen is not pasta. That stuff has its place, especially when we're talking hangovers, but don't try to dress it up. It is what it is."

Pleasure winds into that ache that never goes away. I freeze, staring at her with wonder, but thank God she's too busy pulling plates out of one of the glass-front cabinets to notice. Not one person in the past two years has been able to even come close to affecting me this deeply. I'm both awed by her and undeniably resentful. That place was reserved for E. Not this wounded singer who would likely get back together with her ex given enough time. Most people, once they meet their soul mates, never find happiness with another. She'll be no different. Someday that ass, Kinx, will come to his senses and she'll forgive him.

"How long has your sister been away?" Lucy asks as she spies the chicken fried rice. "Or do her eating habits mirror those of a man who wouldn't know a vegetable if it bit him in the ass?"

"My sister?" I ask before I can process what she's said. Oh, right. "About a week or so. But I've been here off and on." I grab the rice from her and point to a green onion. "There's a vegetable."

She leans over and eyes the onion. "How old is it?"

"A few days, I think."

"You think? Are you willing to risk the certain vomit if it's gone bad?"

"What are you talking about?" I make a show of sniffing the rice as I hold in laughter. I'd seen my parents have a version of this same conversation a dozen times before. "It's fine."

She purses her lips, then pulls out the other two containers of Chinese food. "All right, but if I lose it, you're holding my hair back."

Her dark glossy hair shimmers in the kitchen light, and I have to remind myself I don't have the right to run my hands through it. No matter how much I want to right now.

"Deal?" she asks, turning around.

"Deal." I lose the battle and brush a fallen lock of hair behind her ear. Her body jerks with a tiny shiver that elicits a response from deep inside me. The desire to lift her into my arms and carry her upstairs hits me hard in the gut.

Our eyes lock. I forget everything but the vulnerability shining back at me. Shit. What am I doing? This is not me. Not anymore. I don't do relationships. And this? The undeniable protectiveness I seem to feel for this girl feels entirely too much like something more than a one-night stand. I drop my hand and take a step back. "Go on back to the den. I'll heat this up and bring it in."

She narrows her eyes at me and gives me a look that makes me think she sees right through me.

I shift under the uncomfortable scrutiny of her gaze.

Then she blinks and turns back to the fridge. She grabs a Diet Coke, the one Lillian, my sister, left among the regular ones. "See you in a few," she says, heading back out of the kitchen.

Her hips sway and my eyes stay glued to her rising hemline. Christ. She's intentionally trying to kill me. Damn that skirt.

Five minutes later with two steaming plates of Chinese food, I rejoin her in the den. She's curled up on her end of the couch, fidgeting with her phone. It's buzzing, but she makes no move to answer it.

I set the plates of food on the table and gently pull the phone from her fingers. "Are you expecting an important call?"

She shakes her head, sadness haunting her expression. Anger vibrates through me. Cadan Kinx. He's the bastard who's responsible for the look in her striking eyes. It takes every last bit of strength to not stalk over to the bar and pound my fist into his pansy-ass face. Fucking dick.

I power her phone down. "If you're not going to answer, it's probably better to just turn it off. No need to torture yourself."

"But what about Jax? What if she needs us?" Her voice is small, as if she isn't sure of anything in this moment.

I pull my phone from my back pocket and tap out a text to Jax, letting her know if she needs Lucy to call me. "Is this okay?"

Lucy takes the phone from my outstretched hand. "She's going to think something's going on."

Neither of us says anything. There is something definitely going on, but would either of us act on it? "She's a big girl," I say. "Besides, she's either too drunk to care or she's already home asleep."

"True." Lucy leans back into the couch and closes her eyes. "I can't believe how tired I am all of a sudden."

I hit Send and sink into the couch, closer to her this time.

Her eyes fly open, clearly surprised I've invaded some of her personal space. If she isn't careful, I'm going to invade a whole lot more of it. Given half the chance, I'll do my best to get her mind off that douche mate of hers. At least for a few hours, anyway.

"Eat." I hand her a plate and take the other for myself.

She smiles, and though she isn't exactly the sassy, confident singer she'd been earlier in the night, the tension has drained from her face. Her muscles relax as if she's settling in for the night. She looks comfortable.

I try to ignore how content the scene makes me. It's temporary. She's only relaxing because she has a safe haven for the night. Tomorrow she'll be gone, and so will all the alcohol-induced feelings. Except I'm painfully aware I'm not all that drunk. And neither is she.

She picks up the remote and restarts the movie. She must have stopped and reset it because it starts up roughly where it was when we first left the room. We eat in silence as we watch the protagonist go on date after date, chronicling all her disasters on a blog. She has quite the following before Wes Chadwick calls her to do an interview for a national news outlet about dating after you've lost your soul mate.

I cringe and glance at Lucy, desperate to turn this shit off. Everyone knows it's next to impossible to find a love match after you've met your mate. This movie only serves to torture us into thinking there's a second chance at love. Right. No one can compare to E and everything she was, everything that we were. I take Lucy's discarded plate and my own. "I'll be right back."

She picks up the remote and glances at me, her eyes too bright. This movie is the worst pick ever. But she chose it. "Do you want me to pause it?"

"No," I say more sharply than I mean to. "It's fine." Once back in the kitchen, I take my time rinsing the plates and wiping down the counter, which isn't even dirty. After twenty minutes go by, I have no choice but to return to the movie from hell. I search the fridge for another Diet Coke for Lucy and finally find one in the very back. How long had that been there? Months probably. That case of regular Coke was left over from the surprise birthday party Lillian had tried to throw eight weeks ago. That had ended in a shouting match between us and we haven't spoken much since.

Damn her. Why hadn't she just listened to me when I'd said no celebration? I'd ended up in a cheap bar in Leggett and had woken up next to that girl Cami, who'd already mentally moved to Mendocino. At some point she'd managed to extract my number from my cell phone while I'd been asleep. In the end, I'd had to change my number just to get rid of her. In my mind, the fiasco was all Lillian's fault. I never would have left town if she'd just left everything well enough alone.

The house is really quiet as I move back to the den. There are no voices or background music filtering through the house. Has she paused the movie again? I tense. I cannot watch that crap any longer. I stride into the den, determined to stop the movie, but it's already off.

Lucy stands and holds out a hand to me.

I place the Diet Coke on the table. "That's for you."

"Thanks," she whispers and moves closer. Her fingers brush my arm and slide down to twine with my fingers. I want to pull away, but at the same time, I can't force myself to do it. Her touch is too soft, too comforting, too everything.

"What happened to the movie?" Why did I ask that? I don't give a shit about that movie. In fact, I'm going to smash the Blu-ray into little bits as soon as humanly possible.

She places her free hand on my cheek and trails her fingers across my jawline. "I don't think either of us was enjoying it."

I don't respond. I'm too busy trying to breathe. Her touch is light, tantalizing, and I want her more than I've wanted anything... anyone... in the past eighteen months. The emotional turmoil spilling through me, the guilt, the want, the need, it's all more than I can handle. I know I need to step away from this girl. Leave. Walk out of her life.

But then she rises up on her tiptoes. "Seth," she says and presses her lips to mine.

CHAPTER 7

Lucy

That damn movie. Why had I picked it again? Oh yeah. Wes Chadwick. However, not even Wes's startling eyes and gorgeous body are compelling enough to keep me watching. People lose their soul mates all the time. Whoever wrote this movie clearly had been trying to explore some wish fulfillment. It doesn't happen twice. Everyone knows that. The best you can hope for is some sort of contentment with a person you like well enough to hang out with on a regular basis.

But that all-encompassing love? You only get it once. Pretending it exists outside of the *one* is asking for disappointment.

I grab the remote and push buttons until the screen goes blank. There's no way I'm going to continue to subject Seth to such an awful movie. The despair written all over his face as he left with the plates is too much to bear. My heart breaks for him. Jax told me he'd lost his girlfriend in a horrific accident. He hadn't walked away like I did. Even though it was my choice, I'm still suffering. I don't know what's worse: feeling like half a person or losing myself completely in Cadan's bullshit.

The longer Seth's gone, the more I start to resent the movie for putting that look in his eyes. I'm oddly protective of this guy, and I don't know why. Maybe because he's been so kind to me. Maybe because he's Jax's friend. Or maybe it's because of the way he made me melt when he had his hands all over me.

When Seth finally returns, his jaw is set with barely contained tension. I stand and hold out a hand to him as he sets down a Diet Coke, then I move closer and lace my fingers with his.

He notices the television and turns curious eyes on me. "What happened to the movie?"

Seeing him standing there, filling the space so completely, yet appearing vulnerable and unsure of what to do next, propels me into action. I run my fingertips over his jaw and give a vague response about neither of us enjoying the flick.

At my touch, the uncertainty in his eyes vanishes, replaced by molten desire.

I rise up on my tiptoes. "Seth…"

Our lips meet and it's all heat and fire and raw passion. His hands slip into my hair and tighten, holding me to him in that incredibly sexy, gentle but possessive way.

God, I want him. More than I would've thought possible. He tastes salty and sweet, and I can't get enough. His faint, spicy, masculine scent wraps around me, entrancing me, inviting me closer. I press my chest against his and almost gasp at the rough caress of fabric against my hardened nipples. The halter-style dress wasn't exactly made for bra wearing, so I'd skipped it altogether.

"Lucy," Seth whispers between kisses, his voice rough, full of all the desire I crave.

"Hmm." I moan back as he nips at my neck.

One arm wraps around my waist and he tugs me closer, pressing his groin into me. He's already rock hard. The knowledge sends heat between my thighs. My fingers itch to free him from his jeans, to demand he take me right here and now. Instead, I curl my fists into his shirt and hold on as his mouth works its way from my neck to my exposed collarbone.

"You taste like vanilla frosting," he murmurs against me and tilts my head farther to the side for better access. "It's making me crazy."

"Thank God," I say, breathless.

He lifts his head, his eyes pinning me with their intensity, before he bends and presses his lips to the swell of my breast.

The shock of his hot tongue against my exposed cleavage sends me whirling. I shift my hips against his, trying desperately to get closer. I want to feel every inch of him as he works his tongue lower.

"So fucking beautiful," he murmurs and lifts his head. Holding my gaze, he glides his hands up over my arms to my shoulders and stops at the base of my neck, gently holding the tie of my halter. He watches me, silently asking for my permission.

I answer by slipping my hands under his black T-shirt. When my fingers touch the hard expanse of his warm chest, he sucks in a breath and slowly tugs. The tie comes undone easily. My halter slips down to my waist, exposing me to him. His eyes stay locked on mine for a truly tantalizing moment of self-torture. I bite my bottom lip and shift my gaze to my chest.

Look at me. Touch me, I mentally beg. If he doesn't, I'm going to combust where I stand.

As if he's heard my silent pleas, he gently cups my breasts, running his thumbs over my overly sensitive nipples. My breasts are instantly heavy with lust and craving. I tug his shirt over his head and slide my hands down, trailing them along the indent of his V-line between his waist and hips.

He shivers slightly. Oh, how I want to make him do that over and over again. Tattoos cover both arms and his right shoulder. I want to stop and study each one, but he doesn't give me the chance. He gently pinches my right nipple, and now I'm the one shivering. He kneads the tip until I gasp and then dips his head down, catching the left one between his teeth.

"Oh God." I moan, digging my fingers into his hips. Sparks of pleasure and pain ripple through me as he nibbles and scrapes his teeth over my taut peaks.

Before I know what I'm doing, my fingers are fumbling with the fly of his jeans.

One of his hands covers mine, stopping me. He lifts his mouth from my throbbing breast. "Not yet, babe. Soon, but not yet."

I twist my hand free from his and flatten it against his jeans, running my fingers over the length of his hardness. "I want to feel you. All of you."

His eyes narrow with barely controlled desire. It's the exact reaction I was hoping for.

"Lucy," he forces out through ragged breaths. "If you keep doing that, touching me that way, this is going to be over before we even start."

Before we start? What have we been doing for the last ten minutes?

"Let me worship this sexy body of yours for a while first." He moves my hand back to his hip as he turns us and presses me up against the wall once more. He gives me that devilish smile, then clamps his mouth back over my breast, and I let out a startled gasp of pure pleasure.

"Okay." My voice is almost a whisper as he sucks hard on my nipple and teases the other with his clever fingers.

I give myself over to him and wind my fingers through his thick, bronze hair, holding him to me, afraid that when he stops, I'll never be the same again. The things he's doing to me, the way my body burns for his touch, it's all new. I'd been with Cadan so many times, but it had been different. More of an emotional release after a concert that left us both wound tight. Good, sure. But not hot, needful, or full of this crazy desire to lose myself in someone.

And right now, I'm lost. Utterly and completely.

Nothing matters but the passion crashing over us. Seth is breathing hard when he finally releases my breast. So am I. His hot tongue marks a path back to my lips.

"I want you just like this." He places his hands on my ass once more and lifts me so my legs are wrapped around him, the same way we'd been in the kitchen. When he'd told me he'd been dreaming of me wrapped around him since I first walked away from him at the bar.

Excitement makes my blood pump faster. I want him to take me just like this. Against the wall in an uncontrollable frenzy.

I flatten myself to him, pressing my bare breasts into his chest, and rake my nails lightly along his back. "I'm ready," I say, pulling back slightly to hold his gaze. "Right here, right now."

His emerald eyes glow with green fire. He redoubles his efforts, kissing me thoroughly, and reaches for the zipper of my skirt. In one short motion it's free, and Seth is lifting me off him. My knees wobble slightly as he sets me carefully on my feet. My halter dress falls to the floor, leaving me in my black lace panties and thigh-high boots. I'm almost shaking I want him so badly.

But he's still got his jeans on. I reach for him again, but he sidesteps me and then kneels before me, his eyes level with my sex. "I want to see what's under these," he says, sliding his fingers into the waistband of my lace. Raising his gaze to mine, he slowly works them over my hips and down my thighs until they pool at my feet with the discarded dress. Carefully he lifts each foot, freeing me from my garments.

"Hey," I say softly, surprised I'm not more self-conscious. "You're wearing too many clothes."

He responds by running his hands the length of my boots to my bare thighs. The heat and need intensifies to a pulsing throb as he nears my center. I shift, spreading my feet farther apart to give him access, but his hands don't go any higher. Instead, he feathers kisses down my thigh, stopping at the top of my boot. With steady fingers, a sharp contrast to my own trembling ones, he lowers the zipper of my boot and continues his exploration of kisses down my inner leg and then back up again. He watches my eyes as he rezips the boot.

I raise one eyebrow in question.

"You're keeping these on," he says huskily and repeats the process on the other side.

My right hand is buried in his hair, the other pressed against the smooth wall. I stare out the picture window at the Pacific pounding relentlessly against the cliffs and let out a loud moan of ecstasy as his tongue finally enters me, pleasuring my sex at my most sensitive spot. His hands inch closer, spread wide over my thighs, his rough calluses teasing my tender flesh.

He laps and nips just as he had when he'd kissed my mouth, but this time I'm a live bolt of electricity, sparking all over, pushed to the edge by the bundle of nerves he's commanding. The pressure builds, driving me higher into an unfamiliar realm of sweet torture. My body begs for more, pressing into his mouth, taking everything he has to give.

He pulls back and a whimper escapes my lips as I tremble against the wall, waiting for him to finish what he started. "Seth," I breathe.

"Shatter for me," he whispers, and then his mouth is on me again, his tongue working its magic. I'm wound as tight as I can possibly be, just on the edge, when his fingers plunge into me. I cry out as a long shudder starts from my center and moves through me in waves, crashing hard and thunderous.

When I come back to myself, spent and languid with my release, Seth has his arms wrapped around my middle, his head tucked against my belly, holding on. Only his embrace keeps me standing on my shaky legs. I rest my hands lightly on his shoulders and close my eyes.

"That was…" I can't even come up with a word to describe the magnitude of what he'd made me feel.

"Mind-blowing," he supplies and gets to his feet.

"That will work." I smile at him weakly.

He brushes a damp lock of hair from my eyes and bends to kiss me. The salty taste of his mouth brings the sensations of my orgasm flooding back, and the familiar throb starts up again.

The hungry nature of his kiss enraptures me, fueling a fresh spark of desire. He places both hands on the wall on either side of my head and goes to work once again on my neck, keeping his body slightly away from mine so only his lips are touching me.

But my hands are eager. He's learned every inch of my body. It's my turn. I start by tracing my lips over his shoulder and run one finger down the crevice between his pecs. He stills mid-nibble, and I'm gratified to hear the slight catch of his breath. His muscles clench as he tries to hold himself back. He's beyond need, almost beyond control. I'm certain of it. With one touch, one word, I could have him inside me. Where I know he wants to be.

The knowledge that I hold this power gives me courage, and instead of opening to him, I grab his hips and twist, turning us both so he's now the one leaning against the wall.

His eyes glitter with anticipation. I take a small step back and watch his gaze track my hands as they move to the top of his jeans once more. He keeps his arms loose at his sides and doesn't stop me. Slowly, I undo the button and slip the zipper down, revealing black boxer briefs. His gaze doesn't waver from my touch as his muscles tighten with smoldering intensity. With his shirt long discarded and his jeans open, I can't help but run my hands over his chest, exploring the ridges of his toned muscles. He must work out, but not obsessively so. Just enough to keep himself in decent shape. I love it. He's so different from what I've known in the past. So alive. So incredibly male.

"Lucy?" he says.

I glance up, my hands poised to strip him of the rest of his clothes. "Yes?"

"In about three seconds, I'm going to be inside you."

I bite down hard on my lip, making him groan.

"Jesus. Stop that," he says.

I place one hand in the middle of his chest and push him back against the wall. "You'll give me at least three minutes. There are few things I'd like to see first." Two seconds later, I have him stripped of his jeans and briefs. He's so hard his erection is slightly curved. I take care to not touch him there, knowing that would be his undoing. But I do kneel before him, just as he had done with me, and run my hands over his muscular thighs. He's solid and hot, all male.

I can't help myself. I have to taste him. Have to feel him on the edge just as I had been. Wrapping my hand around the base of him, I lean in, running my tongue along his length. He shudders and his hand curls in my hair, tightening his hold, though not enough to hurt me. I smile and open my mouth, slipping my lips over him, taking him as deep as I can, pleased I don't gag when his tip hits the back of my throat.

"Oh fuck," Seth moans. "You have no idea what you're doing to me right now."

I have a clue, but I don't answer. Instead, I start a slow rhythm, backing off until my lips are wrapped around his tip and then taking him deep, over and over and over again, until his body is rigid from holding himself back.

"Lucy," he gasps. "I want you. I want you pressed up against this wall with me buried inside you when I come."

His blunt words stir the smoldering fire between my legs again, and with one last lingering kiss, I release him. Before I can process what he's doing, he grabs his wallet from his discarded jeans and hands me a foil wrapper.

With trembling fingers, I roll the condom onto him and then brace myself for what he's been promising me all night.

CHAPTER 8

Seth

Lucy's hands are on me, and I'm not sure I'm going to last long enough for her to get the condom rolled on. I should've taken care of it myself. But I couldn't resist the allure of her touch. Jesus, what her mouth could do. With any of the other girls I'd been with in the recent past, I would've just come, let her finish me off, and called it a night. But with Lucy, hell. With her, I want more. I want to own her in a way only a man that's been inside her can. If only for one night.

Her hands release me, and we stand together, frozen in the moment, savoring. At least I am. I doubt she'll give herself to me like this again. Not with her mate circling. But for tonight, she's mine. I pull her close and lean down, kissing her already-familiar mouth. When her tongue meets mine with that incredible intensity, I lift her up and brace her against the wall. Her booted legs wrap around me just as I'd imagined they would. And then I press into her heat, her tight flesh enveloping me. It's all I can do to hold myself back, to let her adjust to my intrusion when all I want to do is bury myself deeply inside her. To claim every inch of her.

She lets out a cry, and I still instantly, afraid I'm hurting her. But she begins to move against me, taking me deeper, moaning with each stroke. I'm overtaken with lust and passion, and finally, after hours of fantasizing about this moment, I take her as I will, thrusting into her, hard and fast, raising her need with each meeting of our flesh.

Her cries grow louder, and I'm all but out of my mind, consumed with something more than raw need. Something more than a night of physical pleasure. I don't know what it is, but I want it. I want her. The realization makes me slow our frantic pace. As I carefully pull out of her, she whimpers and clutches my shoulders in protest.

At the last moment, I slam into her again, filling her completely. We repeat the rhythm together, torturing ourselves, until, on the fourth thrust, she gasps and her muscles tighten around me. The spasms rip through her, and the rapture on her face as she throws her head back nearly makes me come undone. But I hold off, letting her recover for just a moment. Then I move again, making her all but whimper with each frenzied stroke until every muscle goes taut and I'm groaning into her ear as I shudder against her.

We're both breathing hard, sweat glistening on our bodies. She reaches up and places her palm flat on my cheek. Her blue eyes are heavy with satiation. "Seth?"

"Hmm," I murmur and clasp her thumb between my teeth.

"That was incredible."

I nod, not trusting myself to speak. If I say anything, she's going to see right through me. This is a hell of a lot more than a night of hot sex.

"Can you let me down now?"

"Sure," I say, and reluctantly help her to her feet. After disposing of the condom, I return to where she's sitting on the floor. She looks so small and fragile, almost naked except for those boots. I put a hand out, offering to help her up.

She takes it, and when she wobbles on her feet, I pick her up and carry her to the bathroom. The downstairs bathroom is a small one, but it has a shower just big enough for the both of us. I set her down on the vanity, and without speaking, I unzip her boots for the second time, only now I slip them off her feet. Her eyes are big and round as she watches me.

I smile up at her. "Don't want to ruin these."

She chuckles. "No. We don't."

Reaching over, I turn the taps on. Once the bathroom starts to fill with steam, I tug Lucy into the shower, and there, I explore her body again until we both cry out in ecstasy, only this time when we're finished, she smells of citrus-scented body gel.

Hoooonk, hoooonk, honk penetrates my consciousness, and I bolt out of bed. "Holy fuck." I grab my head with both hands, trying to block out the incessant noise. "Keep your pants on."

I glance down, noting my buck-naked state, and grab a discarded towel lying rumpled on the floor. That's when I notice the bed is empty.

Lucy.

Shit. Where is she? The honking finally stops, and I slide to the window just in time to see legs clad in thigh-high boots walking swiftly to the car. Jesus. She's running away just as she had last night when she wanted to get as far away from Kinx as possible. Had the night been that bad?

Dude. Get a hold of yourself. This is the perfect scenario. No awkward morning-after bullshit.

Lucy pauses and glances up at the window. Spotting me, her eyes go wide, then she bites her bottom lip. Desire stirs in my gut, but I do my best to keep my face blank. She's running out on me. No girl has ever tried to leave before I woke up before. Not that I ever bring them home. That's too personal. I wouldn't have last night if we'd had any other option. She frowns, and I don't know why, but I want to chase after her and—

Seriously, dude. Stop it.

Her hand comes up and she gives me a tiny wave. A second later, she's tucked in the car. I stare at the black SUV, focusing on the red taillights as they disappear into the morning fog.

Marty. Bastard. For some reason I hate him more than usual this morning. I slam my fist into the wall, splitting my knuckle in the process. Fuck. That guy is the biggest douche on the planet, and the fact Lucy left with him has me aching to punch the wall again.

Instead, I turn and head for the shower. Not the one Lucy and I shared last night, but the master bath in the room at the end of the hall. I never go in there. Do my best to avoid it at all costs. Even though I'd painted the room white, blocking out the bold sun yellow and tangerine that had once graced the walls, E was still everywhere. The wrought-iron bed she'd picked out, the unmatched nightstands she'd hand painted with wildflowers, the goddamned red velvet pillow I hadn't been able to toss.

I ignore it all, shutting down the part of me that is hers— that will always be hers—and slip into the bathroom. It's easier in here. Whiteness gleams from every surface. It had been our compromise. Whatever colors she'd wanted in the bedroom were fine as long as I had a reprieve of white in the bathroom. Before it had felt clean, sleek. Now it's impersonal. It doesn't stop the memories from trying to slip back in, however.

E using those 1950s hot curlers she'd found at a garage sale. Her Corvette-red lipstick. The two drawers of cosmetics I'd never once seen her use but she insisted on keeping anyway. The sleepy-eyed look she'd give me after we'd been up all night working.

Pain lances through me. It's her contented expression after the all-nighters we'd spent in the studio that I miss the most. The door slams shut on the memory, and I try to think of Lucy, but my pulse quickens and sweat prickles the back of my neck.

The terrible memories of that night come flooding back, and my mind turns hazy as gut-wrenching bursts of metal grinding against metal echoes in my mind. A scream is cut off at impact, and then there's darkness, punctuated by flashes of light. And all I can focus on is the blood. It's everywhere. I can't stop it.

I let out a scream of desperate rage, throw on some clothes, and bolt for the door. Once outside, I take deep breaths of the salted air. In. Out. In. Out. With no memory of heading toward the ocean, I'm at the cliff, crouched down, my elbows resting on my knees. My eyes are open, but I don't see the water crashing over the rocks or the hazy line of the horizon. I see E, her infectious smile, her impossibly curly golden hair, and paint. Lots of paint.

Slowly, I stand, my legs stiff from the cold wind. Then I turn and walk the two miles to my parents' house.

I'm standing on the front stoop, bracing myself for the inevitable questions, when the door pops open.

"Seth!" Mom says too brightly and pulls me inside.

"Mom." Suspicion rings in my tone, but she just smiles up at me, entirely too happy. After staying out all night without calling, I expect at least an hour-long lecture on common courtesy. I'm a grown man with my own house, but ever since I lost E, I've been crashing at my parents' to escape the memories. Since the accident, Mom worries a lot more than she used to. The phone call was her only request. And I'd forgotten. Again.

"Come in here. We've been waiting."

We?

I'd already seen Dad disappear into one of the greenhouses out back. My parents are organic farmers. Two of the best. Together they can grow just about anything. And they do, even when no one else can due to weather conditions. It's their talent. Growing plants.

There's a cinnamon-scented candle burning, and there's a fire in the fireplace.

Shit. These are not the signs of a woman intent on working in her greenhouses all day. No. She has company.

"Honey." Mom tugs me into the kitchen and waves at a middle-aged woman dressed in a bright red dress with lipstick to match. "You remember Francie, don't you?"

I don't, but I nod anyway because I know she expects me to.

"Your father's Navy buddy Don. She's his wife. They visited about three years ago."

A vague recollection of a family dinner comes to mind. "Sure. Hello, Francie. Nice to see you again." I hold out my hand.

She takes it, pumping with surprising strength. The woman isn't an inch over five feet two and can't weigh more than a hundred pounds.

"Oh, my dear. You just get more handsome every year. I bet the girls are lined up a mile long trying to fill your dance card." She gives me an exaggerated wink.

"Uh, maybe not a mile long." Extracting my hand from hers, I give her a tight smile. "Welcome back to Mendocino." I turn to Mom. "I'll be in the kitchen."

Before I can make my escape, she slips her arm through mine, holding me in place. "Francie is actually here to see you."

I stand still and really take a look at the older woman. She's been smiling since I got here, but for the first time, I notice the edge of pain buried behind her facade. I know, because it's the same one I've been wearing for the past eighteen months. Empathy courses through me, and I take her hand once more, leading her to my mother's green-and-white pinstriped couch. "What is it I can do for you, Miss Francie?" I ask gently.

Her big green eyes mist with unshed tears and her hand starts to shake. Unease takes up residence in my chest. I know from experience what's coming, and I shoot Mom a sharp look of admonishment.

"I'm terribly sorry to ask," Francie says, her voice barely audible. She clears her throat, and when she speaks, she's stronger. More sure. "Grace says you're taking a break from your portraits in order to pursue other art interests, but I don't have anyone else I can ask."

"I have friends I can recommend—"

"No," she says firmly. "Thank you, but please just hear me out."

Mom frowns at me. Short of getting up and stalking out, there isn't much else I can do. I nod.

She nods back. "You may know that my Don is starting cancer treatments soon."

I nod again. Seems Dad mentioned something about it.

"Well, I'd really like to get a portrait done of us now, before the treatments progress. Before his body starts changing. I need someone who can see the real us. To really bring us to life." Her voice cracks on the word life. "It might be the last… Well, it's just that now is the time."

A lump of emotion clogs my throat. After the memories that haunted me this morning, this request is too much. I work my throat and force out, "Miss Francie, I wish I could help, but—"

"Oh, dear." She squeezes my hand. "I can see this is hard for you. After Elsa—"

I wince at the use of E's actual name. I don't use it anymore, and everyone around me knows not to.

"I'm sorry," the older woman says. She looks so dejected I don't even know what to say.

Mom scoots forward in the chair she's perched on. "Seth, honey, can you at least think about it?"

I avert my gaze. "I don't think it's a good idea."

"But you have to start painting again at some point."

I jump to my feet, anger boiling up from deep inside me. "Mother," I say in a careful voice. "We've been over this. E is dead. My paintings will never be the same. Without her, the thing that makes them special and unique is gone. Buried with her. You can't know what it's like. Dad is still here, but just try for a moment to think about how you'd feel about growing your plants if he wasn't around to share it with you." My fists are clenched and by the time I'm done, my head aches. If she doesn't stop pushing, I'm going to have to move. Where, I don't know. I can't bring myself to give up my house, and at the same time, I can't bring myself to live there. Hence the reason I mostly live at my parents' place instead of my own.

"Honey," Mom says.

"No, Mom," I snap and turn to Miss Francie. Softening my tone, I say, "I'm sorry, but I can't do this. If you need a recommendation, I have a friend who can probably help you out."

Francie stares at me, her eyes wide and her mouth open in shock.

I can't stay here. Not with this guilt eating away at me. Without another word, I stalk through the house and back out to the street. I'm four hours early, but with nowhere else to go, I head to the edge of town to the only place I ever find refuge. The tattoo shop.

CHAPTER 9

Lucy

I have the key in the lock when I hear the phone ringing inside. Rolling my eyes, I slip into Dad's house… Well, my house now. It's been six months since I lost him and it still feels like it isn't real. He's everywhere here, from the built-in bookshelves lining the living room, to the collection of underwater photography hanging on the wall.

Dad's old answering machine—the one he'd refused to change out for a service—clicks on. His warm voice fills the room. "You've reached the Moores. Lucy and Mack can't come to the phone. Leave us a message."

Tears burn the backs of my eyes and the hollow feeling in my chest intensifies. It's always the same, yet I can't bring myself to change the greeting. I can't erase Dad's voice. It's the same message we've had ever since Mom moved out eight years ago. Dad hadn't even changed it when he'd taken a temporary job out of the country and I'd been forced to move in with Mom and her husband during my last few years of high school.

"Lucy!" Mom shrills into the phone. "Where are you? Are you there? Pick up."

I stare at the blinking light on the machine. How many times has she called since last night?

"Lucile, this is not a game." Her tone is lower, more controlled. Her pissed voice. "Cadan came all the way from Denver to see you last night, and you ran out on him. How long are you going to keep this up? He's not going to wait for you forever, you know. You're messing up your life."

My heart starts to hammer and something breaks inside me. I'm used to her rants. Mom is forever telling me how to live my life. Mostly I've learned to block her out, but this morning, with my emotions all over the place, I can't take it. I can't take her. Blood rushes to my head and I feel like it's going to explode. Before I can stop myself, the phone's in my hand and the words fly. "He won't wait forever? He didn't wait at all, Mother. Jesus fucking Christ. I caught him having sex with two other girls. I wasn't even out of the picture before he started sticking his dick in other people."

"Lucile," Mom scolds. "Don't you dare talk to your mother that way."

I snort into the phone. There it is. The *mom* card. She pulls that one out on a regular basis in an effort to guilt me into her way of thinking. When is the last time she ever gave a shit about what *I* want? "Really? That's all you have to say? Have you even once considered what it must be like for me? To have my soul mate cheat on me? And having to choose between my sanity and my career?"

"Now, honey. I know he made a mistake. But he's sorry. It's hard finding your partner when you're just nineteen. You both have some growing to do. If you do it together, it will mean more later."

"A mistake? That's what you're calling it?" She has lost her mind. I can't believe I'm hearing this from her. And yet, at the same time, it shouldn't surprise me. She has always defended her life choices with the idea that no one should live without their soul mate. "Has Randy made a *mistake*? Did you forgive him?"

Mom doesn't say anything for a minute, and I wonder if I've hit a nerve.

"I'll call you later after you've had a chance to think about the things you've said to me. And if you have any sense, you'll call Cadan. You're not only throwing away the one person who'll love you forever, but there's also a lot of money on the line. You're going to mess up your life if you walk away from him and your record deal."

I clutch the phone until it creaks under my grip. "The *one person* who'll love me forever? Where does that leave *you*, Mom?" Before she has a chance to answer, I gently place the phone back on the receiver. Totally numb, I climb the stairs and head for the shower.

Squeezing my eyes shut, I step under the stream of water. As the spray sluices over me, flashbacks of the night before start to fill my mind. Jeez! What had I done? Had hot sex with an incredibly sexy, gorgeous guy I didn't even know. That's what I'd done. And it had been glorious and exactly what I'd needed to get Cadan out of my mind. Then I'd run out without so much as a good-bye. I figured he'd prefer it that way. But that was before I realized he was watching me from the second-story window.

I'd woken up with the sunrise, an annoying habit I'd developed ever since I'd gotten back home. It's because I like to sleep with the window cracked so I can hear the ocean. If I keep the blinds down, the wind makes them slam against the casings, keeping me awake. Since the house is on the side of a hill facing the ocean, there isn't a pressing need for privacy, but the sun does make it difficult to sleep in.

Once I find my phone and turn it on, I see eight texts from Jax and a dozen from Cadan. The last two were a confirmation from them both that Cadan left town. He's pissed. But who cares? I don't want to see him, and I'm not the cheater.

Though spending the night with Seth *does* make me feel slightly guilty. I hadn't really believed I'd ever be with anyone else. Not even after I'd caught Cadan with the two skanks who'd already worked their way through the rest of the band members.

Angry all over again, I turn the water to scalding. Just thinking about Cadan with them makes my stomach turn. Thirty minutes later, my skin red and tender, I pad into my room and pull on yoga pants, an oversized sweater, and slippers. It's my intention to stay in all day by the fire.

Back downstairs, I rustle around in the kitchen, putting together an omelet. Eggs, tomatoes, goat cheese, and avocado. Perfect. I'm about to crack one of the eggs when the house phone starts ringing again. I let out a long-suffering sigh. Only two people call me on that phone these days, and I want nothing to do with either of them right now.

When the machine beeps, Mom says, "You should probably think about changing the message on the machine, Luce. It's not healthy."

My fist clenches around the egg and... *crack*. The gooey mess drips down my hand.

"But that's not why I called," Mom continues. "Pick up the phone."

I glare at it.

"Lucy, you're being a child. I said pick up the phone."

Not even if Ed McMahon himself were on the other end.

"Fine. Don't talk to me." She's angry now, but when she speaks again, her voice cracks. "What if something happens to me, too? You're going to be all alone. Then what will you do?" The machine beeps, indicating she's hung up.

"Goddammit!" I cry, slamming my hand down on the counter. I accidently hit the bowl and it crashes to the floor, shattering ceramic shards over the tile. The destruction is oddly satisfying. Mom is the queen of guilt and has a way of making everything about her. This latest round about Dad's message is because the sound of his voice makes *her* uncomfortable. She tells me how weird it is every time she gets a chance. I think it's because she still has guilt for leaving him. Not because he's gone.

I creep through the kitchen to the hall closet and pull out a broom. But all I want to do is keep smashing things. I suck in a deep breath. Letting her get to me isn't helping. The walls go up around my emotions as I methodically clean the kitchen floor. When I'm done, I take a seat at the kitchen bar. The layout is such that I'm facing a wall of windows, and the view is stunning. Dad's house is at the top of a cliff overlooking the ocean. Fixated on the rhythmic pounding of waves, I press the Play button on the answering machine.

"Lucy," Mom says.

I hit the Delete button, cutting her off. The machine beeps.

"Lucile—"

Delete.

The next four messages are Mom. As with the first two, I delete before I hear what she has to say. Mom has a habit of calling over and over until I pick up. Considering I was gone for sixteen hours, it's amazing there are only six.

The seventh, however, is Cadan. I haven't spoken to him since the day I walked out on him three months and eighteen days ago. He's certainly tried to get in touch with me, but I changed my number after dodging his calls for two weeks straight.

"Hey, Luce," his tone is quiet, gentle. "It feels like forever since I've heard your voice."

My finger is hovering over the Delete button, but I can't do it. After all these months, I suddenly have to know what he has to say. How could he possibly justify what he did?

"Damn." He sighs. "I miss you."

Tears fill my eyes. It's the first time I've cried over him since I found out about his cheating. I wipe angrily at my eyes and sniff.

"I fucked up. I know that. You have no idea how much I regret my bad choices. Nothing is the same without you."

Of course it isn't. When we sing together, our voices have an effect on people. We touch them deeply, make them feel things in ways they never have before. It's like magic. Apart, we're just two people who can carry a note or two. Our fans have to be disappointed. And even though my heart wants to believe what he says, my head says it's more likely he's only calling because it's affecting both of our careers.

"I know you're not going to like it, but I talked to your mom. Please, Luce, don't be upset about that. I had to get your new number. I have to talk to you."

There's a pause and then he adds, "I'm in California. I took a break from the tour. I can't keep singing without you." There's a click and one final beep.

The tears are flowing freely now, but I do nothing to stop them. The anger I'd been surviving on is gone. Only sadness remains. Pain for what was and won't be again. Cadan had been my best friend, my lover, my partner. Now he's just a cheater and a thief. It's not something I'm going to get over. I'll never trust him again. He trampled all over everything that was important to me.

My cell phone, sitting on the bar, buzzes. I'm almost afraid to look. A message from Cadan will be too much. Another message comes through and I can't help but look.

Jax.

I snatch the phone, desperate to focus on something else.

The string of messages starts with *dude*.

I'm dying.

Help.

Worst. Hangover. Ever.

I chuckle and thank God I stopped drinking before I got drunk enough to suffer her fate. My cheeks heat as I recall what I did instead. I'm both embarrassed and impressed with myself. Jax has been saying I need to get out more. Though I doubt she meant get naked with the first hot guy who showed interest. Crap. She's going to kill me when she finds out. She's told me three times not to get involved with Seth. She's worried about being caught in the middle. But she has nothing to worry about. I already know he's a one-nighter. And I'd made it easy on him.

Bring chai and sweet-potato fries.

Jax's preferred hangover remedy. I text back, *Be there in forty-five minutes.*

Thirty.

Oh boy. She's in bad shape. I run up the stairs, stuff my feet in my running shoes, and fly out the door.

CHAPTER 10

Seth

I can't stop thinking about Miss Francie. The character and the history in her face calls to me, makes my fingers itch to sketch her. And what must Don look like these days? No doubt he's equally as fascinating. I bend over the piece of flash I'm working on and shade in the eyes of a silver wolf.

"Yo, Keenan, what happened after you and Lucy left last night?" Mike calls from the station two booths over. His tattoo gun buzzes under his administration.

I glance up, catching the eye of Sadie Sanders, the girl he's working on. She's a regular. Her arm is half-covered in sunflowers. Mike's been building a garden sleeve on her right arm one bloom at a time.

Her lips turn up in a slow, seductive smile. "Hey, Seth. How about that drink tonight?"

Biting back a grimace, I shake my head, trying for apologetic. "Sorry, Sadie. I've already got plans."

The light in her eyes dims a little. She's asked me out four times now. I've declined each invitation. "Maybe next time."

"Yeah, sure," I lie. Was it so hard for her to take a hint? I don't date locals. Especially ones who were friends with E.

"Well?" Mike presses. "I saw the light on at your house."

He says the last part as a statement, but it's really a question. The house I'd claimed to be my sister's is mine. She stays there when she's in town, but that's rare these days. Most of her time is spent in San Francisco now that she's met her soul mate. She comes home to work on the books for the family business a couple of times a month, but that's it.

"I didn't think she'd appreciate being subjected to Grace and Leo. Besides, Marty was supposed to pick her up."

Mike raises one eyebrow at the mention of my parents. He knows I usually stay in the garage apartment. They never would've known. "Did he?"

"Yeah." I glance away and mumble, "Eventually." I don't need the whole world to know she spent the night. And she doesn't either.

"Oh, did you hear her sing last night?" Sadie gushes. "And then Cadan was there. Omigod, he's hot. I'm so disappointed they didn't sing together. I wonder what happened between them."

Everyone—Mike, Sadie, and John, another artist—turns to stare at me as if I'm supposed to supply the answer. I raise my hands and shrug. "Don't look at me. How am I supposed to know?"

Mike gives me a flat stare. "Maybe because I heard through the grapevine that Marty didn't pick her up until this morning."

"Nice." John gives me a nod of approval. "How was she? If her performance was any indication, I'm fucking jealous, dude. What she could do with that mic…"

"Jesus. Shut the fuck up already." I get up. "I'm going next door. I'll be back after you two find someone else to harass."

They both crack up as they high-five each other. Sadie frowns in my direction, clearly unhappy to be witness to this conversation. I pull on my old, weathered leather jacket and get the hell out of there before they start needling me for details.

Two doors down is a local coffee shop. It's Saturday, so the place is bustling with locals and a few brave tourists up from the Bay Area doing some Christmas shopping in our small artists' town.

I get in line behind an older lesbian couple having a heated debate about what to get Patsy. The taller one insists on a week-end getaway for two at a spa in Calistoga. But her partner shakes her head. "No. I'm telling you, the last time Joan soaked in a mud bath, she came away with a nasty infection on her inner thigh. It took weeks for that thing to heal. She was a total bitch the entire time. Turns out Patsy wouldn't sleep with her until it healed. For the love of God, I have to share an office with Joan. For my sanity, do not send her back to a spa."

"Dammit. Now what?" the taller one asks. "I'm totally out of ideas for her."

"Excuse me."

I freeze and then blood rushes through my veins as my pulse quickens. Lucy. She's two people ahead of them in line, but lets the person behind her order first.

"Have you considered the Times Two music retreat in Calistoga instead? One of the private wineries is hosting the event once a month, and I heard they're booking some really great bands. They have packages from a basic stay to a four-star experience."

The women in front of me start asking questions and scribbling down the information. I'm transfixed, watching her as she smiles easily at them, enjoying the conversation. She looks nothing like the sex kitten she'd been the night before. Now she's wearing black pants and an oversized sweater that hides her curves. Her hair is pulled back with a thin headband, and her face is fresh, rosy from the winter chill. She's fucking beautiful. And I can't stop staring.

It's her turn to order, and she still hasn't noticed me. She's sweet and considerate to the barista behind the counter, even when he forgets to give her back her change.

"Don't worry about it," she says when he rectifies his mistake. Stuffing two dollar bills in the tip jar, she smiles. "I've been there. Thanks for the help."

The clerk gives her a look of gratitude, then his gaze turns to one of admiration as he watches her walk to the other end of the counter to wait for her order. An unexpected jolt of irritation hits me. I narrow my eyes, taking in his lip ring and the amateur tattoos covering his left hand. He's got the same build as her rocker soul mate. I have no trouble seeing him onstage with her, pretending he has some sort of talent with an electric guitar.

"She's adorable, isn't she?" one of the ladies in front of me says to the guy.

"Gorgeous is more like it. What can I get for you lovely ladies this fine December afternoon?" He winks, charming them with his over-the-top delivery.

I roll my eyes and fix my attention on Lucy once again.

She's staring right at me, her face now turning from a rosy blush to scarlet. I can't help the cocky grin I know is spreading over my face. I like that I do this to her.

"Hey, long time, no see," I call.

She averts her eyes for a moment and then raises her hand in greeting.

Oh, hell yeah. I'm going to enjoy this.

I order a plain black coffee in lieu of my regular double-shot latte just so I'm not stuck waiting for it. With cup in hand, I make my way to the bar filled with creamer carafes and proceed to doctor my drink. I strategically take my time and hurriedly put the lid back on when a different barista passes her a cup carrier with four drinks.

"Need a hand?" I ask when she fills the space beside me.

She glances up, surprise in her pretty blue eyes. "Sure. Half-and-half in these two." Waving at the two cups closest to me, she grabs a couple of packets of raw sugar with her other hand.

Neither of us says anything as we stir the drinks. When the lids are replaced, I fall into step beside her and hold the door open.

"Thanks," she says almost shyly.

"No problem." We stand outside the shop and stare at each other as the wind picks up.

After a moment, she visibly shivers. Of course she does; she's only wearing a sweater. No coat. "I better go. Jax is waiting."

"Hangover?" I ask.

"The worst."

"Right. Sweet-potato fries?" I've taken care of Jax at least a half dozen times since the big breakup. It's always the same. Chai and sweet-potato fries.

"I'm headed to get them now," she says.

I shake my head. "Baxter's is closed this weekend. There was some sort of emergency with Jilly's dad. The whole family went."

"Oh no." She bites her lip and noticeably steels herself.

I can't help but wonder what that's all about. Was she good friends with the Baxters? Seems unlikely, otherwise she would've already known. Everyone else did. Including Jax, who probably forgot in her misery.

"Don't worry. I've got a backup plan."

Her teeth are chattering now. I can't stand to see her so cold, so I drape an arm around her shoulder and pull her in close, sharing whatever warmth I can. She's stiff and hesitant at first, but then relents and leans in, her body fitting perfectly against mine. I rub her arm and guide her toward my truck.

She glances over her shoulder. "I'm parked over there."

"I'll drive. Is there anything you need from your car?"

Her steps slow as she worries her bottom lip, but then she shakes her head. "No. I'm good."

"Okay then." A ball of tension in my gut dissipates. Jesus. What is it with this girl? The way she makes me feel by doing absolutely nothing is almost terrifying. Terrifying and miraculous at the same time. Holding the door open for her, I wait for her to climb in before making my way to the driver's side. By the time I'm buckled in, she's already got the fleece throw I keep in the truck tucked over her legs.

"I hope to God this blanket isn't left over from your last one-night stand. But even if it is, I can't make myself part with it. I'm frozen."

My mouth falls open at her casual use of *last one-night stand.* Damn, is that how she sees me? I guess it would be. I laugh to cover the stab of regret. "Don't worry. It's been cleaned since then." Shit! Why did I say that?

She plucks at the fabric gingerly and then closes her eyes. "Thank goodness for small favors."

"I'm joking," I say. "The blanket is new. The heater broke a few weeks ago. The blanket was for Jax before I got it fixed."

"Oh." Her eyes pop open. Is that relief I see on her face? Relief for what? That she's not wrapped up in a skanky blanket, or that I hadn't confessed to participating in nefarious sexual behavior? "That was nice of you."

"It's just a blanket."

She turns to look at me, her eyes searing me with that intense gaze.

"What?"

"It's not. Just a blanket I mean."

The light ahead turns red and I slow to a stop. Lucy smiles at me now, a secret smile, as if she knows something no one else does.

"What are you talking about?" I ask.

She shrugs. "You take care of her. Jax. Blankets. Sweet-potato fries. Not letting her dwell on Brad." Her smile fades and her expression turns serious. "I'm glad you're there for her when I'm not."

I frown. "She's a friend. It's what friends do."

"It's what rare friends do." Grimacing, she turns and stares out the window.

The light turns green, and I step on the gas. The sadness streaming off her makes me want to stop the car and pull her into my arms, but I don't. Something tells me that's the last thing she wants right now. She's blaming herself for not being available for Jax. A few minutes later, I pull to a stop in front of my parents' house. With a twist of the keys, the engine goes silent. We both sit in the cab, not moving, not speaking.

When the silence becomes deafening, she turns to me. "Jax is waiting."

I meet her questioning eyes. "We'll be there soon. Want to talk about it?"

"About Jax?"

"No. About whatever it is that makes you think you're a bad friend."

CHAPTER 11

Lucy

Seth isn't just looking at me, he's seeing through me. Through everything on the surface. Past the stage-performer persona. And he's witnessing that part of myself I keep buried. The knowledge of that makes me want to get as far away from him as possible. It also makes me want to cry and bury myself in his arms.

Since my dad died, I haven't had anyone in my life who could really understand this part of me. The little girl who knows she isn't good enough. Not good enough for Mom to stay. Not smart enough to recognize the changes in Dad when he first got sick and didn't tell me. Not strong enough to leave my boyfriend the first time he betrayed me. And too self-involved to be there for my best friend when she lost the one person she loved most.

Intellectually, I know none of this is really my fault. But inside, down deep, I can't stop the darkness from taking over. The knowledge that I've failed is always there.

"No." I cringe, realizing I'd just validated his statement as fact. "I mean, I don't think that. I'm just glad Jax has someone she can count on."

His hands clutch the steering wheel. I can tell he wants to say something more, but he's fighting with himself about it.

"Everything's fine." I pop the door open, wishing I'd remembered to get my coat from my car. "What are we doing here?"

"Sweet potatoes," he says and exits the cab. He comes around the truck to stand next to me. "I'll make the fries at Jax's house."

The tension caused by his unexpected question eases and a small smile creeps its way back onto my face. "You're too much."

"Come on. Dad's likely in the greenhouse." He holds his hand out to me.

I hesitate. We hardly know each other, and in the light of day, hand-holding seems almost more intimate than the acts we engaged in the night before. The gesture is sweet, and I feel stupid for my reaction. But I'm not looking for a boyfriend. And I'm surprised he hasn't run already. Jax said he's definitely a love-'em and leave-'em kind of guy. It would've been so much easier if I'd chosen my big one-night stand to be someone from out of town.

He raises an eyebrow and nods to his hand as if he's issuing a challenge.

Suck it up, Moore. He doesn't bite. Well, maybe he does a little, but in the best possible way. I glance away, praying he can't read the thoughts on my face.

Our hands clasp, and he tugs me out of the truck and up the front walk. I feel small and feminine beside him. He's not much taller than Cadan, so I'm not sure what the difference is. Perhaps it's the sense that I'm being cared for.

The way he's caring for Jax. Right.

This is about last night. He's just being a friend. A really good one. The kind of friend who comes with history and shared heartache. Jax had told me about the accident, about how he lost his mate. His tragedy is gut-wrenching, losing his girlfriend like that, but loss is loss and Dad hasn't been gone all that long. I'm sure Jax told him all about that too.

Dad was my hero. He was the person I leaned on, the one who was the anchor in my life. Without him, there's a void and an ache inside me that doesn't seem to go away. Ever. I can't imagine what that's like for Seth, but it makes me want to put a smile on his face even for just a brief moment. Maybe he feels the same.

"If we hurry, we might get out of here before Grace finds us," he says.

"Grace?"

"My mother. Leo will be cool, but Grace? She'll fall all over herself when she finds out I brought a girl home."

It's my turn to raise an eyebrow. "I take it that's a rare occurrence?"

"More like a nonoccurrence. I don't date." He says it with finality. Clearly it's not open for discussion.

"Ever?" I press.

"Not anymore." He stops suddenly and looks down at me. "You didn't think we were... I mean, you left this morning without even—"

I hold my hand up. "Whoa, cowboy. I'm not expecting anything. As far as I'm concerned, we're just friends. I'm not the kind of girl who uses sex to find a boyfriend. Not that I want one. I know you're well aware of my current situation. It's enough to deal with the mundane details of life without adding any complications to the mix."

The panic drains from his face, but he's looking at me with an odd expression. I can't quite place it. Uncertainty? Concern? Regret?

"Don't worry about it. We're good," I say. "Now, where are these magical, hangover-curing sweet potatoes?"

"I don't know about hangover-curing, but magical is true enough. My parents' gift is in farming."

I feel my eyes go wide. The result of two mates' hard work is always something special. "Oh, really. Do I get a tour?"

He laughs. "Just a quick one. Remember what I said about Grace. Not to mention Jax is waiting."

I salute him and quicken my pace. "Yes, sir. Show me the goods."

That mischievous sparkle is back in his eyes. "I think you saw quite a bit last night."

"Shut up." I giggle and then clamp my hand over my mouth.

He laughs. "I hope it was worth it."

"Oh, you have no idea," I blurt out before I can stop myself.

He stops and eyes me up and down, his laughter gone, replaced by that hauntingly seductive smile. "I think I can imagine."

Something flutters in my stomach and an echo of our shared desire overtakes me. I lick my lips, suddenly desperate for a kiss.

His eyes shift to my mouth, and I know he's seconds from fulfilling the promise our bodies are making to each other.

I step back and pull my hand from his. "Friends?"

He lets out a slow breath and nods. "Friends."

Our eyes meet and hold. We're lying to each other, to ourselves. But neither of us is willing to admit it.

He waves his hand. "The greenhouse is waiting."

I pull the sleeves of my sweater over my hands and huddle into myself.

"Don't worry. It's warm in there," he says, noticing how cold I am. Though this time he doesn't try to wrap his arm around me.

We bypass the barn-style storefront and head for the back of the property. Three large white greenhouses gleam in the sun that's trying to peek through the clouds. The place smells of salt and earth, that damp soil scent of a dense forest.

"It's wonderful here," I say.

"You haven't seen anything yet," he quips, smiling proudly. "Their skills are impressive."

I believe him, but when we step into the first building, I stand still, awed by the rows and rows of lush greenery and the vibrant vegetables clinging to their vines. "Holy crap."

"Wait until you try some." He leads me up and down the rows until my phone starts to buzz.

"Oops. Jax." I hold the text up to him. "She's lost her patience."

He grabs the phone and texts something back to her. It buzzes twice more. One more message and then he hands it back to me. "Tour's over. The princess is dying."

I laugh and check the phone. "Seth!" He'd sent her lewd messages without telling her they were from him. Now my phone is going off like crazy with WTF messages from her wanting to know what's going on with me. I tap out a quick explanation and give him a dirty look.

Laughing, he grabs my hand again and tows me to the front, where he fills a brown paper bag with sweet potatoes, red and yellow peppers, strawberries, blueberries, and a bunch of other produce that is otherwise impossible to find at this time of year.

I miss out on meeting either of his parents as we run back to the truck and speed off down Highway 1 toward Jax's house.

Along the way, Seth hands one of the bags to me. "Try these."

Inside is a basket of blueberries. It's December, and blueberries are a summer fruit. I'm skeptical.

"Trust me," he says in a low, seductive tone.

There's that challenge again, and so help me, I can't resist when he does that. Not that eating a blueberry is a big deal. It's the current sparking between us that has me squirming in my seat. Just friends. Uh-huh. He's glancing between me and the road, so I take my time inspecting the fruit, then I flick my tongue out, delicately taking in the blueberry.

The truck swerves just a little.

"Whoa," I say, the blueberry tucked against my cheek. "Everything okay?"

He clears his throat. "Yeah, fine. Just a piece of debris in the road."

"Right." I chuckle. I was watching him watch me when the truck started to drift, but I let it go and bite down on the blueberry. Sweet, tangy juice fills my mouth, and I moan with pleasure. "Omigod."

Seth flashes me a self-satisfied smile.

I grab a few more and close my eyes as the juices explode in my mouth. When I open them, we've stopped in front of Jax's house and Seth's eyes are hooded as he watches me.

I can almost see the fantasy running through his head. "Stop that."

"What?" His voice is husky, the same way it had been the night before.

I smirk. "Undressing me in your mind."

My words only serve to put more heat in his eyes.

He's wearing down that friend label awfully fast. I lean in and press my hand to his chest. His heart thrums steadily beneath my palm.

"If you keep this up, we're never going to make it inside."

His hand covers mine, and the gentleness of it takes my breath away. His gaze shifts from my mouth to my eyes. "There's no denying the attraction here."

I nod, not knowing what else to do with that. It's the truth.

"And I'm not going to lie to myself about wanting you."

My breath gets caught in my throat as my pulse quickens.

"Hell, I woke up this morning wanting you, but you'd already gone. The thing is, Lucy, I already told you I'm not the relationship type. If we pursue this, we need to come to an understanding."

I pull away, not exactly sure how I feel about this situation. "Friends with benefits. Is that what you're after?"

"Honestly, I don't know. I just met you last night. Less than twenty-four hours ago. All I know is there's a huge attraction here. We can explore it or not. It's your choice."

"Well… that's quite the proposition," I say with a fair amount of sarcasm. "So much for seduction."

He gives me that sexy half smile again. "If it's seduction you want, I've got plenty in reserve."

My insides melt. Yes. If *I'm* being honest, it is seduction I want. But I'm not ready to say so. Instead, I grab the coffee cups resting at my feet, open the door, and glance back. "I already told you I'm not looking for a relationship. But if you want a friendship that goes beyond platonic, you'll have to work for it."

The truck door slams behind me as I trot up the walk to Jax's house.

CHAPTER 12
Seth

I stare at Lucy's round ass as she climbs the stairs to Jax's apartment. Did that just happen? Since when had I moved from just friends to wanting Lucy in my bed as often as possible? Right about the time I saw her in line at the café, most likely. Or maybe when she put her hand on my heart and I thought it was going to pound right out of my chest. Hell, she'd had a hold on me twenty minutes after we met, fueled by her sexy rock-star persona. Not to mention I can't seem to shake the imprint of her body against mine.

Damn.

I'm not getting out of this in one piece. I should start the truck and head back to the tattoo shop, where she probably won't show up. But Jax is waiting for her fries, and I'd told Lucy I'd take care of it.

With the two bags of produce in my hands, I lock up the truck and head into Jax's house. She lives on the second floor of a duplex her parents own. They live on the bottom floor. I climb the stairs and knock once before letting myself in.

Jax is on the couch with a washcloth draped over her head.

I drop the bags on the bar separating her kitchen from her living room and then go sit on the coffee table next to the couch. "Hey."

She opens one bloodshot eye. "You."

I grin. "Will you live?"

"No," she croaks. "And neither will you if I don't get my fries."

The microwave beeps and Jax cringes.

"Sorry," Lucy says quietly and brings a steaming cup of what has to be chai to Jax. "Here."

Jax takes the cup in hand but doesn't drink. "Keenan?"

"Yeah?"

"Stop staring at Lucy."

Lucy chuckles and heads over to the produce bags.

"Can you blame me?" I whisper.

She puts a hand on my knee and really looks at me. One glance and I know she's suspicious.

I give her my cockiest grin and stand. "Fry time."

"Finally." She pushes herself up and takes a tiny sip of her drink, then immediately starts to gag.

"Whoa." I jump out of the way.

The gagging stops and she collapses back onto the couch. "There's nothing left to purge. I think you're safe."

"Uh, Jax?"

"What?" Her arm is now slung over her head.

"You sure you want something to eat?"

She sighs. "I have to try."

"Okay."

I join Lucy in Jax's tiny kitchen and begin to peel and chop the sweet potatoes. Lucy busies herself cutting strawberries.

"You're not planning on baked fries, are you?" Lucy wrinkles her nose.

"Good God, woman. Don't insult me." This isn't the first time I'd made Jax her fries after a night of indulgence. I reach under the counter and produce a small electric deep fryer.

"Ah." She takes a sip of her drink.

I glance at the two other drinks still in the carrier. "Who are those for?"

"Jax and me. Want one?"

"Are they all chai?"

"No."

She pops a blueberry in her mouth, and a look of pure ecstasy transforms her face. Fuck me. I'm bringing her blueberries every damned day for the rest of my life.

"They're lattes. You're welcome to one if you like."

"Thanks." The coffee I'd gotten had long been discarded, and after staying up half the night, a caffeine boost is exactly what I need.

While I work on the fries, Lucy takes the fruit bowl she's prepared and sits on the couch at Jax's feet. The two whisper quietly. I don't really pay attention until I hear Lucy mention Cadan. The name sends a bolt of anger through me. I don't know what he did to her, but whatever it was, he's hurt her. Badly. He must have. Walking away from your soul mate is nearly impossible.

They'll end up back together eventually. Most do.

The scent of sweet potatoes and oil fills the apartment. I glance at Jax to find she's already looking better. Her eyes lock with mine, then she looks at Lucy. Oh son of a... is Lucy telling her about us? I'll never hear the end of it. Not after I'd promised to stay away from her. It's safe to say I broke the promise with spectacular results.

"Hey, are my fries done yet?" Jax demands.

I turn my attention to the fryer. "Shit!" A few at the top are starting to turn black.

"Need some help?" Lucy jumps up and runs to my side as I'm fishing the fries out with a strainer spatula.

"I've got it." I place the first batch on the paper-towel-lined plate. More than half of them are burned.

"What were you doing over here?" she asks, laughing.

I turn to her and rake my gaze over her body. "Just thinking about that conversation we had outside."

"Oh." She fidgets with the hem of her sleeve and blushes again.

I can't wait to see her entire body do that the next time I get her naked.

Lucy eyes the fries again and then picks up one of the peeled potatoes and begins to slice.

"Well," Jax says from the couch. She's sitting up now with her legs tucked cross-legged. "Isn't this interesting?"

Cringing on the inside, I turn to face her wrath. She knows. I can tell by her tone.

"You couldn't just keep it in your pants for one night? God, Seth. Lucy isn't one of your bar skanks. You can't treat her like that." Her anger seems to have fortified her. The green tinge to her complexion has vanished, replaced by red splotches high on her cheekbones.

"Treat her like what?" Anger threatens to spring from deep inside me. I clutch the plate with the fries and stalk over to her, holding it out. "More is on the way."

She takes the plate but doesn't acknowledge it in any way. "You know what, Seth. Like someone who means nothing but an empty night of pleasure. Like all the rest of them you've burned through since Elsa—" She clasps a hand over her mouth, abruptly stopping her outburst.

"Jax," Lucy says quietly, clearly trying to defuse the situation.

But I've got Jax pinned with my stare. She doesn't seem to be able to look away.

"I'm sorry," she says.

I take a deep breath, fighting for control. I'm seconds from losing my shit. She can yell at me all she wants, but bringing up E? I'm ready to stalk out right now. I would, too, if it weren't for Lucy. "Okay," I force out.

"You don't know Lucy. She's too sweet for you. Jesus, Seth. Why her?"

"Too sweet?" Lucy laughs and guides Jax back down to the couch. "Have you not been paying attention to my life these last few years? I've been dating a rock star and have been on tour. Nothing about my current life has been sweet."

Pain starts throbbing behind my left eye. "Jax, let it go." I really don't need this shit right now.

"Oh, Lucy, please," Jax says, ignoring me. "You make it sound like you were living that movie *Almost Famous* or something. We both know you spent most of your time writing songs when you weren't onstage. Not exactly the stuff gossip rags are built on."

Jax's dismissal of her life rankles, but I'm too busy focusing on Lucy to say anything.

Her entire demeanor shifts and a cold expression hardens her face. "Stop it," she says in a quiet, steely tone. "I'm done with people treating me as if I either don't have a brain or am too naïve to understand the implications of my actions. Well guess what, Jax? I came on to Seth. Not the other way around. So if you want to yell at someone, start with me." Her fists are balled on her hips. "I'm not the sixteen-year-old girl both you and my mom seem to think I am. It's been over four years. I've seen a lot, done a lot, and have changed a lot. It's time to start seeing me for who I am now. Not then."

Jax's mouth drops open in a shocked *O*, and I get the impression outbursts are rare for Lucy. Jax finally spits out, "You think I treat you like your mom does?"

Lucy shrugs, but the movement is forced. "Sometimes. You both have a way of invalidating my truths. Though admittedly, she's way worse than you are."

Tears fill Jax's eyes and she sinks back down to the couch, clearly shaken by Lucy's words.

"I'm going to go," Lucy says. "You need to get back on your feet, and I think I need some space." She turns to me. "Seth, can you give me a lift back to town?"

"Sure. Give me a sec." I return to the kitchen to clean up my mess. When I'm finished, I hold out a hand once again.

Lucy takes it and pointedly turns to Jax. "See? My choice."

"Okay, Lucy. Fine. You're a dirty whore and you want me to stay out of it. I get it. Just remember, I told you he'd break your heart. They all do sooner or later." She rolls over and faces the back of the couch.

"Ouch," I say to Jax. "Don't you think you're being a little harsh?"

Lucy shakes her head and whispers in my ear. "This is about Brad. Not me and you. Try not to start anything until she's ready to talk."

She's right. Jax is generous, kind, supportive and an all-around perfect friend... except when she's hurting. Then she's mean, selfish, and petty.

I grab my keys. "Feel better, Jax. I'll come by tomorrow to make sure you made it through."

She doesn't turn over, not even when we pause at the door.

"You're welcome," Lucy says, clearly frustrated with her friend. "It's not every day someone brings you chai, coffee, and potatoes for fresh fries. Enjoy them."

Jax manages a small grunt of gratitude as we escape out the front door.

Once we're back at the truck, Lucy slumps against the side, holding her head in her hands. "Could that have gone any worse?"

I step in front of her, my feet straddling hers, and wrap my arms around her. I tell myself it's to comfort her, to keep her warm, but I know the real reason. Five more minutes of not touching her and I might lose my mind.

She presses her head against my shoulder and lets out a sigh. "That makes me zero for three."

"Huh?"

"On the list of most important people in my life, I'm currently not speaking to the top three." Her grip tightens on my shoulders.

"Cadan, Jax, and...?" I ask, even though it's not really any of my business.

"My mom. She's on Cadan's side."

"I see." I don't really. Mom loved E, but I'm her son. And no one could come between us. "Well, I don't think the Jax thing is permanent. After she recovers, you'll talk and everything will be fine."

She sniffs and pulls back, wiping away a tear. "You're right. It's just a lot, you know?"

I pull her in for another hug, hating that anyone has caused her pain. My protective streak takes over, and the desire to take her home, to keep her safe, almost overwhelms me. I release her, fighting my instincts every step of the way. "I do know. Let's get you home, okay?"

CHAPTER 13

Lucy

Why was Jax so mad that Seth and I hooked up? They're just friends, aren't they? A horrible thought comes to me.

"You and Jax," I ask Seth tentatively, "you've never hooked up, have you? I mean, like we did last night."

He jerks and glances at me, his face full of incredulity. Abruptly he pulls the truck into a small gas station and stops. "Seriously?"

I want to curl into a ball and hide under his spare blanket. Instead, I meet his outrage head-on. "You saw the way she acted back there. How am I supposed to know she's not one of your one-night stands? You already told me you don't do relationships. I'm just trying to get a grip on what's going on."

His jaw works as he tries to form words. Then he clamps his mouth shut and puts the truck in drive without saying anything.

"So that's it then?" I can't let this go. Jax is far too angry and he's too defensive.

"That's what?" He keeps his gaze steady on the highway in front of us.

"You and Jax have history." I say it with finality as if it's fact. "You should have told me."

He speeds up as he goes around a corner, not quite driving recklessly, but close. I clutch the door, my body stiff with tension. Cadan drives like he's invincible and it's always scared me. But the way Seth is driving, it's more like he can't wait to get to town to just get rid of me. And that makes me more angry than scared. I turn and stare out the window for the rest of the ride.

When we finally stop in front of the coffee shop, Seth turns the truck off and turns to me. "Lucy," he says with a sigh. "Jax is just a friend. We've never been together. You can believe me or not, it's your choice. Frankly, I'm insulted you assumed the worst about both of us. But since we don't know each other very well, I can understand why you might be suspicious. Jax is acting very strangely. And it's true I have a reputation, but I'm honest and if you ask me something, I'll tell you the truth."

"I… well… okay. I didn't—"

He holds up a hand to cut me off. "There's one last thing. We talked about exploring this attraction as friends, right?"

I nod.

"Well, to me, my friends are everything. So if we're going to be friends, I want a promise you're not going to push me away when things get hard." He's gazing at me so intently I fight not to squirm in my seat.

"What makes you think I'll push you away?" The implication irritates me. I'm loyal almost to the point of being destructive. It's why it took me so long to leave Cadan and why Mom and I are reaching critical mass. I spent far too many years trying to please her, knowing that what she wants for me and what I want for myself are never going to be the same.

His eyes go soft and he places his hand lightly on my knee. "From the outside looking in, it seems an awful lot like you're running from everyone."

Anger boils up from somewhere deep inside, and despite the chill in the air, my entire body goes hot. "I'm not a runner." My tone is low and measured. "You don't know my circumstances. After one day and one night together, this is what you come up with? Until you know the details, maybe you should keep your psychobabble bullshit to yourself."

He leans back against the door, clearly stunned by my outburst. Then he starts to chuckle. "Fair enough, Lucy Moore. Fair enough." He holds his hand out to me.

I take in his easy, relaxed manner and can't decide what to think. Clearly he's a loon, but then so is everyone else I know. I clasp his hand in mine.

"Here's to getting to know each other." He shakes my hand slightly, but mostly he's just holding it.

The anger fades, and as I look at his handsome face and the vibrant tattoos, I realize I do want to know him. The real him. Not the person who runs from commitment. "To getting to know each other."

He gives my hand a final squeeze before pulling away. "Have a nice evening, Luce."

"Wait just a minute," I say. "Give me your phone."

Seth reaches into his pocket and hands it to me without question.

I punch in my cell number and hit Send so it will show up on my phone and then program my information into his. "There." I hand it back to him. "Now we'll have a better shot at that getting to know each other thing."

Studying his phone, he quirks an eyebrow. "You gave me your number."

"Yeah." I frown. "So?"

"You told me before that only Jax had it. I thought I was going to have to work a lot harder than that." He winks and pockets his phone.

I roll my eyes and push the door open. "Just don't abuse it."

"Later," he says.

"Later." I slam his door shut, wondering what exactly later means. Later tonight? Later in the week? Or just a random later, as in, see you when I see you? Probably the random one. I sigh, realizing I want it to be later tonight. But I'd sooner volunteer to stay at Mom's house for a week, enduring her incessant Cadan talk, than tell Seth that.

I hurry back into the coffee shop to get out of the wind and order myself a replacement latte for the one I'd left at Jax's house. With a coffee cake and latte in hand, I hurry off to my car, ready to get home and curl up in front of the fireplace.

Buckled in, my latte in the cup holder, I rub my frozen hands together and rush to start the car. Nothing. I turn the key again. The car is completely dead.

"Shit!" I grab my latte, my phone, and the jacket I'd left on the passenger's seat, then head back into the coffee house to call Triple A.

An hour later, a man with his belly pushing his pants down shows up in a tow truck. He determines it's not the battery and speculates it's an electrical problem. "Need a ride somewhere?" he asks.

His truck is full of so much debris, I wonder how he even sits in it. I shake my head. "No, thanks. I've got it covered."

He nods and carts my car off to the nearest repair shop in Fort Bragg.

I stand on the street, staring at my phone. I could call Jax. Even though we had a fight, she'd come get me. But she has a nasty hangover, and I'm not certain she can drive without vomiting.

There's Marty, Jax's brother, but he's likely at work. Everyone else I know is either at work or has moved away. There are the guys from the band. I have Mike's number. Or I could call Seth.

My finger hovers over Mike's name. I hit Seth's instead.

He answers on the second ring. "Miss me already?"

"Why yes," I say. "I'm soaking in my hot tub and thought, who can I call who would make this experience that much more enjoyable?"

There's a moment of silence, then he clears his throat. "Is this an invitation?"

"What do you think?"

"I'll be there in ten minutes."

"Great," I say smiling. "Pick me up at the coffee shop on your way."

"Uh, what?"

"Oh, I meant I was wishing I was sitting in the hot tub. Really, I'm at the coffee house trying to figure out how to get home. My car died. But since you're clearly not busy, maybe you wouldn't mind giving me a ride?"

He laughs. "You could've just asked without all the buildup, though I am enjoying the visual of you naked in that hot tub."

"Who said I was naked?"

"Oh. I guess I filled that part in myself."

I shake my head. "So, do you have a few minutes to run me home?"

"Yeah, but I warn you, I don't have my swim trunks, so if you want to use that hot tub, I'm going to have to go commando."

"Oops. I guess this is a bad time to tell you I lied about the hot tub."

"It doesn't exist?" There's mock horror in his tone.

"Nope."

"Fuck."

"Sorry," I say. "I'll make it up to you."

"I like the sound of that." Someone calls his name in the background. "Hold on, Luce."

I go back inside and order him a latte while I wait. If he's coming to get me, it's the least I can do.

"You there?" he asks.

"Yes."

"Okay, I've got a walk-in. Head over to the tattoo shop and when I'm done, I'll get you home."

"Sounds good. And, Seth?"

"Yeah?"

"Thanks."

With coffee in hand, I head up the street to wait for him. The Tattoo Shoppe is in a nondescript building with only the neon sign to distinguish it from the real estate building next door. Inside, the place is spotless and artwork covers three walls. The front is a wall of windows.

"Can I help you?" a pink-haired woman with three eyebrow rings asks.

"Hi, I'm here for Seth."

She glances over her shoulder. "He's with a client. You're welcome to wait over there." She waves toward the four hard plastic chairs near the front door.

"Tish!" Mike stands up and glances at me. "That's Lucy. Send her back."

She gives me a dirty look. "She's fine where she is."

"Tisha, goddammit. Stop being a bitch." Mike walks over to me. "Hey, don't mind her. She hates everyone, especially those who have a thing with Seth." He winks and nods toward the workstations behind the reception desk. "Come on back."

"A thing with Seth?" I ask.

Mike laughs. "We heard his end of your phone call."

"Shit."

"Eh, he's a good guy, even if he tries to tell you otherwise." He waves me toward a padded drafting chair. "Take a seat."

Seth waves from his station across the room. He's busy working on a woman who appears to be my mother's age. She's getting an ankle bracelet tattoo.

"Hey, Lucy," Mike says as he pulls up a chair next to me. "Nice set last night."

Pleasure winds through me. "Thanks. It was fun."

"Yeah, until Kinx showed up." He snarls. "What an ass."

I automatically start to apologize for whatever he did, but stop myself just in time and scowl. "What did he do this time?"

Mike gives me a look of respect. "Can't say I blame you for ditching him. After he realized you'd left, he kept demanding we tell him where you went. He got super pissed when we told him we had no idea. He was a real dick, and then he and his entourage took the stage and spent the rest of the night playing his new songs for the crowd. The worst part is they loved them."

My heart starts to pound and I'm convinced I'm going to have a heart attack. "New songs?"

"He said they were for his new album. He dedicated one to you."

An ache forms in my stomach. I don't want to ask, but I have to know. "Which one?"

Mike scratches his chin as he tries to remember. "Hmm, not sure what it was called. But it was a ballad. Slow and soulful. Damn, Lucy, it was good, but it would be fucking awesome if you sang it."

The tears sting the back of my eyes and I blink hard. "'Alone in the Dark'?"

"Yeah, you know it? I mean, I can't stand that guy, but that song…" He shakes his head. "The lyrics, man, they're something else."

"Yeah, I know it." Pain bursts in the middle of my chest. My heart is breaking, and there's nothing I can do to stop it.

"Lucy? You okay?" Mike asks.

I shake my head. "Sorry." My cheeks are wet with tears now, and I angrily wipe them with the back of my hand. "I didn't mean to—"

"No. Damn, I'm an idiot. Hearing about your ex has to be hard. Especially…" He's uncomfortable. No one ever wants to talk about soul mates when things go bad.

Seth stares at me from across the room, his tattoo gun clutched in his hand. I force a smile to let him know I'm okay. After taking a moment to just breathe, I turn to Mike.

"Dude. I'm sorry," he says.

"No, don't be. It's not Cadan I'm upset about." I let out a hollow laugh. "Well, it is, but not for the reason you think. I've come to terms with our break. It's what I need and I'm better for it. This—" I wave to my face, knowing I must be splotchy with the effort to stop crying. "This is because that song, 'Alone in the Dark,' it's mine. I wrote that about my dad right after he passed." My voice breaks, and I clear my throat. "It's about Dad, and Cadan stole it from me."

Mike stands up, knocking his chair over in the process. "Are you fucking kidding me? What do you mean he stole it?"

I clutch my hands in my lap. "He told the record company he wrote it, and I don't have any way to prove he's lying. It's further complicated by the fact we're both under contract, and

I bailed. The record company isn't interested in what I have to say. If I fight, they'll sue me for breach of contract."

By now Seth is done with the tattoo he was working on and is standing beside me, a murderous expression on his face. "He stole the song you wrote for your dad? Did I hear that right?"

I nod and stand because with both of them hovering over me, it makes me too vulnerable. "Yes. Now you know why I left." I can't stand the way they're both looking at me. It's worse than when people find out about the cheating. The pity, the horror that the person who was my soul mate had taken something so personal, was too much for them to process. "He's a selfish bastard who only thinks about what's best for him. It's over."

Mike eyes me with skepticism, but Seth's expression clears and he says, "Good. Then there's nothing stopping me from taking you out tonight. Ready?"

"A date?" I give him my you've-lost-your-mind look. "I just want to go home, take a long hot bath, and curl up by the fire."

"Sounds like the perfect date to me," Mike says with a wicked smile.

"What?" Then heat floods my face as I realize what I said. "Oh, shut up."

Seth laughs. "Sounds kind of girly to me. I was thinking more like shots and a hot tub, but your way will work."

I roll my eyes, my mood lifted by their easy banter. "Are you available to take me home now?"

Seth glances to Tish, who is sending me death glares. "When's my next appointment?"

She casts a bored glance at the appointment book, and without looking back at him, she says, "An hour."

"Thank you, Tish," he says dryly and then puts an arm around me. "Let's go."

I pick up the latte and hand it to him. "This is your thank-you present."

He takes it and smiles down at me. "That's very sweet, but I can think of a variety of other ways I'd prefer—"

"Stop," I say and turn to Mike. "We do not have something going. Don't pay attention to anything he says."

"Sure." Mike raises his eyebrows at Seth, clearly not believing me. "I saw nothing, heard nothing."

Seth just grins.

I shake my head and take off for the door, Seth a half step behind me.

Once back in his truck, he turns and says, "Where to?"

"Head south on 1. It's about ten miles."

He still hasn't started the truck. "Ten miles on 1?" His tone is hesitant, sort of cautious.

"Is that okay? I can pay for the gas." Highway 1 to the south is pretty windy. The speed limit fluctuates from fifteen miles per hour on up to fifty-five. Ten miles can take up to a half hour depending on traffic.

He starts the truck but doesn't put it in gear.

"Seth?"

"Hmm?" He turns and catches me staring at him. "Oh. No, I don't want any money. It's fine. Sorry, I just remembered something I was supposed to take care of."

"I can find someone else. Jax or maybe Marty."

"No," he says with finality and puts the truck in gear. "Jax needs to recover and Marty... forget about him. You don't need to deal with his shit today."

"Okay," I say cautiously. Marty isn't exactly my favorite person, but that's only because I've known him since I was five and after all these years, I still haven't heard him say one decent word to Jax. "Bad blood between you and Marty?"

He starts backing out of the space. "Something like that." His mood has done a complete one-eighty. He's gone from the sexy, innuendo-slinging flirt to the closed-off, noncommunicative male in sixty seconds flat.

He's silent for most of the ride toward my house, not even acknowledging me when I point out we're about a mile away. Was it something I said? The length of the drive? Had I asked too much?

"Seth, is something bothering you?" I finally ask.

At my question, he seems to make a concerted effort to relax his shoulders. The tension in his face melts away as he turns to me. "No. Nothing to worry about."

I want to ask what's going on, but we just met last night and I don't want to pry. It's odd, though. I feel as though I've known him forever. Maybe it's the combination of sharing his bed and him now knowing about Cadan. Or maybe just because he's been so nice to me, and I'm not exactly used to that. "It's the gray house on the right," I say.

He nods and pulls over in front of the closed wooden gate, letting the truck idle.

"Thank you so much. I owe you one," I say as I climb out.

He shakes his head, subdued. All traces of the easygoing guy I'd spent the day with are gone. "No, you don't. I'm just happy you're home safe. Have a good night, Lucy."

"You too."

He nods and pulls out onto the empty highway, doing a U-turn to head back into town.

I watch him go, still puzzled as to what happened. Had his one-night stand walls finally slid into place? Sadness washes over me. He's the first person, besides Jax, that I'd truly felt comfortable with in a very long time. Maybe I can still convince him we can be good friends.

When his red truck finally disappears into the distance, I open the unlocked gate and slip inside. From the front of the house, there's a peek of the ocean, and I just stand there for a few moments, staring out into the vast greatness of the churning water and wishing Seth had stayed. I know he had to go back to work, but I don't want to be alone tonight.

A shiver creeps up on me and out of the blue I get the feeling I'm not alone. I freeze and glance around. Then panic takes over and I start to shake.

Right there on my front step is Cadan.

CHAPTER 14

Lucy

Cadan's leaning against the lamppost, clearly waiting for me to notice him.

No! Dammit.

I steel myself. "I thought you left. Don't you have a show to put on?" My words come out clipped, full of anger.

He studies me, his sandy hair blowing in the breeze, and he looks so fucking perfect, like one of those metrosexual fashion models. Then he steps off the stoop and moves toward me.

I take a step back.

"Whoa," he says softly. "Don't run. Not now."

My hands ball into fists. "I'm not running. I'm just trying to stay away from you."

Hurt crosses over his face as he frowns at me. "Luce. Don't do this. Babe, we need to talk."

"We don't." I pull the house keys out of my pocket and make a move to slip past him, but he cuts me off, blocking my way.

"You can't keep shutting me out."

Rage bursts forward in my chest, and before I can stop myself, I throw my hands out, knocking him backward. "I can do whatever the hell I want to. You forfeited the right to have any say in how I behave the day you stole Dad's song!"

He stumbles back, almost losing his balance, but recovers easily enough. His eyes widen with sudden understanding. "Is that what all this is about? The song?"

I let out a frustrated growl. "You self-centered bastard. You know what that song means to me, and you sold it to the record company without even asking me. You recorded it. It's on the fucking radio now. It was mine. And *you* took it." Tears spring to my eyes, but for once it's because I'm so incredibly angry. Not heartbroken.

His mouth drops open. Then he closes it. I can tell he's working to come up with something to appease me, but it's not going to work.

"Go back to whatever hotel you're calling home these days, Cadan. I don't want you here." This time I manage to push past him. I almost have the door open when his arms snake around me from behind. I still and it takes all my effort to not jam my elbow into his stomach. "Step back."

"Lucy," he whispers in my ear. "I'm so sorry, baby. I only took that song to the label because it's so good. I wanted you to sing it on the track, but then I messed up and you left. I own that. I know this is my fault. Let me make it up to you."

The words sound just like every other apology he's ever given me. I can't believe I've fallen for his bullshit a hundred times before. Not this time. He's gone too far. "You took the song because the label was pressuring you for new material, and you didn't have any of your own. How else do you explain your name on the credits?" I twist out of his arms, glaring at him.

He holds his hands up in surrender. "They just assumed. I never said it was written by me."

"Everything is always someone else's fault," I yell at the top of my lungs. "I'm not going to forgive you for this. Not now. Not ever. Leave, Cadan. I don't want you here."

He actually takes a step back, shocked at my outburst. I'm not a yeller. I also don't make a lot of waves, which may be part of the reason we've reached this point. Standing up for myself hasn't exactly been my strong point.

"Lucy," he says softly. "Listen. I know you're upset. I get it. I didn't before, but I hear you loud and clear. Let me make it up to you."

I let out a huff of frustration. "You can't. Just go," I say, calmer now. "Please. I need this time to myself."

Cadan's eyes narrow. "To yourself? Really? Is that why you left with that guy last night? And why you didn't come home? I know you weren't with Jax."

He can't know for sure, but I was gone for hours while Jax was still at the bar, drunk as hell. He stuffs his hands in his pockets. "What happened?"

"That's none of your business."

The expression on his face morphs from mild curiosity to outrage. "You slept with him? That's it, isn't it? You fucked this guy. What the hell is this? Your twisted way of getting back at me?"

I stare at him, dumbfounded. Has he lost his mind? I left him three months ago. And he'd cheated on *me*. Was he so self-absorbed that he thought I'd be sitting around pining for him? "You've got to be kidding me. Jesus, Cadan. When are you going to realize I don't belong to you?"

"You're my soul mate," he says through clenched teeth.

"You're a dick. Leave or I'll call the cops." I won't. At least I don't think I will. A police scandal is the last thing either of us needs.

"I know you better than that," he says, his voice calmer. "Let's go inside so you can warm up. You're freezing."

I'm so mad I haven't even noticed the cold seeping through my clothes. The wind is picking up and I can hear the crash of the waves on the rocks intensifying. A storm is coming, and I feel as if it's brewing from deep inside me.

Cadan holds out his hand for the house key. I stare at it, knowing no matter what I do, he's not going to leave until he gets what he wants. Only I'm not exactly sure what it is he wants from me. For me to return to the band? To write him more songs? To be the soul mate I'm supposed to be? I can't do any of those things and remain myself. If I give in, I'll be lost, living in a world that caters to him and what he wants.

"Lucy?"

I raise my gaze to his worried one. I can't stand the hidden manipulation I see there. As if in a trance, I raise my hand and drop the house key into his.

He smiles and then turns to unlock the door.

"I'll be right back," I say.

Turning, he raises an eyebrow. "Where are you going?"

I nod toward the garbage bins. "I need to roll those out before the rain starts."

"Okay. I'll see you inside." He disappears into my house as the first drops of rain fall on my head.

"Asshole," I say and spin on my heel. I bypass the garbage cans and his Mercedes rental and head straight for the highway. If he's staying, I'm going. I don't care if I have to walk the entire ten miles to town. Anything is better than enduring what's waiting for me inside.

Once I'm outside the gate, I break into a jog, careful to keep to the shoulder. It won't take long for Cadan to start to wonder where I am. And considering he has access to a car and I don't, the likelihood that he'll find me is high. If I can make it to the small convenience store a mile down the road, I might have a chance. Bessie, the store owner, was a good friend of my dad's. She'll let me hang out in the back if necessary.

The rain starts coming down at a steady rate, and it doesn't take long for my clothes to get soaked through. I'm cold, angry, and pissed that I'd let Cadan get to me. The frustration only makes me run faster. And to add insult to injury, as I round a corner, a line of cars shoots past, spraying a wall of water at me.

My only salvation is that none of them was Cadan. Or if one was, the rain is so heavy he didn't notice me.

My teeth are chattering by the time I get to Bessie's, but instead of walking in, I bang on the door and poke my head in. "Bessie?"

"In the back," she calls.

"Do you have a towel?" I don't want to track in the mud clinging to my tennis shoes or drip a river of water on her hardwood floors. "I ran here and I'm soaked."

"What? Are you nuts?" She stalks out of the back room, her hands on her hips. "You could've been killed out there."

I grimace, knowing she's right. "I have an unexpected visitor. And unfortunately he won't leave, so I had to."

She tucks her gray curls behind one ear and smoothes her red apron over her round belly. "That good-for-nothing two-timer is here?"

She knows my life well. I nod. "And my car died. It was either be stuck in the house with him or come here. Is this okay?"

The anger melts from her face and she holds out a hand. "You know you're always welcome. Come on in the back and dry off."

I leave a soggy trail behind me as I follow her.

She pulls out a chair at what appears to be a break table and waves for me to sit. Then she bustles to a supply closet to grab a towel. "Is Jax coming for you?"

I shake my head. "I haven't called her yet."

"I'm sure she'll be thrilled for some girl time. If not, you'll stay here."

Bessie's offer is sweet. But with her daughter and son-in-law and their four kids, her house is already bursting at the gills. I need to find somewhere else to go.

With a tap of my finger, I call Jax. The phone rings once before it goes to voice mail. Damn. She declined my call. Her voice comes on the line, requesting I leave a message. "Jax. I'm stranded and desperately need a ride. Call me."

I end the call and try again, just in case. Two rings this time and then it goes to voice mail again. I frown at the phone, frustrated. Is she that mad at me? Seth's at work; I can't bother him again. Mike is there too. Shoot.

"Bessie," I call and head for the front of the store, but just as I slip through the door, the bell rings, indicating a customer.

"Excuse me," says an all-too-familiar voice.

I duck back into the storage room, my heart pounding practically out of my chest. Cadan is already looking for me.

"How can I help you?" I hear Bessie say.

"I'm looking for someone. You might know her, she lives down the way. Lucy Moore?"

"I know Lucy," she says. "Haven't seen her today though. On a day like this, I'd expect her to be tucked up in her house."

"Yeah." Cadan sounds confused. "She should." There's a pregnant pause. Then he says, "Well, if you see her, please let her know I'm worried."

Bessie doesn't say anything. A moment later, the bell chimes on the door again.

"Need a ride somewhere?" a voice says from behind me.

"Holy hell," I say, clutching my chest. "Holt, you scared me."

He smiles. "Gran said to take you to town." Holt can't be a day over seventeen. He's tall and lanky with recently straightened teeth.

"You're all grown up," I say.

"Getting there." He jerks his head toward the back door. "Come on. I've got to meet my girl. I'll drop you on the way."

"Thanks." I smile up at him and then rush into the store to thank Bessie.

"You can't keep running forever," she says.

I bite my lip. "He's not taking no for an answer."

"That's tough. But you'll need to find a way to make him understand sooner or later."

"I wish I knew how."

CHAPTER 15
Seth

I'm pissed at myself. As soon as I'd found out Lucy lives south on 1, my entire mood had shifted. It's always rough passing by 128, the highway we'd been on the night of the accident. I should have told Lucy. Instead, I'd abandoned the pleasant flirtation we'd had going and turned into a moody dick. So much for that possible date later.

The clock ticks loudly in the silent shop. Mike's in the back grabbing more supplies for his station, and Tish is sitting at the desk, staring at me. It's uncomfortable to say the least. It's my own damn fault, though. Never mess around with anyone you work with, even if you were both so drunk you barely remember what happened. I have the feeling she remembers a lot more than I do. It was just once, months ago, but she still hasn't let it go.

"What time was my appointment supposed to be here?" I ask.

"Twenty minutes ago." She smacks her gum and pops a bubble.

"Okay." I turn to my sketchbook, meaning to finish a drawing of a phoenix I'd started a few days ago, but I can't concentrate. All I see is Lucy's face. My fingers twitch to sketch her. Charcoal. I rummage around in my drawer and come up empty. "Shit," I mumble and stand up abruptly. "Tish?"

"What?" She gives me a hostile look that I patently ignore.

"Text me if my appointment shows up. I need to run home for a moment."

"Whatever." Grabbing a magazine, she spins in her stool to face the entrance.

The rain is coming down in sheets now and it seems crazy to go out in the weather just to get my charcoal pencils, but there's a driving force inside me. That creative fire that comes so rarely these days. I have to draw. And I can't wait.

By the time I get to my truck, I'm drenched. The windshield wipers work overtime as I creep through the city streets, but I move forward with single-minded determination. My house is close, but the storm makes the visibility almost zero. No wonder my appointment hadn't shown up. I'm so focused that by the time I get home, I don't even notice I'm flying up the stairs until I reach the sunroom door.

Then I freeze. Water drips down the side of my face and splatters on the hardwood floor. I don't come up here anymore. I'd forced myself to enter twice. Neither time had ended well.

My pencils are on the other side of the door. That driving force is getting stronger. I don't think I can turn around now even if I want to. I grab the handle and twist, waiting for the panic to set in. It always does.

But this time, with the sheets of rain obscuring the view and my mind on the charcoal, it doesn't come. Not even when I walk to the center of the room and eye the oil paintings lined up against the wall.

They're all there. The last dozen or so E and I worked on. Flashbacks of her standing in this room, a paintbrush in her hands, her long blond hair piled into a loose knot on her head as she laughs at her own jokes, filter through my mind. That joy I'd always felt with her around slams into me. I let the emotion fill me up, reveling in the long-forgotten state of being. This used to be my life, so full of hope and wonder. Now the room is dank and dusty, holding everything I loved about her locked away.

All too soon, the soul-crushing ache I'd lived with the last eighteen months takes over, knowing the person who made me whole was gone. Those long days of creating together, bringing something meaningful to not only ourselves but the world around us, had vanished that awful night.

Why?

The question haunts me now just as it had then. There is no answer. There's only silence.

I blink, and the visions of her are wiped away, leaving me in the dark room as the wind blows, rattling the glass. Why am I here?

The charcoal. Lucy. It should feel wrong to be in this space while my mind is on another lover, but it doesn't. Instead, the urge to sketch grows. If only those portraits weren't staring at me. The ones still waiting for a few minor finishes. The ones they'd never get now.

I move mechanically to a shelf full of supplies and pull out a drape. I should have covered them long ago, if for nothing else other than to preserve the art against the sun. Once I have the drape in place, the memories of E dim, and Lucy's image fills my mind again.

The image of her standing on the stage, feet shoulder-width apart as she sings seductively into the mic, fights with the one of her eyeing me shyly in the truck when she thinks I'm not paying attention.

My easel lies abandoned on the floor, knocked over in a drunken rage the last time I'd ventured up here. Now I bend and pick it up, positioning it in the corner so all I have to look at while working is the rain splattering on the glass. I rip a handful of damaged sheets off the sketchpad, wadding them up as I go. Once I have a fresh, unmarred surface, my hand closes around the charcoal and I begin to sketch.

The world fades away, and all I hear is the splatter of raindrops mixed with the faint sound of the pencil against the paper. It's soothing as my creative self takes over, seeing only Lucy and the angles of her body, the striking intelligence shining through those eyes and the hidden vulnerability. It's that above everything else that draws me to her. The sheen of strength masking all the emotions underneath.

Time ticks away as I fill half a dozen sheets with various poses, all ones my mind has been locking away for just this moment, I realize. She's become my muse, the one I can't walk away from. What's happening to me right now isn't the same as what E and I had. Together, we'd brought magic to a piece; it came alive under our ministrations, revealing something to the subject. No, this is revealing what's inside me through a subject. In a way, it's almost more personal. It's raw and though it's her image, it's all about what's going on inside me.

A dam breaks, and my walls come crashing down. I'm all in, adding stroke after stroke, shading and erasing, pouring myself into this piece in a way I can't with my tattoos. It's freeing and also terrifying because I don't know if I can go back.

But for now, I just draw.

Hours later, with over a dozen sketches hung around the room, my hand begins to cramp. I know if I don't stop, I won't be able to work tomorrow, so even though I'd rather stay up all night in the sunroom, I put my charcoals away and step back.

Pleasure seeps into all those broken crevices inside me. I created something. Something just for me. It's not for anyone. It's an expression of what I feel in this moment. My heart thumps a little faster. I'm alive for the first time since I lost E.

And it's thanks to Lucy.

The overwhelming urge to see her takes over. Should I call? Head over to her house? The rain is still battering our town. I shouldn't go anywhere, but I'm afraid if I call I'll only hang up utterly frustrated. After spending the afternoon and the evening with her image in my head, I want her. Want to experience her gentle yet demanding touch, see her smile, hear her soft laugh as her breath tickles my neck.

Hell. I'm hard just thinking about her. I pull my phone out and send her a text.

Would you mind company?

My phone buzzes a few moments later, but it's not Lucy. It's Tish.

Your appointment is finally here… five hours late. Want to take it? Or should I send him home?

I glance at the clock. It's eight p.m. The shop closes at nine. My first thought is to tell her to send him packing. But then my rational mind takes over. It's December, not exactly a high-traffic season, and a job is a job. I could use the cash.

I'll be there in less than ten.

Fine.

I take a moment to wash the charcoal remains from my hands, then grab a raincoat and head on back to the shop. The street is empty with only the lights of the tattoo parlor and the coffee shop glowing in the night. After stopping in for a latte, I jog up the street and slip into the shop, ready to work.

"Hey, Tish," I say. "Did Mike already leave?"

"Ten minutes ago when he found out you were coming back."

I nod and glance around. "Where's my appointment?"

"Bathroom." She grins. "Wait until you see who it is."

"Who?" I ask as I settle in at my station.

She shakes her head. "You'll see."

I roll my eyes and check my phone. Lucy still hasn't answered. I glance at the storm brewing outside and start to worry. No, she's at home where I left her. She's probably just not near her phone. If I still haven't heard from her by the time I'm done, I'll give her a call to be sure she's okay. Right. That's why I'll call. Not because I'm aching to see her. No, not at all.

"Hey, man."

I lift my head and have to fight back a scowl. *Shit.* Cadan Kinx. What the fuck is he doing here? I keep my expression neutral and nod to the chair. What I really want to do is throw his ass out, but he hasn't done anything to me and we have bills to pay. "Hey."

"Sorry I'm late. I had some business to take care of." He gives me that million-dollar smile he no doubt uses on all his groupies. The ones he's busy banging instead of hanging out with his girl. Ex-girl that is. What a fucking loser.

"It's fine. Did you have something in mind?" I ask.

He nods and pulls out a piece of paper with a crude sketch of a dragon. "I know it's rough, but judging by the piece on your arm, I'm guessing you can turn this into something badass."

I narrow my eyes at the dragon spiraling around my arm. "I didn't ink that."

"Sure, sure. That makes sense. But you can do something with it, right?"

"Yeah, but I'll need a little time to work it up. We might be able to get the outline drawn, but we don't have enough time to finish tonight."

He raises an eyebrow. "What if I pay you double?"

"Sorry," I say without even considering it. "I've got somewhere I have to be." I don't, but I plan on being at Lucy's. Or at the very least, making sure she's all right with this douche hanging around.

He raises his hands in mock defeat. "Okay. I'll be in town a few days anyway. We can finish tomorrow, right?"

I give a noncommittal shrug. The idea of working on this guy makes my skin crawl. It shouldn't. He's done nothing to me. It's because of what he's done to Lucy. After today's work session, I'm feeling more territorial than I had after we'd spent the night together. I can't explain it, but it's as if I'm connected to her in some way. Not like with E, not in the magical sense. No, this is something else on a pure primal level.

I get up and walk to Mike's station, pretending to look for supplies. I need to get away from Kinx before I say something I'll regret. Their relationship isn't any of my business, no matter how much I'm starting to realize I want it to be. Twenty-four hours ago, my life had been uncomplicated and void of all emotion.

Now Lucy has changed everything.

I turn back to Kinx. "Where is this going to go?"

"Right here." He thumps his chest over his heart.

Great. Now I have to stare at his ugly ass half-naked. "Take off your shirt," I order.

After discussing size and placement, I grab a fine-point Sharpie and go to work, turning his crap drawing into something that doesn't suck ass. Ten minutes later, I'm ready to get started.

"Hold on a sec," he says. "I've got to make a phone call."

I sit back in my chair, my fist clenched around the tattoo gun. I grab my own phone. Nothing. Not even a text from Jax. I send her one asking if she's surviving.

The phone buzzes back almost immediately. *I'm alive, but feel like a total bitch. Have you spoken to Lucy?*

I type back. *No. Why?*

She called a few times but I didn't answer. Now I can't get a hold of her.

I frown and type back. *Kinx is still in town.*

WHAT???

He's at my shop now. I dropped Lucy at home hours ago. She should be there.

I'll keep trying.

I want to ask her to let me know Lucy is okay, but I don't. She'll only ask questions I don't know how to answer.

The phone buzzes again. *Call me as soon as he leaves.*

Will do.

Kinx strolls back over with a frown on his face. I'd heard him talking, but hadn't been able to make out the words. Had he been speaking to Lucy? If so, it hadn't gone well.

"Let's get this started," he says, all of his charm gone. "I have to meet someone after."

I lay the transfer of the dragon over his chest and then peel it away. He studies it in a handheld mirror. "Make it vibrant, all right?"

"Sure." I grind my teeth and go to work.

From the way Kinx sits back in his chair, relaxed, you'd think he's an old pro at this, but I don't see evidence of a tattoo anywhere else. At least not on his upper body. Usually I love working on a new, blank canvas, but I can't stand touching

Kinx. I'm jumpy, and after a while, the gun almost slips from my hand.

"Dude," Kinx says with a scowl. "What's up?"

"Sorry, man. Long day."

He glances at it. "Oh, yeah. Before you're done, I want initials on the tips of the wings."

I freeze. "What?"

His lips turn up into a slow shit-eating grin. "L and C."

Fuck! Their initials. He means this to be a soul mate mark. One to tell the world he's taken. And he wants me to do it. I put the gun down. "That's something you should have told me before we started."

"I'm telling you now."

Cocky bastard. There is no fucking way I'm finishing this. "Sorry, too late."

He stands and walks over to a large mirror on the wall. "No it isn't. There's plenty of space." He strides back and sits down. "Put them on."

Anger shoots through my veins. I'd managed to keep it at bay while I was focusing, but the impulse to kick the shit out of him is back. I'd gotten a fair amount done. The entire outline of the dragon plus his face and wings are done in detail. It still needs to be colored in, though. There is room for the letters. But I'll be damned if I do it.

"It's late," I say and stand. "You'll need to get it finished another time."

"Dude. I'm not leaving until you ink the initials."

I finish cleaning up my station. "You're going to be here a while then."

"What the fuck, man? I'm not paying for this until it's done."

"Fine." He owes me a few hundred at this point, but fuck the money. I wouldn't take it from him if I were starving.

He glares at me while I wrap his skin with ointment and a bandage. "What time are you available to finish this tomorrow?"

"I'm not."

"But I'm leaving town. You have to fit me in."

"No. I don't." Entitled little bitch. "You didn't make an appointment. Find someone else."

His jaw tightens, and for a second, I'm positive he's going to take a swing. But then he stalks to the door, and just before he walks out, he says, "Stay the fuck away from her."

CHAPTER 16

Seth

"What?" I snap, more pissed than ever. The sick son of a bitch set this up. He'd come to me on purpose.

His eyes narrow. "I know she spent the night with you. This is a small town. Word gets out. This"—he points to his chest—"is to let you both know who she belongs to."

My entire body tenses. "Lucy doesn't *belong* to anyone, least of all not some chickenshit singer who can't even write his own songs."

He closes the distance between us. "What the fuck did you just say to me?" Kinx says, his eyes aflame with crazy-like rage. He leans forward, his jaw jutting out.

"You heard me." I cross my arms over my chest. "It's pretty fucked up to steal a song she wrote about her dead father. That's shitty low."

"You don't know what the hell you're talking about." He's vibrating with the urge to beat the shit out of me, but for some reason he holds back.

Too bad. I'm dying to rough up that pretty boy face of his. "Maybe you should leave."

"Fuck you." His eyes flash with pure hatred. "Lucy will never leave me. I know all about you and your mate. It didn't take more than ten minutes on the Internet to put the pieces together. I bet you wish you'd never taken a drink that night. What will Lucy say when she finds out?"

On reflex, I reach out and grab him by the shirt, dragging him to me. "Don't ever talk to me about E."

"You must hate yourself." He nods sympathetically, not fighting my hold at all. "I would, too."

I yank him closer, his face so close to mine I can see his pupils dilate. My entire being longs to crush him.

"Do it," he taunts. "Take a swing."

His words bring me back to myself. He's not worth it. I push him backward. "Get out."

He gives me a self-satisfied smile, straightens his shirt, and strolls out into the darkness. I close the door, lock it, and slump down into one of the hard plastic chairs. "Fuck."

"Holy shit," Tish says softly.

I jerk my head up, having completely forgotten she was there.

"That was Cadan Kinx." Her eyes are wide with a mix of shock and excitement.

I let out a heavy sigh. "I know."

"And you had a thing with his soul mate." She raises her hand to her mouth, giddy with the gossip.

"Tish," I say as I stand, "do me a favor and keep this all to yourself, all right? Lucy's had a rough few months with losing her dad and all. This drama is the last thing she needs."

Disappointment crosses her face, and not for the first time, I wonder how I ever ended up sleeping with such a shallow person. My stomach turns at the thought. "Yeah, okay," she says. "I can do that."

"Good. It's late. You can go on home."

She grabs her purse, and for the first time since the night we'd spent together, she doesn't try to manipulate me into a late-night invitation back to my place. At least that's one good thing to come out of all of this.

I lock the door behind her and immediately call Jax.

She picks up on the first ring. "Tell me everything."

"You first," I say. "Have you heard from her?"

"No. I can't get her to pick up."

"Fuck."

"Seth, what's happening?" Worry seeps through her tone.

"Kinx was here to get a tattoo. I was pretty far into it when he decided to tell me he wanted their initials. I…" Do I really want to tell her this part? No. "It's a dragon." I take a deep breath. "He told me to stay away from Lucy. He knows we spent the night together."

"Omigod! Seth, Jesus. I told you not to mess with her."

"Not now, Jax. This is serious. He's acting like a psycho, and I'm worried about Lucy."

"He won't hurt her."

"Maybe not physically, but he's already done a number on her emotionally."

Jax is silent for a moment. Then she says, "Come get me. We need to find her."

"I'm on my way."

Seven minutes later, I'm idling in front of Jax's apartment. She must have been watching for me because she runs out the door before I can even get out of my truck.

"Go to the club first," Jax says.

I glance at her. "Are you sure? Her car broke down. Don't you think we should try her house?"

"She's not there." Jax presses a button on her phone. Lucy's voice fills the cab. "Jax. I'm stranded and desperately need a ride. Call me." Jax hits another button. "Never mind. Holt is giving me a ride to town. Call me back."

"Did she? Call you back, I mean?" I ask.

"No. At least, I don't think so. I turned my phone off, so if she did, she didn't leave a message."

"Jax," I say, exasperated. "Why are you so mad at her?"

"I'm not!"

"You were." I turn onto the highway and speed up.

She closes her eyes. "I was just feeling sorry for myself. I drank too much and didn't get to have my one-night stand."

I smile at her. "That's a good thing."

"No it isn't. I'm going to die an old spinster."

I hate that she's so down on herself. "Not possible. You can have any guy you want."

She huffs. "Easy for you to say. I just wanted one night, preferably with someone I trust." She lowers her voice, and I can barely hear her last words. "Lucy got the one I wanted."

My breath catches in my throat. The silence hangs in the air. I glance over at her, but she's staring out the passenger's window. "Jax?"

"What?"

"Did you just say what I think you said?"

She doesn't answer. And I don't push her. She'd said she'd wanted me to be her one-night stand. And that's why she was so pissed earlier. Unease grabs hold of my gut and doesn't let go. Jax is my friend. Just about the only one I confide anything of importance to. Sleeping with her is out of the question.

I pull to a stop in front of the bar and put the truck in park. "I think we need to talk about this."

"No we don't," she says and grabs the handle, her face pinched in anger. "I just thought you should know what was bugging me. It's over. That ship has sailed. I won't make that mistake again."

I place a hand on her arm, stopping her. "*Why* are you mad?" I ask softly, genuinely confused. "I thought we're friends. You know I don't want to do anything to mess that up."

She turns, unshed tears shining in her eyes. "I just don't get it. You sleep with everyone and anything. Even that bitch who works at your shop. But not me? Why *not* me? All I wanted was a little fun. I'm not looking to have a relationship or anything, but I sure as hell don't want to get it on with a random stranger. I need someone I trust. And you're it. Don't you get that?"

I sit back in my seat, feeling as if I'd been gut-punched. "But we're friends."

"I know. That's the whole point," she says with conviction.

"I don't... shit." I run my hand through my hair. "Okay, let me try to explain this."

She folds her arms over her chest and waits.

Good God. This is exactly why I avoid romantic relation-ships. Had I completely misread what's going on here? "I've never considered pursuing a sexual relationship with you because I value your friendship. Those other girls, that's purely physical. Just a moment in time to forget… everything. Then it's over. But you, you're my best friend. I don't want to fuck that up."

She doesn't say anything, just sits there studying me.

"But I guess I might have anyway? Because of Lucy?" I glance at the bar's front door, hoping she's in there. Even now, sitting here with Jax, my mind is on the petite brunette, wor-rying about her.

"Yes. No. I mean, I don't know." She lets out a breath. "I didn't expect a relationship with you, except friendship. I just don't understand how you can treat people that way. Using them and then moving on. And what about Lucy? It sure as hell looks like you care about her from this end."

Frustration replaces the unease eating away at my stomach. "Look, *I* don't even know what I feel for Lucy. I can't even believe we're having this conversation. And that's bullshit anyway. I'm honest with everyone I've been with. It's their choice what they want to do. Hell, you just said you wanted the same thing. Double standard, much?"

She unfolds her arms and puts her hands in her lap. Staring at them, she says, "I didn't mean it like that."

"Shit, Jax, this is what I don't want to happen." I suck in a breath, prepared to be completely honest. "I like you. A lot. And you're gorgeous. But since E, I haven't wanted a girlfriend. Haven't even been able to comprehend a relationship. Not like that, hence the one-night stands. And you deserve better than that." I reach over and brush a lock of hair out of her eyes. "You are not a one-night-stand sort of girl, no matter how much you think you want to be."

"You're probably right," she says on a sigh. "But does that mean you used my best friend? Because she's not a one-night-stand kind of girl either."

"I don't know. Hell, we just met, and normally for me, last night would've been the end of it, but today something happened. I spent the day in my artist's loft." I shift forward and lock my gaze on hers. "Working."

Her eyes get big. "You painted today?"

"Sketched. With charcoal." I glance away, far more uncomfortable talking about my art than why I didn't try to seduce my best friend.

"What did you sketch?"

For whatever reason, I think it's important that she knows, so I say, "Lucy."

"I see." She bites her bottom lip.

"I don't think you do."

"You like her." Jax's voice wobbles. "Everyone does."

That's when realization hits me smack in the side of the head. Jax doesn't have a thing for me. She's jealous of Lucy. "Hey," I say softly and hold out my hand. "Come here."

She stares at it, then tentatively places her hand in mine. I tug her over and wrap my arm around her, giving her a half-hug. "You know you're beautiful, right?"

Laughing, she thumps me on the arm. "Don't start hitting on me now, Keenan. It's gross."

"Not on your life. I just wanted you to know that if you want a night of wild abandon, I know a few guys who'd be more than willing. Nice ones who will take care of you."

"The moment's passed," she says stiffly.

"I figured as much. But I wanted you to know they exist. And about Lucy?"

"Yeah?" She tilts her head to really look at me.

"She's pretty messed up right now. Me and her, we're not that different, and that might be part of why I'm drawn to her. But she'll never replace you. Got it?"

She forces a smile. "Yeah." Then she blushes. "I don't know what got into me."

"I think it was about half a pint of tequila."

"Oh God," she groans. "Don't say that word ever again."

"As long as you don't try to get in my pants again." I grin and wink at her.

She looks me up and down, then gives me a pouty smile. "No deal. You can't ask a hot-blooded girl to agree to such hard-core demands." She laughs and her eyes sparkle with mischief the way they usually do when we're joking around.

I chuckle. "Okay, perv. Keep your fantasy, but don't be surprised when the tequila shots show up in the near future."

"Oh, damn you." This time when her hand reaches for the door handle, she jerks and opens the door. "Let's go look for your muse. She's got to be here somewhere. There aren't many other places in town she could be."

CHAPTER 17

Lucy

Sitting in a booth, I swirl my straw around the cherry bobbing in my ginger ale. Even though I'm not hungover from the night before, alcohol is the last thing I want right now. Actually, I'm dying for a hot chocolate and a hot bath, but I'm not getting either anytime soon.

"So what do you think?" Mike asks. He'd called while Holt was giving me a ride to town to ask if I'd be available to discuss singing in the band on a permanent basis. Without anywhere else to go, I'd suggested meeting at the bar to discuss it. And luckily when he found out I was carless, he'd agreed to give me a ride home later. We'd been in the bar ever since.

I glance at the notebook in front of me. It's a song list he wants the band to consider. One of them happens to be one of mine. It's about meeting your soul mate and sticking with them no matter what. Everyone thinks it's about Cadan and how love conquers all. It isn't. I wrote it after my Mom found her mate and left Dad. "Sure, I can sing these."

"Even that last one?" He studies me with a concerned expression.

He's asking about "One Last Step." My song. I shrug. "Sure. I like that song." And I do. It helps me work through the conflicting emotions that have plagued me since the divorce.

It starts running through my mind, and before I realize it, I'm humming the melody. It's familiar and brings me a sense of comfort.

Mike starts a slow background beat with his hands against the table and hums along with me. I smile. It's been months since I've sung anything of mine, and the melody winds through me, taking hold the way it does when I'm singing something I've created. I can't help myself. The words come spilling out.

You take the road less traveled
You say you know your way
But we both know there's more to living
Than the path you chose yesterday

As I'm singing the last verse, peace settles in my bones and my soul fills with a pure, euphoric state. My tone smoothes out, harmonizing with a voice I know better than my own. I turn in my seat and meet Cadan's eyes. He's crouching near me, singing the verse softly, emotion radiating from him. The love is overwhelming, and it's spreading to everyone in the room. They've gone silent as they wait for us to finish the song, to give them what they crave. A few minutes of joy, of love, of contentment. I let everything go and lose myself to the words and him.

Take my hand now, baby
Don't be afraid to meet me halfway
Take that one last step, baby
And meet me halfway

Everything Cadan and I experience when we sing together is amplified to the audience, even when we don't intend it to be. Most say it's a mind-blowing experience that's like a natural drug. It's what makes our concerts sell out in less than three minutes when they go on sale. Or when they used to go on sale, before I left.

I abruptly clamp my mouth shut and ignore the pleas from the bar patrons.

"Luce," Cadan says, his eyes pleading. "Can we talk?"

I shake my head. "Now's not the time."

"Please, love. There are things I need to say."

"Don't call me that." I try to snap at him, but it comes off as weak, like I don't mean it. Sadness immediately replaces all the music-filled places in my heart.

He holds his hand out to me, his expression understanding. "I'm sorry. You're right. Just a few minutes and I'll let you be. I promise."

I meet his eyes and see the person I met three years ago. The one I knew before the record deals. Before he was the rock god everyone catered to. None of our bandmates or roadies are here. No managers, no handlers, no one. It's just me and him. He does nothing to hide the vulnerability written all over his face, and it nearly breaks me. As much as I hate him, I still love him. I will always love him. And no matter how far I go, no matter how much distance is between us, it will never go away. It's at the core of me.

Reaching out, I close my eyes as I slip my hand in his. His fingers are warm and clasp protectively around mine—gentle, yet firm. My traitorous body longs to be near him, to be touched by him, but my heart is breaking with the bittersweet reality of what lies between us.

He tucks my hand between both of his, holding on as if I'm someone to be cherished and protected. The way he hasn't held me in months.

"Lucy?" Mike says. His hands are fisted and he's casting murderous glances in Cadan's direction.

"What is it?" I ask him.

"Are you sure you want to do this? Talk to him, I mean?" His tone implies he thinks I should run in the other direction. He's right. I should. It's what I've been doing. But it's also clear Cadan isn't going to go away until he's had his say.

I nod, fighting back tears. This is something I have to do.

"I'll be right here if you need me."

"Thanks," I choke out, overwhelmed by his concern, and then force myself to step closer to Cadan.

Cadan wraps a protective arm around my shoulders and regards Mike with disdain, but he doesn't say anything as he tugs me off to another table, one in a quieter corner where we can talk. He pulls out a chair for me and scoots his close so our shoulders are almost touching.

After being away from him for so long, my instinct is to lean in. I stop myself and move my chair to the left, pointedly putting some distance between us. He opens his mouth to talk, but I hold up a hand, stopping him. "Whatever you do, do not start singing or I'm out of here. Got it?"

He gives me an incredulous look as if I've offended him, but then he starts laughing. "Fair enough."

The singing is my downfall. How could it not be? That's when I go all mushy inside. His voice is a drug to me, and when I join in, we pull everyone under with us. It's both the most amazing and the most terrible thing that can happen to a person. When trust is broken, as mine has been over and over and over again, it's torture to be so connected and yet not be able to give oneself over to the emotion.

If I go there one more time, I'll be broken. I turn swiftly so we're facing each other and then stare him hard in the eye. "Tell me why you did it? The real reason this time."

"The song, you mean?"

The fact that he has to ask makes me want to weep. I nod and finish with a sad shake of my head. "I already know why you slept with the skanks. Ego and opportunity."

"Luce." He huffs out a deep breath. "I don't want to fight."

"Neither do I. Don't you think that's part of the reason I've been avoiding you?"

"I thought you were pissed."

This time I let out a humorless laugh. "I am. Honestly, Cadan, I don't know what else there is to say."

The silence stretches between us. I can't take this. His proximity wears on my resolve. I want to touch him and share an inside joke. Write songs. Sing. Dance. Do all the things that were *us* before he turned into a first-class bastard. I'm just about to get up and bolt when his hand slips over mine.

Reflexively, I wind my fingers through his, wanting that connection. He's who I'm supposed to be with. The one who's supposed to make me whole.

"I never apologized," he says, regret clear in his voice. "Not really."

"No, you didn't." I stare at our joined hands. Nothing about this is right. I know it in my heart. Gently I pull away. "The thing is, Cadan, you're not good for me. I crave these little moments. The ones that feel so right. But they're always fleeting, and my heart is left trampled and bruised. Only the bruises never seem to fade. Not even when you're this person, the one who is sweet and considerate. When you're as you are now."

"I haven't been with anyone since you left." He says the words as if he hadn't even heard what I said.

I raise one extremely skeptical eyebrow. Jeez. The urge to punch him makes my fingers curl. "What am I supposed to say to that? Congratulations?"

"No." He runs a frustrated hand through his dark blond hair. It's a little longer than it had been when I left, and honestly, it looks good. "I needed a reality check, some time to get my head on straight. You leaving made that happen. I know I fucked up. Multiple times. God, how I fucked up. The life does something to people. Makes them feel like they're greater than they are."

"You mean makes *you* feel like you're greater than you are. I was there, too, remember? I have fans. Guys hitting on me who'd be more than happy if I pulled them backstage. Yet you didn't see me fucking random people right under your nose for months on end."

"No? What about that guy you left with last night? Seth?" He spits his name out with utter disgust. "Jax's friend, right?"

What? How does he know Seth's name? Had Jax said something in her drunken stupor? I stand and glare down at him. What I did with Seth is none of his damned business. "This conversation is over."

He jumps up and blocks my way. "Wait. Jesus. I'm sorry. That was uncalled for. You're right. I was a total self-indulgent asshole."

"Was?" I say, totally put off by his accusation. After I'd caught him red-handed, the truth had come out. He'd been sleeping around on me for months.

"Hey, I bailed on the tour. I'm here. Trying."

I refrain from rolling my eyes. Though I understand that for him, there is no bigger gesture. He lives for the tour, for the audience.

"I'm not the same without you, Luce. Everything means less. You gotta give me a second chance."

He seems so sincere, so lost, that I sit back down. But I don't know what to say. I can't give him what he needs. Not without losing myself.

Relief washes over his features as he settles in next to me again. "What can I do to make it up to you? To earn your trust again?"

"You can start by telling the label that song is mine." The anger and disappointment I'd been carrying around all these months floods my senses. He'd hurt me more than he knew by cheating, but when he stole my song and recorded it without me, he'd taken a piece of my heart that belonged to my dad. I couldn't forgive what he'd done. Not unless he made it right. "I want it back. Then we'll talk."

"I've already told them," he says softly.

My heart starts to pound, and I'm sure I haven't heard him correctly. "You did?"

He nods.

"And?" What if they didn't care? Was it lost to me forever?

"They want you to come in and record it."

Shit. I was afraid of that. I stand again, ready to leave. "I can't do that. I can't sing with you. Not while things are like they are. And not that song. Not now. Maybe not ever."

As I turn to go he says, "Luce, they want you to record a solo version of it."

I freeze. When I'd left, the label had been less than happy. I'd offered to do a solo album, but they'd told my agent something about me not having the stage presence for a solo act. Now, since I ditched the tour, I'm in breach of contract. It doesn't make for a pleasant negotiation process.

But if what he says is true, I have a chance to rectify that with a song that means the world to me. "Since when?"

"Since I told them you wrote it. They're pretty pissed I took credit for it."

"Why? Why did you tell them?" But I already know the real answer. He did it because the label is going to drop him anyway if I don't come back. The Cadan I know would never sacrifice his career by owning up to anything.

"Because, Lucy…" He grabs my hand and presses it to his heart. "I love you. Like I said, nothing's the same. I miss sharing the stage with you. I miss you. It turns out it means little without you by my side."

He's saying everything I've ever wanted to hear. Hope blossoms in my chest, but I'm not convinced. I probably never will be. "And what if I say no? What if I never come back? You risked your career for me."

He closes his eyes, and when he opens them, they're filled with pain. "It's a chance I had to take. I couldn't live with myself if I didn't make this right."

I can tell this is tearing him apart. He's made big mistakes, and he seems sincere no matter what his initial motivations were. But I've left that lifestyle and found I'm happier staying out of the spotlight. Yes, I enjoyed performing the night before, but that was just to the local crowd. It was fun, void of any pressure from the labels and the bean counters. I'd been singing for me, not everyone else.

I nod, accepting his explanation, even if I am still skeptical. "I don't know what to say."

"Say yes. Say you'll come back with me and record your dad's song. After that, we'll figure it out."

I hesitate, wanting to say yes. Wanting to ease his suffering. It's our soul mate connection. I can't help it. This is the reason I've refused to even talk to him. Being around him makes me weak. I shake my head. "I need time to think about it."

The breath he'd been holding comes out in a whoosh as he stands and crushes me into a hug. "That's better than no."

"Yeah," I agree, and hug him back, tears stinging my eyes. This will never work.

He tightens his hold on me until our bodies are pressed together. I let him, knowing full well it'll only make saying no harder. He's strong and familiar and everything I'd always wanted.

Until last night happened.

CHAPTER 18
Seth

Jax pulls me through the rain into Raven's Tavern. The first thing I notice is Mike sitting by himself at the bar. I gesture to him. "That's strange. Mike never comes here unless he's playing." I scan the room for the rest of the band, but come up empty.

That is, until I notice Lucy wrapped in the arms of that douchebag Kinx. "Fuck me."

"Is that an invitation?" Jax asks, laughing. "I thought we already covered that topic."

I all but growl and turn her shoulders until Lucy is in her sight line.

"Aww, shit," she whispers. "Why can't he leave her alone?"

"Because he's trying to get her back," I say, resentment burning a hole in my gut. And by the looks of it, he's off to a better than decent start. "Let's go."

"Go? Where?" Jax turns around, her eyes crinkled in confusion. "We're not leaving her here with him."

"Really? Looks like she's doing fine to me. Besides, weren't you the one not even answering her phone calls a few hours ago?" Suddenly, I'm pissed at Jax. If she'd been there for her friend, Lucy would've likely been tucked into Jax's apartment instead of standing over there plastered to the devil incarnate.

"Hey." Jax punches me in the arm. "Don't get snippy with me just because you've fallen for her after one night of whatever you two got up to."

I narrow my eyes. "I have not fallen for her."

"Right. That's why you spent the day in your artist's loft instead of at the tattoo shop." She gives me a saccharine-sweet smile and then heads off toward Lucy.

I immediately make my way to the bar and slump down next to Mike. "How long have you been here?"

"Since I left the shop." He picks up a shot glass full of whiskey and downs it.

I raise a curious eyebrow. "How many of those have you had?"

"A few."

"I better catch up then." I wave the bartender down and order a shot of my own. "Were you playing or something?"

"Nope. Trying to convince that gorgeous brunette to become a permanent member of the band."

The bartender slaps the shot glass in front of me. I lift it and study the liquid sloshing against the rim. "You asked Lucy to be a member?"

"Yep."

I can't help but glance back at her. Jax has an arm around her shoulders and is dragging her away from Kinx. Good. I'll have to send her a giant thank-you bouquet in the morning. "What did she say?" I ask Mike, nervous energy making it hard to breathe. Why do I care so much? I barely know this girl.

It's the art.

That's what I tell myself. Something about her opened up a part of me that I thought had died the night I lost E. That's all it is. And I don't want to lose that.

"Nothing. Her ex showed up and lured her away before we could work anything out."

The bartender asks if we need anything else. We both order another round of shots.

"So why are you drinking?" I've only seen Mike drunk once before. That was the night his girlfriend dumped him for his best friend. Make that *ex* best friend.

"Fuck, dude." He shakes his head. "I was just sitting there with Lucy, and we were talking about the band playing one of her songs. So she starts singing it, right?"

"And?" I stare into the whiskey, contemplating if I really want to drink it.

"Next thing I know, Kinx is there. And he sings the last few bars of the song with her."

"Okay." Yep, I'm definitely going to need this shot.

I pick it up, but then Mike says, "You've never heard anything like it, man. Or more accurate, felt anything like it. Their voices, they do shit to a person. Make you feel shit you don't want to feel."

Slowly, I lower the drink to the bar. "What do you mean? I've heard it's more like a shot of joy right in the arm."

He lets out a huff of laughter. "That's one way of putting it. I swear they were only singing together for a few seconds, but in that time more memories than I can count came flooding back. Memories I've worked hard to let go of. The ones that remind you of what it's like to give a shit."

His words filter through my haze and a cold dread slides down my spine. "Jesus."

"Yeah." He raises his glass, salutes me, and downs the whiskey. The shot glass slams against the bar and he stands. "Do yourself a favor. Run if those two ever team up again."

"Headed somewhere?" I ask, trying to ignore his last remark. The thought of Lucy going back to Kinx makes me physically ill. I grit my teeth. I'm way too invested in this girl.

"I have to get out of here."

"Hey," Jax says from behind us.

Mike grunts at her and heads toward the door.

"Where's he going?" Lucy asks.

I shrug. "Home?"

"I'll be right back," she tells Jax and runs after him. Kinx watches her from his place across the room. He's scowling, glancing back and forth between me and Mike. It takes a shit ton of effort not to head over to him and slam my fist into his nose.

"Stop," Jax says and waves the bartender off when he tries to pour me another drink.

"Why? You can drive my truck."

"Not the alcohol, you idiot. Though you clearly don't need any more of that tonight. I meant stop glaring at Cadan." She turns and rests her elbows on the bar. "He's Lucy's mate, and she'll decide what's best for herself without any input from you."

I know she has a point. But the primal need to protect Lucy is overpowering my rational mind. "He's a douche."

"I know."

"Does Lucy?"

"Yes." Jax pats my arm the way a patient mother would pat her child. "Why do you think she left his ass in the first place?"

Lucy and Mike are standing near the door, their heads bowed as they talk. He's a foot taller than her with jet-black hair. Even Mike would be better for her than Kinx. At least Mike respects women. He's a serial monogamist. But his last girlfriend did a number on him when she left him for a chick.

It's that soul-mate connection. No one can compete with that shit.

Lucy tugs Mike back over to where we stand at the bar. "Mike can't drive. I've confiscated his keys." She holds them up, letting them dangle in front of Jax. "Can you take him home?"

Jax grabs them. "Sure." Turning, she gives me a sidelong glance. "You can't drive either, can you?"

"Nope. But I'm walking distance." One of the perks of living right in town. My gaze lands on Lucy, and my mind flashes back to the night before when I'd had her in the shower and the agonizing way she'd trailed kisses down—

"All right," Jax says. "Come on, Luce. I'll give you a ride, too."

The three of them head for the door with Mike swaying between them. I guess he'd had more than a few. An invisible force sends me trailing after them. The last thing I want to do is go home to an empty house, but if I stay in the bar, I know I'm going to lose my shit on Kinx.

Jax reaches for the door, but before she can grab the handle, it bursts open on a gust of wind. "Holy shit," she says and shoves it closed. "Is there a high-wind advisory in effect?"

The bouncer nods. "Probably why there aren't very many people out tonight."

"Crap," she says and looks at Lucy. "Do you want to stay over? The ride to your house might be a little hairy."

Before Lucy can answer, I step in front of all of them, my shoulders tense. "No. I have more space. Everyone can come back to my house. You can stay there."

Jax gives me an odd look and then shrugs. "Okay."

"Dude," Mike says, rubbing his eyes. "All I want is my own bed."

I scowl at him. "Forget it. Jax isn't going to drive in this just because you're being a pussy."

Mike mumbles, "Whatever, man. As long as you have food. I'm starved."

Lucy opens her mouth, closes it, and after a pointed look from Jax, she nods.

"Good." I pull the door open, and the four of us huddle under the protection of the balcony. Sheets of water pour from the skies. Dammit. Just getting the block and a half to my house is going to be bad enough. "Jax? Will you be able to drive my truck? Visibility looks nonexistent."

"Yeah," she says in that soft voice I hate. It's the one full of pity. The one that says she knows why I'm being so adamant about this.

"All right, then. Mike, where'd you park? Do we need to move your car?" There are meters, and if he's parked on the street, he'll get a ticket in the morning.

"It's at the shop," he slurs.

"Great," Jax says and rolls her eyes. "He's totally sloshed."

"What? I'm not drivin'." Mike squares his shoulders and takes off into the night.

"Oh, man." Jax presses her lips together in annoyance. "Is he heading to your house?"

"I hope so," I say and hand her my keys. "You and Lucy take my truck. We'll meet you there."

She wraps her arms around herself and shivers. "You sure?"

"Yeah. He's a mess. I can't let him wander around by himself." Those last shots must've hit him hard.

"Okay, see you in a few." She waves me off with a worried expression.

I turn my back and ignore her. It's not the rain she's concerned about. Not with us walking, though it's fucking cold and I want to kill Mike. No, she's concerned about my state of mind. I can't say I blame her. Storms usually set me off. Tonight I'm a little calmer, but I'm not at all sure I want to analyze why.

Pulling the collar up on my jacket, I jog out into the punishing rain and am instantly drenched. "Fucking Mike," I mutter as my teeth chatter. At least some of the buildings have second-story balconies for a short reprieve. But that doesn't last long, and soon enough I'm back in the storm, blinded by the rain. He couldn't have gone far. Car lights flash over the street as a vehicle moves slowly in my direction. I recognize the familiar hum of my truck and wave Jax on, but I doubt she can even see me. The truck is inching along the road, spraying water from the wheels.

My gut seizes, and all the shadows morph into another time, on another road where the rain batters the redwoods.

Elsa's shoulders are tense and her knuckles have gone white from gripping the steering wheel.

"You look like my ninety-year-old grandmother," I say, laughing.

She's pressed forward, peering out the window, going all of twenty miles an hour. "Shut up, Seth," she snaps. "It's your fault we're on this damn road."

I just grin, thinking of all the ways I'm going to coax her out of her bad mood when we get home.

"Why did you have to go out tonight? God. I told you it was going to storm." She slows as she heads into one of the hairpin turns of Highway 128.

I don't say anything, hoping she'll let it go. No such luck.

"This is like the third night this week. It's bad enough that you go out, but you guys don't even think to set a designated driver. And then I have to pick your ass up."

"Babe." I lean my head against the cool door, trying to stop a minor bout of nausea. I'd definitely had one beer too many. "I already told you, I had to go. It was Marty's going-away party."

"Seth!" she yells, her dark eyes flashing with anger. "There were strippers there. And you're drunk. Again. You don't even like Marty."

"He's Jax's brother. I had to go." But inside, I'm wondering why. She's right. I don't like him. He's a dick. Jax hadn't even been there. My other friends were, though. And since I work from home, I rarely see them. I'd gone for them, not Marty.

"Don't lie." Her tone is low and full of ice now. "This was my night to stay in with the girls. Not drive all the way down to Boonville to pick your ass up. And in this weather, too."

"Calm down, will you?" The rain starts to pick up the closer we get to Highway 1. "You can rip my head off when we get home."

"Don't tell me to calm down." Elsa speeds up, knowing the road is about to straighten out, and then glares at me. "I'm tired of this shit. I have a life too."

"Oh come on. Give me a break will you? I don't give you a hard time when you go out."

"Ha! Really? Wasn't it just last week you were having a fit because I went up to Fort Bragg for a spa day with the girls?"

Now I'm pissed. "Not this again. Can you drop it already?"

"No, I won't drop it," she says, mimicking my inflection, and then huffs. "It's okay for you to get drunk with the guys, but it's not okay for me to get a manicure with my girlfriends?"

"It's not the manicure. It's the facial, the massage, and the two hundred dollars' worth of shit you buy when you do that."

"It's my goddamned money!" She gets really quiet, then says, "At least I'm not spending it on strippers."

I close my eyes, exasperated, and clutch my pounding head. "How many times do I have to tell you, I didn't spend money on the strippers? They weren't my idea."

"But you knew they would be there and you decided to go anyway." All the accusation is gone, replaced by hurt.

Shit, now I feel like a total ass. She wasn't mad I was out with the guys. She was mad because of the entertainment. "Babe, I—watch out!"

Elsa gasps and swerves to miss the pickup that's coming head-on into our lane, but she's too late. The truck clips her small Honda on the driver's side and then everything is just a memory of her screams combined with metal crunching and then the horrific sensation of the car hydroplaning. We hit the guardrail, and metal scrapes against metal until it gives way and the car freefalls into the ravine.

I don't remember anything after that except the blood. And guilt.

"Seth?" a husky female voice is calling my name.

I blink. My body is ice-cold. "It's too late," I say, still seeing E's bloody body in my mind.

"Are you all right?" Small hands wrap around my arm.

I wipe the wetness, a mix of rain and salt, from my eyes. Lucy.

She tucks herself against my side and wraps her arm around me.

"You shouldn't be out here," I say as I let her tug me along.

"Neither should you."

Her teeth are chattering by the time we burst into the kitchen of my house. The place is quiet except for the creak of footsteps overhead. Someone's upstairs. I stand there, still dazed by the flashback, seeing nothing.

Then Lucy steps in front of me and stares up at me with those brilliant blue eyes. She's drenched, her hair flattened to her head, but she doesn't seem to care at all. My world spins with the images of E, the blood, and the terror I never seem to be able to let go of. But when Lucy places a light hand on my cheek, everything fades and all I see is her. After a moment, she silently takes my hand again and leads me up the stairs.

CHAPTER 19

Lucy

The gusts of wind drive against Seth's truck, and even going ten miles an hour, the vehicle seems unstable at best. I have no idea how Jax can see anything out the windshield. The rain is coming down too hard for the windshield wipers to keep up. But it's only a few blocks, and after narrowly missing a black sports car, she comes to a stop in front of Seth's house.

We sit in the truck with the heater running, waiting for Seth and Mike to show up.

"Jax?" I ask.

"Hmm?" She peers out the windshield.

"Why did Seth lie about this being his sister's house?"

She freezes and then turns, grimacing.

I raise an eyebrow, waiting for her to answer. When she doesn't, I say, "Well? What's that about? Is he afraid his one-nighters will turn into stalkers?" I'm curious. If that's the case, why had he brought me here? Because I'm Jax's friend?

"That could be part of it. He definitely doesn't like attachments, but it's not the main reason." Her expression turns sad. "And really, that's his story to tell. Not mine."

"It has to do with the accident, doesn't it?" Deep in my gut, I just know he lived here with his soul mate. The place has too many feminine touches to be a twenty-three-year-old's bachelor pad.

"Something like that."

We're quiet as the rain batters the truck, each lost in our own thoughts. It's hard enough being away from Cadan, but that's my choice. I can't imagine how I'd survive if I lost him completely. For better or worse, he has a part of my soul. For Seth to lose his soul mate so young—I can't even imagine the devastation.

"Hey," Jax says and rubs on the fogging window. "Is that Mike?"

Before I can answer, she's out of the car, running across the street toward Mike, who appears to be trying to force his way into the wrong house. Where is Seth? He'd been right behind Mike.

I jump out of the truck and scan the area. Nothing. Within seconds, I'm soaked through. Damn. Jax and Mike stumble toward me with Mike's arm draped over her shoulders. "Where's Seth?"

Mike doesn't even acknowledge I've spoken.

Jax hands me Seth's keys. "Can you find the house key and unlock the door?"

I fumble with the key ring, trying to get my frozen fingers to work. After three tries, I finally find the correct one and hold the door open for them. I follow and stand dripping just inside the door as Jax pulls Mike to the breakfast table. He sits and grins at her stupidly. "Hey, Jax?"

"Yeah?"

"Wanna help me out of these clothes?"

She laughs and heads out of the room. A few seconds later, she comes back with a stack of towels and throws one at his head. He catches it but makes no move to actually dry off. After tossing me one, she wraps hers around her dripping hair and then shakes her head at Mike. He's eyeing the way her shirt is clinging to her body.

"Dude, stop," she says and rolls her eyes.

As she walks by, he grabs her hand and yanks her toward him. "Thanks for saving me from the rain."

She slides into his lap playfully and banters with him about getting out of their wet clothes.

"Hey," I call. They both turn and glance at me as if they'd forgotten I was here. "Where's Seth?"

Mike shrugs and hugs Jax closer to him. She frowns but makes no move to remove herself from his lap.

"It shouldn't take this long for him to get here," I say and open the door.

"Where are you going?" Jax asks as I head out.

The wind whistles with the roar of the storm and I call out, "To find Seth." The door slams behind me and cuts off Jax's response.

Jesus, it's cold and utterly horrible out. Ice-cold rain drives into me sideways as I trudge down the street, searching for Seth. It's too dark to see much of anything. Where is he? There's no use calling out; he wouldn't be able to hear me over the storm. I trace the steps toward the bar but don't see him anywhere.

Shit!

What happened to him? My heart speeds up as I get closer and closer to the bar. Panicked now, I run across the street, splashing though a puddle that turns my feet to ice. He has to be here somewhere. Just has to be. Nothing is open, and the streets are deserted. But I press on. I can't go back without him. I won't. After circling the block twice, I finally spot him. He's hunched over, leaning against a door as if he's having trouble breathing.

"Seth!" I continue to call his name as I run to his side. Then he straightens and looks at me with haunted eyes, ones full of anguish.

My heart squeezes and feels like it's breaking in two for whatever it is he's seeing. "Seth," I say again and wrap my hands around his forearm. "Are you all right?"

He mumbles something about it being too late. He's completely lost in another time, and I wonder if he's even seeing me at all. But he lets me guide him toward his house, and that's good enough for now.

By the time we step inside, I'm shivering uncontrollably, frozen to the bone. Seth has gooseflesh covering his arms, but

I'm pretty certain he doesn't even realize it. He stands in his kitchen glancing around, but doesn't seem to focus on anything.

The pain lining his face touches that raw part of me that's been aching for Dad ever since he passed six months ago. Seth is clearly still grieving and it breaks my heart. Slowly, I step up to him and cup his cheek.

Recognition replaces the agony in his deep-green gaze. And all I want to do is take care of him. To do my best to keep that haunted look from his eyes.

I don't know where Jax and Mike have gone, but it makes little difference. My only concern is Seth. I lace my hand in his again and gently lead him upstairs. The room we'd stayed in the night before has a light shining under the door, so I bypass it for the next room. As soon as we walk in, I know this is Seth's room. Seth's and his mate's. I freeze and the breath leaves me as my lungs constrict. No wonder he never brings anyone here. The walls are white, but there's color everywhere else. The poppy pillows, the floral nightstands, the bright yellow lamps. I'd bet my last dollar his mate decorated this room.

"This way," Seth says and leads me to the master bathroom. Relief washes through me. White tile everywhere. No traces of the ghost that still haunts him.

Seth stops in the middle of the room and stares down at me. I can't quite read his expression. He's intense, but not with desire. Just emotion.

"You're cold," he says.

"So are you." I am cold, but I'm far more worried about what's going on with him than my own comfort.

"Shower." He reaches over and turns the taps on, letting the water heat up. But he doesn't move. He just keeps standing there watching me. The depth of sadness radiating off him caresses me, sinks into me, and makes me want to take care of him.

With my fingers trembling, I reach up and work my way through the buttons on his shirt. My fingers start to regain some of their feeling as I fumble through the task.

I want to strip my own clothes off and jump in the shower, letting the heat drive away the effects of the storm. But taking care of Seth is more important. I want to see that light in his eyes again. Hear the laughter in his voice. Somehow find a way to show him he can love again. Once the buttons are undone, I push his shirt over his shoulders and then tug the white tee over his head.

To my surprise, he places his hands on my hips and runs them up along my sides, taking my sweater with his motion. A second later, I'm topless, standing only in my bra and black pants.

There's nothing romantic or erotic about either of us undressing the other, just a tender understanding of one human being needing another. We finish stripping each other and then Seth tugs me into the blissful, hot stream.

I stand in front of him, my back to his chest with his arms wrapped around me. We stay there until the cold is driven from our bodies, if not our hearts. We don't speak. Not even when Seth gently washes my body with shower gel, and then I do the same for him.

Once clean, he stares at me, his eyes soft with tenderness and vulnerability. I stare back, lost in the moment until the water turns tepid. Releasing me, he turns the knobs to off. I hadn't been self-conscious before, but I am now. I don't know why, but the fact that we'd taken care of each other seemed almost more intimate than what we'd shared the night before. Almost. Wrapping my arms around my chest, I turn away from Seth, hoping he'll disappear into the other room long enough for me to find a towel.

"Here," he says and gently wraps a bath sheet around me.

I clutch the ends together and send him a grateful smile. "Thanks."

The sweet look on his face melts away all my apprehension, and the tension eases from my shoulders. "You're welcome," he says softly. "I'll find you a robe."

Then he's gone, and all I can think about is the way he'd been watching me. Cadan has never looked at me that way, as if I were someone to be cherished. The closest he's ever come is while we're singing and have that magical connection. But I'm certain it has everything to do with the way the music makes him feel, not the way *I* make him feel.

While waiting for Seth, I towel-dry my hair and then wrap my body back up in the towel. The house is quiet, eerily quiet. Where are Jax and Mike? A knock sounds on the door.

"Yes?"

"I've got a robe and some socks for you," Seth says from the bedroom.

I open the door and smile at him. He's wearing straight-legged sweats and a black T-shirt. No socks. I stare at his feet. "Your toes are going to get cold."

He doesn't say anything, and when I look up, he's gazing at me, his brows drawn together with indecision. Handing me the robe and socks, he says, "I can't sleep with socks on."

"Oh." I clutch the robe to my chest. "I'll only be a minute, then I'll get out of your way."

He frowns. "Out of my way?"

"So you can get some sleep." I slip the robe on and turn away from him to pull the towel off. Once the robe is cinched, I hand him the towel. "I'll go find the guest room or the couch. Thanks for letting us stay. It's ugly out there."

I'm almost to the door when his hand wraps around my wrist, stopping me. My pulse skips a beat, and I take a moment to collect myself. What is it about this guy? His very presence turns my insides into all kinds of crazy.

"Stay," he says.

"Uh…" Is he propositioning me? There's no denying I'm attracted to him, but having a repeat of the night before seems like a bad idea. Especially after the way I'd found him earlier.

"To just sleep," he says. "Nothing else. I promise."

I glance at his king-sized bed and raise an eyebrow. "You're sure?"

He nods and tugs me to the bed. "I'd really like you to stay."

"Okay." Nervous anticipation zings through me. How would we spend the whole night together in the bed with me only wearing a robe and not end up sleeping together? It seems impossible, but I can't stop myself from climbing in the bed.

Seth crawls in after me and rolls onto his side, tucking me close. His arm slips around my waist, and he rests his hand between the folds of the robe, on my bare stomach.

I sigh, instantly warm and comfortable in his bed. In his arms.

"Good night, Lucy," he whispers in my ear.

"Night, Seth."

CHAPTER 20
Seth

Out on the street with the rain pounding away at me, I'd been right back there with E that night. The pain and anguish ripped through my gut as if I were experiencing the accident all over again. This wasn't the first time I'd had a flashback so intense, but it's the first time in a very long time.

Then suddenly, Lucy had been there, a beacon in the sea of my anguish. And she'd brought me home, brought me back to myself by just being there. The way she'd let me hold her in the shower and then again in my bed had restored something vital in me. I'd barely even been a walking shell of a person since the accident. But now a small trace of acceptance starts to take up residence in my gut. I'll never get over losing E. I know this down to my core. I only hope I can learn to live with it. And last night, in Lucy's sure arms, something broke loose. For the first time in months, I felt like I could breathe. To just relax with someone else. I can't let her go.

The predawn light filters through the blinds as light rain patters against the windows. Lucy's soft body is still snuggled against mine. Her deep, rhythmic breathing, indicating she's still sound asleep, is more comforting than I care to admit. I want her to stay. I don't want to know what the day will bring. I'd rather stay right here with her warmth keeping the darkness away.

I lie next to her, taking in her silky dark locks splayed across my pillow, and force myself to not run my fingers through her hair. They twitch with the urge, but I don't want to do anything to wake her.

The minutes tick by as I watch her and I pray the moment never ends. I'm content, a state of being that is so wholly foreign I almost panic. I don't deserve this. But then Lucy shifts and rolls over to face me. Her eyes are hooded, heavy with sleep. Sultry. My gaze shifts to her lips, and my mind turns off. I want her.

She chuckles and sweeps her hair to the side, tucking the strands behind one ear. "Well, good morning."

I smile. "The best."

We stare at each other, not moving. My body goes taut with desire. And it has little to do with the fact the robe she fell asleep in is gaping open to reveal the creamy slope of her breasts. Though that doesn't hurt. No. It's the easy intimacy. And the way she puts me at peace by just being present.

"I'll be right back." She scoots to the edge of the mattress and swings her legs out of the bed. A shiver visibly shakes her. When she cinches the robe closed, the fabric stretches across her round ass and I consciously hold back a groan. Damn.

After a few minutes of the water running, I can't help myself. I have to be near her. Padding into the bathroom, I grin, catching her brushing her teeth with a bit of toothpaste and her finger. "You know, that extra toothbrush is still in the other bathroom."

She spits and rinses then turns to me. "I didn't want to wake Mike and Jax since I plan on climbing right back into that bed." Her gaze runs the length of my body, pausing briefly on my chest. Then she raises one eyebrow. "Are you joining me?"

This time my groan is audible, and her smile widens.

She reaches out and strokes one finger over my abs. "See you in a minute."

I can't keep my eyes off her as she saunters back into the bedroom, the silk robe showing every delicious curve. Sweet Jesus. Last night she'd been gentle, soft, and… solid. An anchor. My anchor. This morning, she's sultry Lucy. The one I met at the club. The combination makes my chest ache with something between awe and fear.

Standing at the sink, I press my hands to the marble and hang my head, taking a minute just to breathe. I have to let whatever is happening inside me go. She has a soul mate, and no matter how much I want her, she's going to go back to him eventually. He'll get his shit together one of these days, and she won't be able to help herself.

I should leave. Go down and make breakfast for everyone. Spending the morning loving her will only make it worse. I make up my mind to do just that, but when I reach for a towel after brushing my teeth, her discarded clothes catch my eye. The black lace bra I'd carefully stripped from her is lying on top of her sweater. The swell of her breasts is fresh in my mind and my fingers ache to touch her.

Screw breakfast. I can't leave her alone in my bed. Who am I kidding?

"Hey," she says, her eyes glinting with desire as I head back into the bedroom.

I smile seductively, mentally peeling back the blankets covering her bare body.

She laughs, a low, husky sound that makes me instantly hard. I could listen to her read a grocery list and die a happy man. "Jax calls that smile you're wearing the panty-dropper."

"What?" I half-choke, half-laugh, then clear my throat. "Is that a trait shared by others, or only specific to me?"

She smirks, then runs her pointed tongue over her bottom lip. "Hard to say. It's the first time I've experienced such a phenomenon."

Holy fuck. She's hot. I mentally calm myself before I throw the covers back and take her right here and now. Sitting on the edge of the bed, I run my fingers along her jawline, letting them trail softly down her neck.

She takes in a sharp breath as I feather my thumb over her pulse.

"I want to kiss you right here," I say.

She swallows. "I'm not stopping you."

The want on her face only makes me more determined to take my time. Watching her desire build is doing strange and wonderful things to both my mind and body. "In a moment," I whisper and slide my hand down, dipping my fingers into her cleavage.

Her chest rises as she arches into my touch.

God, I want to take her breasts into my hands, clasp her taut peaks between my teeth, and tease her until she's writhing beneath me.

But that slow tremble taking over her body is too alluring.

I take my time, exploring the satin feel of her skin as I slowly peel back the blankets.

"Seth?" she breathes.

"Hmm?" Cupping her hip with one hand, I slide down and press a kiss to her inner knee.

She responds by spreading her legs, giving me full access. "I want you."

Satisfaction fills me to my core. I want this girl to want me. Want her to want only me. Shit. This is intense. I shouldn't have these feelings. I don't want them. But I can't help myself. "You've got me," I say and kiss my way up her inner thigh. I pause and gently blow against her sex.

"Oh," she moans and her hips rise slightly.

I tilt my head up and smile in smug satisfaction. She wants me just as much as I want her. Her eyes flutter open, intense with need. She doesn't say anything, just winds her fingers into my hair and applies the tiniest bit of pressure. Not a demand. A request. And I'm all too happy to oblige.

Her sweet scent assaults me as I taste her, licking, sucking, teasing, using her moans of approval to unravel her secrets.

"Seth," she gasps and tightens her grip on my hair.

I redouble my efforts, determined to coax her to climax with just my tongue. She bucks beneath me and I grasp her hips, stilling her, forcing her to give me complete control.

Her cries grow louder, her entire body sparking like a live wire.

"Take me," she forces out. "I want you inside me."

Holy fuck. I want that, too. But I can't bring myself to pull away until after she comes completely apart. I pulse my tongue against her faster.

Her cries turn into high-pitched gasps as her body goes taut and then stills beneath me. Deep personal satisfaction fills me, and while her limbs go limp, I gently kiss my way up and over her left hip. She stirs beneath me, and I continue my exploration until I have one of her nipples right where I want it, clasped lightly between my teeth. Wrapping her legs around me, she lets out another gasp and grinds into my ever-hardening erection.

"Now," she demands, pushing at my sweats, lowering them as far as she can reach. I want to resist, drag this moment out for as long as possible, but when her small hand slips over my cock, I lose all sense of self-control and grab a condom from the nightstand.

"Now?" I ask to confirm. Or was I trying to buy a little time?

She grabs the condom from my hands, rips it open with practiced skill, and then rolls the latex on me.

"Now," she orders and tilts her hips up, pressing herself against me.

I could so bury myself into her heat and take her fast and hard. It seems to be what she's demanding. But I have other plans. I pull back slightly and position myself right at her opening, gently teasing.

Her nails bite into my shoulders and she lets out a strangled growl. "Seth, dammit, you're driving me insane."

I can't help the smug smile that claims my lips. I'd gladly drive her insane for the rest of the day, if only I could hold out that long. But the way her tongue dances wickedly over my chest and the shocking darts of delicious pain from her nails raking over my back have me pressing into her, slowly, inch by inch, her heat driving me out of my fucking mind.

"Oh, God," she says and gasps as I bury myself deep inside her and still, waiting for her to adjust to my intrusion. And then when she rocks her hips, I pull out just as slowly, torturing myself. My body shakes with the effort to hold myself back, and when I meet her brilliant blue eyes, full of so much lust, I let myself go and thrust hard and fast, watching as her eyes close from the intense pleasure.

The way she arches her body into mine, so completely lost in the moment, it's the most beautiful thing I've ever seen. Something breaks free inside me. An overwhelming urge to make her mine, to bind my soul to hers, takes over. To some-how, through our physical joining, make a connection that's impossible to break.

Her eyes open, and our gazes lock as I once again thrust deep, making her gasp.

"More," she says breathily. "Much more."

Those words are all I need to hear. In one swift movement, I grasp her wrists and hold them over her head, pausing just long enough for her acceptance.

Though she doesn't speak, the way her body quivers in anticipation and her legs tighten around my waist, I know she's as into this as I am. I bend my head to hers and whisper, "Today, you belong to no one but me."

I pull back and stare into her wide eyes. She nods once and then our bodies begin to move in unison, matching each other's every thrust in raw, unabashed need. It's not just sex anymore. She's in my heart now. I'm sure of it. And right now, even though I know it will be my undoing, my heart is bursting with the joy of it.

"Lucy." I groan and quicken my pace, slamming into her.

"Seth," she answers on a shortened breath and lets out a cry of pleasure. Her body spasms as she tightens around me. "Now. Come with me."

I thrust one more time, deep inside her as she shudders beneath me, and finally lose myself in her.

CHAPTER 21

Lucy

I lie spent in Seth's arms, my limbs languid with the aftermath of incredible sex. But I know that no matter how much I want to tell myself what we did means nothing, my heart says otherwise.

Today you belong to no one but me.

His words keep running through my head. At the time, it had been sexy as hell. But now it's terrifying. Had he actually meant anything by it? Or was he just caught up in the moment? Sex makes people say crazy things. Especially hot, mind-blowing sex.

And holy freakin' cow, had it been mind-blowing. I never thought sex could be better with anyone than it was with Cadan. With him, sex had been almost magical, but it all revolved around a release of our connection. A way to purge some of the intense emotions that lingered after we'd put on a show. My attraction to him was only that intense if we'd been working together. But with Seth? Damn. All we needed was each other and boom. Instant sparks.

Why was that?

Seth presses his lips to my temple. "Are you ready for breakfast?" he asks as he runs his fingers lightly over my bare spine.

"Yeah." My voice is so low with uncertainty that he shifts and rolls me to my side in order to look me in the eye.

"We don't have to get up," he says. "I'm happy to stay right here for the rest of the day."

I want to deny him and leap out of the bed, but I can't. I'm frozen with the knowledge that once I get up, everything will change. Cadan and the label aren't going to leave me alone. And if I don't go back, I'll lose the right to record my own songs. They still think I signed that publishing contract. I can't work with Cadan and be with Seth at the same time. And I'll be damned if I set myself up to hurt Seth. He's been through enough. "I think Jax and Mike might come looking for us sooner or later."

He sighs. "Yeah. Probably."

Reluctantly, I extract myself from his arms and shiver with the loss of his warmth. Wrapping myself in the robe, I glance back at him. He's propped up on one elbow, studying me.

"What?"

Shaking his head, he gets up and walks around to where I'm sitting and holds his hand out. "Come on. The shower is waiting."

I quirk one eyebrow and try not to stare at his naked torso or his well-defined abs. "Planning a repeat performance of this morning?"

He grins. "Well, I'm thinking I'll change the moves up a little."

I can't help but laugh and take his hand. If I have to give him up, I might as well enjoy him while I can.

It's late afternoon by the time Jax drops me off at my house. "See you tomorrow?" I ask.

"Sure. Call me when your car is ready."

The shop said the starter had gone out and they'd had to overnight the correct replacement. "Thanks."

I'm already out of her car when she says, "Luce?"

"Yeah?"

She glances down at her hands folded in her lap. "Don't hurt him."

"Cadan?" I say, caught off guard, and then bite my lip at the incredulity on her face. "Oh, you mean Seth."

She rolls her eyes. "Dude. You just spent the last two nights banging my best friend and now I barely recognize him."

"Your best friend?"

"Well…" She closes her eyes and grimaces a little. "He's the one I spend most of my time with these days. Sorry. It's hard when you're not around."

I wave a hand and try to ignore the slight ache in my heart. I wasn't anyone's person anymore. I'd been Dad's. And I'd thought Jax's. But Dad's gone and Jax has moved on. That leaves Cadan, and I don't want to be his person. At least I don't think I can survive being his person. "Don't worry about it. I get it."

She gives me a small smile. "So, about Seth."

"What about him?" Now I'm just irritated and feeling utterly alone. "I thought you said he's the player type. Right? Shouldn't you be warning me to stay away from him or something?"

She sits back in her seat and lets out a long breath. "I tried that already. It didn't work. And now I don't know what's going on, but Seth isn't himself. Or at least not the Seth he's been the last eighteen months. Around you, he's almost his old self."

"So? Maybe he's like that when he's with other girls too." I shrug her concerns off. We've only known each other a few days. An intense couple of days, but still.

"Maybe," she says. "But I don't really think so. Just try to let him down easy when you go back to Cadan."

I open my mouth to protest her remark about Cadan, but then close it. No one believes Cadan and I won't end up together. It's useless to argue. I nod. "It's not like we even have a relationship, but I'll talk to him."

"Thanks."

I stand on my porch as she backs out of my driveway and disappears down Highway 1. Before I go inside, I wander around to the back deck. Rainwater is pooled on the chairs, and the skies are still overcast from last night's storm. The gloom matches my mood. I lean forward on the deck railing, losing myself in the surf churning below. This spot, right here on Dad's deck, is the one that usually calms me, brings me peace when everything else is unsettled.

But not today. There's a war going on inside me. My connection to Cadan when we sing together. The way we seem to see into each other's souls and know each other so well. It's unlike anything I've ever experienced with anyone. I don't know if I can give it up forever. Yet, I can't be with him either. Not with the way he is now. Selfish, self-centered, and arrogant.

And then there's Seth. I've just met him, and while I know whatever we might have together will never be as intense as the soul connection I have with Cadan, he makes me feel things I've never experienced before. Wanted, respected, maybe even cherished.

Or was that just the kind of lover he was? Maybe in a few weeks he'd turn into every other guy I knew and move on to someone new. *Today you belong to no one but me.*

Today. Yeah. That said it all.

When the chill from the ocean is too much to bear, I let myself in the back door and head straight for the fireplace. The wood is already stacked, and all I need to do is light the fire starter. Before long, heat fills the living room and the wood crackles under the flames.

In the kitchen, I start simmering a cup of milk for homemade hot chocolate. The familiar pang of loss hits me hard and tears sting my eyes. How many times did Dad and I stand in this spot making hot cocoa together on a cold winter night?

The shrill of the house phone snaps me out of my memory, and without thinking, I grab the receiver. "Hello?"

"Lucile Marie," Mom says.

Shit! I bite back a sigh. "Hi, Mom."

"Don't *hi* me. Where have you been? I've been trying to reach you for hours."

My teeth grind together as I clench my jaw. "I was with Jax." It's sort of true.

Silence.

"Mom?"

"Cadan is here."

This time I can't stop the sigh. "And?"

"You're ruining your life."

The phone creaks as my hand tightens around the phone. "If that's all you wanted to say, Mother, I've heard it before. I've got something on the stove. I'll talk to you later."

"Lucy? Wait."

I debate pretending I didn't hear her, but can't bring myself to hang up. She's still my mother, after all. "I'm here."

"You'll be here Friday, won't you?"

Friday is Christmas Eve and her house is the last place I want to be. Her husband will spend the entire day talking about how screwed up the music industry is and tell me what a shame it is that music is my talent. Then he'll move on to everyone else who has ever wronged him. The bitch fest will go on until he finally passes out from too much rum in his eggnog. And Mom will take every chance she can to get me to go back to Cadan. She'll preface her argument with all the money I'll be giving up and how stupid I am for throwing my life away. "Yes," I say because she's the only family I have. Being alone on Christmas for the first time since I lost Dad is unthinkable.

"Four o'clock." There's a beep and then the line goes dead.

"Bye," I say, staring at the phone, and then I throw the cordless on the counter. Ugh!

I grab my phone and start texting Jax, but before I can hit Send, a message comes in.

Seth. *Need someone to keep you warm?*

A strangled laugh bubbles up from the depths of my throat. I type back. *Why, Seth, are you trying to invite yourself over?*

Only if the answer is yes.

I stare at the message, not sure what to do. After the call from Mom, I feel more alone than ever. Jax would let me rant to her over the phone, but she has to work at Mendocino Cuisine waiting tables.

My phone buzzes. *Or maybe dinner?*

Whoa! Is Seth Keenan asking a girl out on a date?

His answer is almost immediate. *Damn right he is. You don't want to crush a vulnerable man, do you?*

No. I definitely don't want to do that. Come over. Bring dinner. The second I hit Send, a weight lifts from my chest. The pressure from my mom and Cadan vanishes as I look forward to an easy night with the sexy guy I can't seem to stay away from.

Be there in an hour.

The milk is steaming on the stove, but instead of tossing in the chocolate, I turn the stove off and head upstairs. I have a date.

CHAPTER 22
Seth

Did I really just ask a chick out on a date? That's probably not what Jax had in mind when she'd grilled and then berated me for getting involved with her best friend. The one who was still tied to her soul mate. But dammit if I couldn't get Lucy out of my head. And the fact that I always want to paint after seeing her has me texting against my better judgment.

After she'd left this morning, it was all I could do to get Mike out the door so I could spend the day in my studio. My fingers had ached with the need to paint. And after I'd put the finishing touches on one of the portraits, I sent that text without thinking it through.

I don't chase girls. Not like this. Hit on them? Flirt my way into their beds? Hell yes. But dating was out. Not my style.

Whatever it is with Lucy is different. The sheer fact that just being around her stirs my passion for painting is enough to make me pursue her for as long as she'll let me. I'll deal with the fallout later. The only thing I know for sure is I can't stay away.

I shower quickly, and with my hair still damp, I grab my keys and head over to the Seafood Café. My buddy Dean is the chef here. What he creates with his wife, Ashley, is almost better than sex. A solid second for sure. I bypass the busy entrance, shaking my head at the amount of patrons who came out on a Monday night in December for his famous lemon-grass halibut, and use the back door to walk right into the kitchen.

He grins and waves me over to where he's sautéing some mussels. The mouthwatering scent of garlic and coconut permeates the air, and my stomach growls.

"Hey, man. What's going on?" he asks.

I clap him on the back. "Any chance I can con you out of two takeout orders of whatever your special is tonight?"

He quirks a curious eyebrow. "Your sister in town?"

Lillian and Dean used to date before he met Ashley. While she adores his food, she's not too excited about seeing her ex so happy when he's the one who dumped her. I shake my head. "No. Not until later this week."

He raises his other eyebrow. "Date?"

I give a noncommittal shrug.

"Oh, ho! Keenan has a date," he says with a grin. "About damn time, man."

"It's no big deal." I shift uncomfortably. What Lucy and I do or don't do together is no one's business but ours. Dean isn't likely to talk, but I'm conscious of the fact she's a public figure. And the last thing she needs is reporters sniffing around if anyone hears she's seeing someone. Or even appears to be seeing someone.

"Right," he says and bobs his head, indicating he doesn't believe me for a second. He knows me better than almost anyone. A date is unprecedented.

"The meals?" I prompt.

He laughs. "Yeah, sure. It's halibut tonight. Go have a drink at the bar. I'll have Ash bring them out to you."

"Thanks." I head to the bar, but I don't drink. I'm driving, and ever since that horrific night, I haven't touched one ounce of booze and then slid behind the wheel. Not once.

In the twenty minutes it takes for the food to arrive, I fend off not one but two locals who clearly would like nothing more than to take me home with them. A week ago, I'd have already ditched dinner and had my tongue down the brunette's throat. Tonight, I'm less than interested. Downright annoyed actually.

"Pardon me, ladies," Ashley says, squeezing by them. "This man has a date waiting."

One of them gives me a look of pure disappointment. The other shrugs and immediately moves on to start flirting with the bartender.

"Thanks, Ash."

She smiles and puts the bag on the counter. "Anytime, Seth. Anytime. Now, go on and have your mysterious date before Dean's curiosity gets the best of him and he demands all the gory details."

I chuckle. "It's driving him crazy, isn't it?"

She nods and leans in for a half-hug. "Bordering on obsessive. Go. Have fun."

I hug her back and kiss her on the top of her head. "You're the best."

"I know." She gives me a gentle push toward the door.

"Wait." I pull out my wallet. "I need to pay the bill."

She shakes her head. "Not tonight you don't. It's on me."

I'm holding my credit card out to her, but she pushes it back. And knowing there's no way I'll win the argument, I stuff the card and wallet back in my pocket. I'll settle up later. One way or another.

The drive down Highway 1 seems to take forever. Just my luck, I get behind the one driver who is clearly a tourist on the Pacific Coast Highway. He slows to a crawl around every corner and slight bend. Though it's probably for the best. I'm so anxious to see Lucy that if I'd been given open road, I more than likely would've ended up at the bottom of a cliff.

The lights shine bright from her gray seaside home. I pull to a stop in her gravel driveway and take a moment to collect myself. Suddenly I'm filled with nervous energy. What am I doing here? Setting myself up for disaster. That's for certain.

With food in hand, I stride onto her porch, and before I can knock, the door swings open. Lucy's face brightens with a smile as she leans against the open door, dressed in a flared skirt, leggings, and a form-fitting T-shirt. Her feet are bare except for the bright pink toenail polish that hadn't been there this morning.

"Hi," I say as I lean in and brush my lips over hers.

"Hey." Her smile turns mischievous and then she grabs my shirt and yanks me inside.

"Whoa. Did you miss me already?" I laugh at her.

She shakes her head. "No. But one more minute on the porch and I was going to turn into a Popsicle."

We're standing in the foyer in front of the staircase. To the left is a short hallway into what appears to be the living room. To the right is a dining room table. I set the food down and pull Lucy into my arms, kissing her deeply and so thoroughly she's breathless when I finally let go.

"Oh," she says, her face flushed. "Hello to you, too."

I grin and head through the dining room to her kitchen. "Wine?"

She grabs the bag of food and follows me. "White or red?"

"White."

She opens the refrigerator door and hands me a full bottle of sauvignon blanc, followed by a corkscrew.

"Perfect," I say.

While I open the wine, she turns to pull dishes from the white cabinets. As she reaches up to grab them, her T-shirt rides up, exposing the creamy flesh of her lower back. In an effort to control myself, I turn toward the window for something else to focus on. "Jesus, Lucy."

"What?" She spins around, holding the plates to her chest.

"This view is fucking amazing." The night is crystal clear, and the moon lights up the Pacific.

"Yeah," she says. "This was my dad's house. He was an oceanographer before he retired. Being close to the ocean gave him peace."

The look on her face is so sad and tender I want to forget about dinner, pull her into my arms, and hold her until the pain fades.

But she grabs two wineglasses and holds them out to me. "You pour. I'll set the table."

Dinner it is. Moments later, the lemon-grass halibut is resting on a bed of rice and smells like heaven on earth.

Lucy sits across from me, a fork poised in her hand. "This is amazing."

Not as amazing as she is.

Her eyes sparkle with joy as she raises her wineglass in my direction. "To new friends."

I set my fork down and grab my glass but don't raise it yet. "Is that what we are?"

Uncertainty flickers in her expression. "Aren't we?"

Her pouty frown makes me want to forget the food and show her just how friendly I really want to be. But I've opened the door to the conversation no guy ever wants to have. Dumbass. Why did I ask that? "Of course we're friends. But I don't usually share my bed with friends, so this is new for me."

She lets out a startled laugh. "You mean you're not friends with any of the girls you've slept with? Ever?"

I shrug and give her a chagrined smile. "Only you."

"Well..." She picks up her glass again and holds it out. "Then this really calls for a toast."

Raising my glass, I nod. "To you, the singing pixie with a fiery voice."

She pauses and then giggles.

Holy shit, I've never heard a sweeter sound. So far I've seen sassy Lucy, sexy-as-hell Lucy, rock-star Lucy, and supportive Lucy. But this Lucy? The one that's relaxed and completely unguarded? This is the one I want the most.

"And to you, the man with the gorgeous ink." She casts a glance at my arm, eyeing the vibrant green dragon.

It's my design, but Mike inked it. I clink my glass to hers, and we watch each other as we both take a sip. After a few bites of fish, I put my fork down and lean in. "You were amazing on that stage, you know."

Her cheeks redden, but she gives me a pleased smile. "Thank you."

"Tell me you're going to be a regular with the band. That you'll be back on that stage next week."

Her eyes cloud over and she hangs her head, staring at her food.

"Lucy?" I reach over and gently clasp her hand. "You were born for that stage."

Her head snaps up and her fire is back. "That's what everyone says. But what if I don't want that life?"

I release her hand and sit back, studying her. "What life? One that puts that sexy smile on your face? One that clearly lights you up on the inside? I saw you on that stage. There wasn't anything about it you don't love. And I'm pretty sure if your ex hadn't barged in, you would've stayed on that stage until the bar closed."

Her lips quirk up in a small smile before her expression turns serious again. "The other night, that's not real. That's not what being in the music business is about. All they care about is charts and how many seats can be filled. The label, the producers, the managers, they manage to take everything that's good out of it. I can't even record my own damn songs." She bites her lip as if she's said more than she wanted to. "Sorry. I don't mean to sound ungrateful. People would kill for the opportunity I'm throwing away."

The troubled expression on her face and the way she pushes her food around her plate makes me want to stuff my words back down my throat. Too late now. "That's not ungrateful. Sounds like you've found out what you don't want. But that doesn't mean you have to give up music, does it?"

She lets out a long sigh. "No. But almost everything I love about it is tainted now. The audience wants to see me sing with Cadan. And since I'm still under contract with my label, I can't record anything new unless my lawyer manages to get me out of my contract. Which isn't looking likely. Everything is a mess right now."

"And you left because of your ex?" Jax told me he was a cheating bastard, but I get the feeling there's more to it than that.

"You could say that." She grabs the wine bottle and refills her glass. After a sip, she peers at me. "What about you? How does a painter go from having work in galleries around the country to trading it in for a tattoo gun?"

I choke mid-sip and my eyes water as I cough.

She raises her eyebrows, waiting for me to answer.

Shit. I guess I deserve that. I'd pried into her life and what she plans to do with her gift. It's only fair she should get to ask about mine. I clear my throat. "Elsa and I painted those pieces together."

Her expression turns soft, sympathetic. "Elsa was your soul mate?"

"Yes." It's my turn to stare at the food. "After the accident… Well, I was pretty beat up." It takes me a moment to find the courage needed for what I want to tell her. I rest my right arm on the table in front of me and run my hand over the dragon scales. "The accident was pretty horrible, and a piece of metal was lodged in my forearm right here." I reach over and take her hand. Pressing her fingers to my arm, I guide them over the expertly camouflaged scar.

"Oh wow," she says with a gasp. "I can't believe I didn't notice it before."

We've only known each other for a couple of days, but we'd spent a lot of time exploring each other during that time. I shrug. "I do my best to avoid letting anyone touch the scar. It's too painful."

She pulls her hand back as if she'd been burned. "It's still sensitive after all this time."

I shake my head. "That's not what I meant."

"Oh." The look on her face says she knows exactly what I mean. "I'm sorry."

"Don't be. But it was painful for a few months, so during that time I didn't paint, even though it was all I could think about. I wanted to work, to block out the awful memories, but I couldn't. Then when I healed, I found out blocking the memories were impossible. Every time I started a piece, I'd only see her. I had over two dozen pieces started when I finally gave up. The tattoo thing is just a way to stay creative and to make some money. It was never my passion."

"But you're good at it," she says.

I smile at that. "How do you know?"

"I saw the back piece you did for Jax. It's amazing." She takes a bite of her halibut and another sip of wine.

Good. She's eating again. And for once I was able to talk about Elsa without feeling as if I'd been sucker punched. I stare at her. What is it about this girl?

She catches my eye and raises one eyebrow. "What?"

I shake my head and let out a low chuckle. "You know, I have absolutely no idea."

CHAPTER 23

Lucy

The night Seth brought dinner to my house marked a change in our relationship. We went from two strangers who couldn't keep their hands off each other to two people who were rapidly becoming close friends. It was more than confusing because we were still wildly attracted to each other, but we both knew it couldn't last. Not with the uncertainty of my future hanging over our heads.

Still, Seth and I spent the next three nights together. It's surprisingly easy when we're just hanging out and amazing when we're in bed together. Not to mention he seems to be able to make me laugh when no one else can.

On Friday morning I wake to the sound of light rustling. Or is that scratching? I pop one eye open, and the first thing I notice is Seth is gone from my bed. I open my other eye and my gaze follows the sound.

Seth is sitting in my bedside chair, smiling at me. He has a pencil in his hand and is studying me while he sketches.

Joy fills my heart. The mere fact that he feels comfortable enough to work in front of me, heck, to draw me, is overwhelming. "Morning," I say shyly.

"Morning." He's focused, his eyes darting back and forth from me to his sketchpad.

I lie there, waiting for him to finish, wishing we could stay in this moment forever. I like being his muse, love sharing his passion with him, if only by being his subject.

"What's that look?" he asks, his brows pinched in concentration.

"Look?"

"The one you were just giving me. Your mood changed, but I'm not sure to what."

"Oh." I sit up, pulling the sheet with me to cover my chest. Then I stop. "Is this okay?"

He laughs. "Of course. I've got what I need." He continues to work on the sketch, though, shading and smudging his lines. "Now, what were you thinking about?"

"You." I wave at him and me. "This. The fact that you're drawing here. It makes me feel... special, I guess. I get the feeling you don't work much in front of other people unless it's for tattoos."

He pauses and then nods. "That's true. Elsa..." He closes his eyes and takes a breath. When he opens them he gives me a sad smile. "Elsa is the one who got me started drawing, you know. I always associate it with her. Or always had, but lately, it's different. It's something I'm compelled to do, and while she's always with me, it's nothing like it was before."

"It fulfills you," I say.

"Yes. But it did then, too."

"Sure. But it's not the same, is it? I mean, when I sing with Cadan, there's magic there. It feels so *right*. Like a calling or something."

He purses his lips together and slowly nods. "Yeah. It was like that with E."

"And now? I bet it's more personal. Like it's something you do just for you because it gives you joy, but not in a mystical sense. Cosmic forces have nothing to do with it. Right?"

Again, the slow nod.

"That's how it is for me with the singing and songwriting. I pull something from deep inside that really only has meaning to me. It's a true expression of myself—not shared with anyone." I sit up straighter. "It's great when someone else gets something out of it, like when an audience is really enjoying themselves, but it's just different. It's for me first. Not them. And I know that sounds selfish."

"No, it doesn't," he says and puts down the sketchpad. "It's the truth. And it's pure."

"I don't know about that." I laugh. "I don't see myself as pure."

His gaze dips to my barely covered chest and he grins.

"Hey, we're talking here," I say with a chuckle.

"Right." His desire-filled gaze locks on mine. "You were saying?"

I swallow and force myself to not yank him back onto the bed. "Just that when we offer our art without that soul-mate connection, we consciously give something of ourselves without it being pulled from us. I'm not saying our soul-mate gifts aren't pure or less worthy. Just different. Like when I sing with Cadan, the effect is what the audience needs or wants. But when I sing by myself, it's an extension of what's going on inside me. Weren't the paintings you did with Elsa similar?"

He stands and rubs his stubbled jaw. "Yeah. Sometimes. Our commissions were, for sure. And paintings we were compelled to paint but didn't know why. They always had more meaning to the final owner than they did to us. The stuff I do now… yeah. It's an artistic expression that is only mine. I hadn't thought of it that way before."

"Does that make you feel sad? Like you're letting anyone down?"

He sits on the bed next to me. "No. But it's different for me. I don't have a choice anymore, do I? Is that what you think?"

"Sometimes." I let my head fall back against my headboard. "Is it okay for me to walk away, knowing how much joy people get from our songs? Or knowing how deeply touched people can be?"

"Yes," Seth says with conviction. "It's not fair for you to sacrifice your own well-being and sanity just so a bunch of strangers can experience the magic for a couple of hours during a concert. The weight of the world is not on your shoulders, Luce."

"I know." I close my eyes and see an entire hospital ward of sick children, their sweet expressions shining back at me. Those are the ones I ache for.

"Come on." He wraps his hand around mine. "I think it's time for breakfast."

"Shower first," I say.

His grin is back. "Even better."

We're emerging from the shower together when the house phone starts to ring.

Seth wraps an arm around my waist and pulls me back against his chest. His lips brush over the nape of my neck and he murmurs, "Let the machine get it. I think I'm going to keep you locked away in your bed all day."

A tingle runs from the base of my neck down to my center. "Excellent idea."

But then the old recorder beeps, and my lawyer's voice floats up from downstairs. "Lucy, I'm sorry to call you on Christmas Eve, but the label is getting antsy. They're demanding you return to the studio by January second. If you don't, they'll definitely move forward with the lawsuit." His voice goes soft and truly apologetic. "I'm sorry it's come to this. Give me a call and let me know what you decide."

A chill runs through my body, and I start to tremble despite Seth's arms wrapped around me. I'm going to have to give him up.

"Shit," he says and lets me go. A second later he wraps my fuzzy robe around my shoulders. "Are you all right?"

Shaking my head, I push my arms into the robe and cinch it tight.

"Luce?"

I glance up at Seth. He's already stepped into his jeans and his green eyes are filled with worry.

"What can I do?"

"I…" Oh my God. What am I going to do? I have no choice. If they sue me, I'll lose Dad's house. They won't just sue me for the advance; they'll sue for loss of income. My life will be in shambles. Angry tears spring to the surface, and I slam my hand against the bathroom door. "Those bastards!"

Seth doesn't move. He doesn't try to calm me or comfort me. He seems to know that's the last thing I want right now.

I turn to him, frustration making me shake. "I have to go back." I'd known this all along, but it's finally starting to sink in. I'm truly trapped.

He takes a small step forward, a haunted but determined look on his face. Slowly he raises his arm and holds his hand out to me.

I take it, and though the solid weight of his hand in mine is welcome, it only makes me feel worse. Once I go back, there will be no more Seth. I'll be sucked back into Cadan's world no matter how hard I try to stay away from him.

"For how long?" he asks.

"I don't know. Six months to two years. It depends on how long it takes to record the new album, and then there will be the tour. The more successful the record is, the longer it will be." A pit forms in the depths of my stomach. I'm not quite sure whether it's the dread of going back to a life I now know I don't want or the fact I'll be leaving this man who has become more than a lover. Somehow in the last week he's become just about the only person who helps me feel normal.

He pulls me into his arms and tucks my head against his chest. "If they sue, what do you stand to lose? Is it worth hanging on to?"

A sob clogs my throat as I pull away. Waving a hand around the room, I gesture to the house.

Recognition dawns in his expression. We're both silent, then he says, "Let's get breakfast."

"I'm not really hungry."

"I know, Luce." He gives me an ironic smile. "Humor me anyway."

I nod. "Let me get dressed and I'll be down in a few minutes."

Seth shifts forward and tips my face up so I have to meet his intense gaze. Then he leans down and kisses me, tenderly at first, but then our joining turns heated, desperate. It's almost as if he's saying good-bye already. I cling to him, wanting to get lost in everything he has to offer. But then reality slams into me, and I know I have to let go. In less than two weeks I'll be back in LA with Cadan, working on the album, and Seth won't be there to save me.

I pull myself from his embrace and cross my arms over my chest. "Go on down. I'll be there in a minute."

He gives me a long look. Then he pulls his T-shirt over his head and disappears down the stairs.

My hands are shaking. I close my eyes and sink down onto the bed, clasping them together. My life since leaving Cadan has been so normal. Lonely at times. And certainly there'd been a piece of me missing, that part of me that comes alive while singing. But that seemed to come back while singing with the band last week. It turns out I don't need Cadan to find joy on the stage. It's different, not as intense or emotional. But damn it's fun.

I could live life finding meaning in less intense ways. If only Cadan hadn't signed that damned publishing contract. If my songs and Dad's house weren't on the line, I'd walk and let them do their worst. But they are and I can't let them go. Those two things are all I have.

With a deep breath, I finish getting dressed, stuff my feet into a pair of fur-lined boots, and make my way downstairs. "Hey. What's cookin'?" I peek over Seth's shoulder and grin. "Waffles?"

"And bacon."

"Good gracious. I'm keeping you."

He hands me a steaming cup of coffee and his lips quirk into a smile. "That's the plan."

I laugh at the absurdity of our conversation and add, "I can stick you in my suitcase."

"Really? Smuggling? Wouldn't it be easier if I bought my own plane ticket?"

I hold my cup up in a mock toast. "Touché."

The waffle-iron light goes off, and Seth busies himself with removing a golden waffle and starting another one. He opens the oven and the entire kitchen fills with maple-bacon scent.

"Damn, Seth. I'm drooling over here," I say from my seat at the kitchen bar.

"Again, that was the plan." He sets a plate in front of me along with butter and real maple syrup. "I would, you know."

I tear into a piece of bacon, and after swallowing, I ask, "Would what?"

"Go with you if you wanted."

Startled, I suck in a piece of bacon and start to choke.

He pounds on my back, clearly holding back laughter.

My eyes water as I get myself under control. I clear my throat. "What?"

"If it would make it easier for you, I'd come visit you while you're recording."

Panic snakes its way into my core, settling like a stone in my gut. "You want to come with me?" I can't deny I want him to do just that. Though he and Cadan within a thousand feet of each other sounds like a nightmare.

"Not the entire time." He laughs. "Just when you need a break. Or a really great distraction."

I laugh with him. "Is that all you guys think about?"

"Yes," he says solemnly and then narrows his eyes with suspicion. "It seems you've been thinking about it a lot lately as well."

My laugh turns to a giggle. "True. I'm not immune to your considerable charms."

He chews on his own piece of bacon, nodding. After swallowing, he answers, "That's fairly obvious." His eyes sparkle, and I make a conscious effort to remember this fun, easy moment. He doesn't really expect anything from me, just as I don't expect anything from him. It's fun to tease each other, though. Damn the future. We have right now.

As we're finishing off the waffles, the phone rings again. I groan. "That ring is never a good sign."

"Your mom?" Seth asks. Besides my lawyer this morning, she'd been the only one to call on the house phone since Seth had started hanging out with me the last few days.

I make a face and answer it.

"Lucy," Mom says by way of greeting.

"Hi, Mom." I make a conscious effort to keep the irritation out of my voice. I'll be seeing her in six hours. What could she possibly want that couldn't wait?

"Good, I caught you." There's a clinking sound as if she's preparing herself an iced drink. "Make sure you leave early enough to beat the traffic. And when you get to town, I need you to stop at the store and pick up a prescription for your father. They close at two today, so don't be late."

I tense, white-hot anger rushing to my head. "Randy is not my father."

"Luuuucy…" Mom drags out my name in exasperation. "Why do you always have to be difficult? Randy is part of this family. It's time you started treating him that way."

I say nothing, fearing my next words will start World War III. The silence stretches between us until finally Mom says, "It's Christmas Eve. Try to be on your best behavior."

The line goes dead. I set the cordless carefully back on the receiver and stand in the kitchen, my head bowed, trying to contain the rage consuming me.

Seth runs a light hand down my arm. When he gets to my fingers, he squeezes lightly and then moves to the sink and proceeds to do the dishes.

When the urge to scream fades, I move to Seth's side and start drying the dishes he's placed on a towel next to the sink.

"Tell me about him," he says in a soothing tone.

I huff out a disgusted laugh. "He's a controlling ass."

Seth shuts the water off and turns to me. "No. I meant your dad. Not your mother's husband."

"Oh." Thinking about Dad calms me and fills me with a sense of home. I move to the French doors and wave at the ocean. "Dad said life was like the vast ocean. Turbulent, beautiful, calming, devastating. And he said to truly live, one needed all those things."

Seth, still standing in the kitchen, leans across the bar, balancing on his elbows. "I'd say you're living life to his terms."

This time my laugh is real. "Everything except the calming part."

"I thought that's what we're doing together."

I turn to scoff at his assessment, but then stop. Outside the bedroom, that's exactly what we're doing. At least he calms me. I'm not sure how I affect him, but he seems happy enough to just hang out with me. "Could be."

"What else? Tell me what life was like living with him." He gazes at me intently, so interested. It's not something I'm used to, and I find I have to look away to get my bearings.

"Well…" I stall, letting my memories flood back. I feel my lips crack into a small smile. "Dad was a gentle giant. Tall and foreboding to those who didn't know him, but a giant teddy bear to those who did. He was quick with a kind word, the first to offer support even if he didn't agree with my choices, which for a while there was often. And he wasn't afraid to tell me when he thought I had my head up my ass."

Seth chuckles. "Sounds like someone I'd be friends with."

I eye him, taking in his ink. "He would've hated your tattoos. Though he wouldn't have held them against you."

"That's good to know." Seth moves from behind the counter, takes my hand, and pulls me to the couch. We sit side by side, our knees touching. "What would he say about the choice you're facing now?"

I lie back against the couch cushions and blow out a breath. "I don't know, Seth. I really don't. He'd hate what Cadan has done and likely would threaten to hunt him down and beat the crap out of him. He wouldn't, but he'd really want to. What I do know is he'd support whatever decision I make."

Seth leans back, mimicking the way I'm sprawled out. "Even if it meant losing this place?"

"Yes," I say without hesitation. "He always said home is where you hang your hat. If he had to give up this place to keep me from drowning in Cadan's crap, I believe he would. The problem is, I won't give it up. Not ever."

"I understand." His tone is so low I barely hear his words.

I know he's talking about his place with Elsa even though he hardly ever stays there. I still can't believe he said her name. Jax said he hasn't referred to her by anything other than E since the accident. Did it mean anything? Or was E a term he only used with friends? Either way, I'm grateful he opened up to me about her. I squeeze his hand.

He leans over and kisses me gently. "Why don't you skip your mom's and come to my place for dinner?"

I shake my head and give him a sad smile. "Thanks, but no matter how much I don't want to go, she's still my mom. I'll stay a few hours and then come home."

"Really?" He raises his eyebrows. "It's a two-hour drive to Santa Rosa. I thought you'd stay there."

"Oh, God no." My heart speeds up just thinking about it. Not after what happened when I lived there. "I only go over there on holidays for Mom's sake, but that's it. Randy and I, well, we don't get along."

He frowns, worry lines appearing around his eyes. "It's supposed to storm again later. I'd feel better if you were traveling with someone."

He's so sweet to be worrying about me. Rain is the last thing I'm worried about at the moment. If Randy and I get into it again, I'm not sure I'll be able to hold back. "Who's going to come with me? Jax has to work, and even if she didn't, she has her own family stuff." I pause and eye him, then grin. "Unless you're volunteering?"

"I..." He shifts uncomfortably.

Laughing, I stand up. "Kidding. I wouldn't subject you to them on a regular night, much less Christmas Eve. It's okay. I'll survive."

His worried expression doesn't ease, but he nods anyway. Then he gets up and says, "Will you do something for me?"

He's so serious that it unsettles me a bit. I nod. "Sure. Anything."

"Call me if it gets bad." Stepping close to me, he rests his hand on my cheek. "It's time you had someone in your corner."

His concern and the tenderness of the moment overwhelm me, rendering me speechless. When was the last time anyone cared how I was feeling? A lump clogs my throat, and instead of answering, I wrap my arms around him and press my face into his shoulder. Finally I whisper, "I will."

CHAPTER 24
Seth

After I reluctantly leave Lucy's house, I'm supposed to head to Jax's to drop off her Christmas present, but I take a last-minute detour to the three-story farmhouse I can't bring myself to live in. My sister's car is parked just ahead of me, and for once I'm not irritated she's here.

She moved in when I refused to live here after the accident. It was Elsa's family house, and she left it to me in her will. Her mom had passed a few years before she did. If she'd had any family left, I would've given it back. But she didn't, and Lillian said someone had to take care of it if I wouldn't. The truth is I'm grateful she did. At the time, I'd hated her for it. I hadn't wanted anyone in Elsa's space.

"Hey, loser," Lillian calls from the door. "Are you going to get your ass in here or do I need to drag you out of your truck by your ear?"

I glance at her and chuckle. She'd do it, too.

"Is that a smile I see?" She says it mockingly, but I know her better than that. There's hope warring with suspicion in her eyes.

I climb out of the truck and meet her on the steps. "No. Must be a figment of your imagination."

"Really?" She follows me in. "And are the dark strands of hair and second toothbrush in the bathroom a figment of my imagination as well?"

"No." There's a fresh pot of coffee in the carafe and I pour myself some, then hold the pot up, silently asking if she'd like a cup.

"Yes, please," she says and sits at the kitchen table.

With two steaming cups of coffee, I join her. "Where's Trace?"

"At his dad's. Where's your new girlfriend?"

Trace is her soul mate. They met four months ago, but none of us have met him yet. I'm starting to think she's made him up. I raise an eyebrow. "You sure he's a real live person? You haven't resorted to a blow-up mate, have you?"

She reaches across the table and smacks my forehead. "Shut up, you perv. If you must know, he's coming up tomorrow. You'll meet him then. Now. About this girlfriend of yours…"

"I don't have a girlfriend," I say stubbornly.

Lillian's pale green eyes narrow. "Well, whatever you're call-ing her, there's someone. The signs are here and I've seen you smile twice in the last five minutes. Spill it."

I stand and head toward the door that leads to the living room.

"Hey! Where are you going?"

"You'll see. Come on." I wave a hand and disappear through the threshold. Halfway up the stairs, the pounding of her feet on the steps tells me she's following. There's a slight pause when I keep going up to the third floor. I resist the urge to glance back at her. If I do, I might not go through with this.

I stop at the top of the landing with my hand on the door-knob. I feel rather than hear Lillian come to a stop behind me.

"Are you sure?" she asks.

"Yeah." I take a deep breath and open the studio. The pun-gent odor of oils assaults us. The room full of glass windows is freezing, and Lillian lets out a small gasp, rubbing her arms.

"Where's that space heater you used to have up here?"

"It died." I stride across the room and pull back the curtain designed to protect the paintings from UV light. "This is her," I say almost to myself. "Lucy."

Lillian carefully makes her way toward me and spends long, agonizing minutes studying the abstract painting I'd worked on the past few days. Then she shifts and stares intently at two more. When she looks up at me, she has tears in her eyes. "Who is she?"

My nerves are raw, and suddenly I regret bringing her up here. I shove my hands in my pockets and hunch my shoulders. "Does it matter?"

She takes two steps and stops right in front of me. Her lips are set in a determined line. "Of course it matters. She got you painting again."

I walk over and turn around the last painting Elsa and I had worked on together. It's a small cottage on the edge of a cliff with an intricate garden full of rhododendrons, camellias, and daffodils. The sky is darkened purple and gray as a storm rolls in. The sea rages below in the perfect juxtaposition of tranquility and impending disaster.

"You finished it," Lillian says on a whisper.

I nod and can't stop the tears from burning my eyes. Blinking them back, I steel myself. "She always said this is what she perceived life to be. Wonderful and devastating at the same time. That one can't really experience life without both. I didn't really know what she meant before."

Lillian touches my arm. "What are you going to do with it?"

"Put it in a gallery, I suppose. Elsa worked on it, too. Its true owner is out there somewhere." That's how our paintings worked. If we painted something together, eventually it would make its way into the hands of whoever needed it most.

"Does this mean you're going to show again?" Her eyes are wide with disbelief.

"Yeah," I say, running a hand through my hair. "I think I have to."

"Wow." Lillian goes silent as she wanders around the room, taking in the other half-finished pieces. Pausing, she picks up one of an older couple. "Isn't this Dad's friend?"

I nod. After I'd started painting again, I couldn't get Francie's request out of my mind. It's a Christmas surprise.

"That's really sweet of you."

I shrug.

She turns and gives me a hard stare. "And none of this is because of this new girlfriend?"

"She's not my girlfriend," I say again. "She's… Hell, I don't know. A friend for sure. She's a singer. She and her mate, that's their connection—"

"She has a mate?" Lillian cries. "Seth! You can't get involved with someone who's bound to break your heart. What are you thinking?"

Her words hit me deep in my chest and fear rolls through me. I know she's right, but I won't stay away. I can't. "I already said she's a friend. And you don't have to tell me about the power of mates. I think I have enough experience to know she'll go back to him eventually."

She nods sadly. "They all do."

"It doesn't matter anyway," I lie. "You know I don't do relationships."

"Yes, you do." She shakes her head. "Jax, me, the guys at your shop. Mom and Dad. You have relationships with all of us. And what you had with Elsa, not every soul-mate partnership has what you two had. If there's anyone in this world who does relationships, it's you. You're just too scared to try again."

Anger flares to life deep in my chest. "Don't talk to me about scared. Jesus, Lillian. You don't have a clue what it was like when she died. To be the one who held her as the life literally bled right out of her. All because I'd insisted she drive me home from that damn party. She asked me not to go. I was too stubborn, and she died because of it." I narrow my eyes at my sister. "Don't ever talk to me about being scared again. You have no idea what being scared is."

"Oh, don't I?" she yells back. "How about watching your baby brother almost drink himself to death? Or watch him cut out everything… or everyone… who was important to him. Including me." She's standing there shaking, her face red and fists clenched. "What I see now is a man who has found his way back to his gift. But believe me, it won't mean anything unless you find someone to share it with." She sweeps past me, heading for the door.

I grab her arm, stopping her. "Lillian," I say and wait for her to look up at me. Tears glisten in her eyes, which are almost identical to mine. "I didn't cut you out."

"You did," she insists.

"I didn't mean to. You did what I didn't have the courage to do." I wave my hand around the room. "You took care of this place. You were close to her when I couldn't be. When it hurt too much to think about it." I tug her to me, wrapping my arms around her. "Thank you."

Her hands clutch at my shoulders and she lets out a muffled sob. "It's about time, you big doofus."

I chuckle and tighten my grip. When I let her go, she wipes at her eyes and pushes me away. "That's enough. Now, tell me about this girl."

I glance once more at the abstracts. Lucy's eyes are huge, her mouth distorted as she sings, and color is everywhere. It's beautiful and disturbed at the same time. I love everything about it. "Downstairs," I say and pick up the portrait of Don and Francie.

She nods, and a minute later we're sitting in the kitchen with fresh cups of coffee.

"Spill it," she says and stirs sugar into her cup.

"What do you want to know?" I hold my mug with both hands and gaze out the window at the horizon. Another storm is definitely rolling in. And all I can think about is Lucy driving alone on the two-lane highways on her way to her mom's. God I wish she had someone with her.

"First, who is she? And second, what is it about her that got you back in the studio?"

I shift my gaze from the storm clouds and smile at my sister. Her eyes light up with pleasure, almost tearing the smile from my face. Have I really never smiled around her since Elsa's accident? Jesus. I'm a dick. I force my smile back in place, if only for her benefit. "Well, she's Jax's best friend."

Lillian lets out a gasp. "Lucy Moore?"

"The one and only."

"Holy shit, Seth." She bites her lip and gives me a grimace. "You don't really believe she'll leave Cadan Kinx, do you? Their music is… damn. Magical."

"Don't remind me," I huff out. "I know. But here's the weird part. It was her singing that snapped me back to myself." She opens her mouth to speak, but I hold a hand up, stopping her. "Not her and Kinx's songs. Last week she sang on her own at the bar as a birthday present for Jax. And damn if she wasn't mesmerizing."

Lillian's expression turns to one of pity.

"Stop looking at me like that." I scowl at her. "The point is that she was up there enjoying the hell out of herself. She was doing what she does best on her own terms, just for the love of it. She was so alive. I wanted that. At first I thought I just wanted her. But I wanted what she had. Passion for her gift."

Lillian leans back in the chair and really studies me. "That's great, Seth. Really. But tell me something."

"What?"

"Have you or have you not been sleeping with her?"

Heat crawls up my neck as I clamp my mouth closed. This is not a conversation I want to have with my sister.

"Aha! I knew it." She stands up, a knowing grin on her face. "Singing wasn't the only thing that touched you." She makes disgusting kissing noises and mimes making out by wrapping her arms around herself.

"Stop it. You're embarrassing yourself." I get up and grab my coat from the hook near the door.

She drops the act and shakes her head at me. "Just sayin'."

I roll my eyes. Grabbing the painting once more, I ask, "You want a ride to Mom's?"

"Sure." She grabs her own coat, hooks her arm though mine, and tugs me out the door. I turn and look at the house. For the first time since the accident, it almost feels like home again.

CHAPTER 25

Lucy

The two-hour drive to Santa Rosa goes by far too fast. I suspect it has a lot to do with the trepidation I have for returning to my mother's house. I don't want to spend the entire time defending my decision to leave Cadan. And I really don't want to have to make nice with Randy. My skin crawls with the thought.

As I take the exit for the pharmacy, my phone buzzes for the fifth time in ten minutes. A quick glance at the screen reveals Mom's name. Crap. How'd she get this number? Cadan probably. "I'm driving!" I yell at it. "And it's raining. Compulsive texting isn't going to make me answer you any faster."

A few blocks down, I pull into the parking lot and scan the messages:

Where are you?
Don't forget Randy's meds.
We also need milk. Skim.
Call when you get close.
What time can I expect you?

"Holy crow." I delete all the messages and tap in one to let her know I'll be there in fifteen minutes, then turn the phone off and toss it into my purse.

There's a line of retirees stocking up on blood pressure and cholesterol meds before the pharmacy closes for the holiday. The delay puts me back another ten minutes, and when I pull to a stop at Mom's house, she's standing outside in the rain, her arms crossed over her chest. Her salon-dyed auburn hair is already stringy from the rain, and her satin blouse has rain splotches staining it.

I take a deep breath, grab the meds, the milk, and Mom's Christmas present, and paste a smile on my face. "Merry Christmas," I say as cheerily as I can muster.

She uncrosses her arms and places both hands on her hips. "I was worried."

I bite back a snarky reply and brush past her toward her front door. She can stand in the elements all day if she wants. I'll wait on the covered porch.

"You didn't call." She follows me onto the porch and smoothes back her damp hair.

"Mom." I sigh. "I sent a text when I got to the pharmacy. After that I was driving. You do realize there are laws against using the phone while driving, right?"

"Don't be difficult. I have something to tell you."

"Okay." I shift and lean against the side of her house. "So spill it."

"I invited—"

The door swings open and Cadan strolls out, wearing designer jeans and an expertly tailored sports coat. "Lucy! Merry Christmas." He wraps his arms around me and kisses me on the cheek, lingering longer than is polite for a simple Christmas hug.

My mind whirls while my body automatically relaxes, feeling completely comfortable in his arms. Irritated with my physical response, I stiffen and pull out of his embrace, trying not to scowl. Fighting in front of Mom will only make matters worse. She'll take a side. His. "Cadan," I say, eyeing him, "this is a surprise. I thought you'd be with your family."

"I am." He nods in my direction. "I can't spend Christmas away from you."

My jaw tenses. I can't believe I didn't see this coming. I should have. It's exactly the kind of thing both of them would do. He's going to milk this for everything he can. "What about your mom? She can't be happy you're here instead of back east."

"Lucy!" Mom scolds me in a hushed whisper. "Stop berating him. He came to surprise you."

I narrow my eyes at him. No he didn't. He came to ambush me.

He smiles for my mother's sake and shakes his head as if I'm being amusing. "Mom and Dad went on a cruise to the Caribbean. She's been dreaming about it for years."

"A gift from you?" I know he bought her the tickets. His parents, while they do fine, don't have money for extras.

He shrugs. "It's nice to do something for them once in a while."

"Aren't you just the sweetest," Mom gushes. She gives me a dirty look as she takes his arm and pulls him back into the house. "Lucy, get in here and be pleasant to your father."

That uncontrollable anger rushes to my head again. The pressure is so great I'm certain my head is going to combust right there on her porch. How dare she refer to him as my father? Dad passed only six months ago. I almost turn around and leave right then and there, but Cadan extracts himself from her grip and is by my side almost instantly.

His expression is full of concern as he leans down and whispers, "Nothing she says can change the truth in your heart. Ignore her."

"What if I can't?" I ask, shaking from sheer frustration.

"Then I'll take you home right now."

He seems so sincere I almost take him up on it. But then I'd be stuck with him for two hours in the car. Not to mention if he drove me back, one of our cars would be left here. "No," I say. "Let's just get this over with."

"Lucy, Cadan," Mom calls from her tract home. "Get in here. You're letting all the heat out of the house."

I let Cadan take my hand as we head inside. My chest constricts the way it always does when I come back to visit. It's hard to breathe. "Has he started drinking yet?" I whisper to Cadan.

He nods. "Whiskey and Coke. I think he's on his second."

"Shit."

Cadan squeezes my fingers and gives me a sympathetic smile. "I'm here."

As much as I don't want to rely on Cadan for this, I'm relieved he's here. Once Randy has another couple of drinks, I'll need a buffer.

We walk through the formal living room and dining room, stopping when we come to the opening of the family room. The kitchen is to the right, and Mom is busy stirring something on the stove. Randy is sprawled in a lounge chair, wearing sweats and an NFL T-shirt. Classy. I ignore him and place Mom's gift on the kitchen table. "What can I do to help?" I ask.

"Get Randy a glass of water and bring him his meds."

At least she didn't call him my father. Cadan, knowing my mother's kitchen almost as well as I do, pulls out a glass and fills it while I put Randy's meds on the counter. "How many of each?"

"Just open the bottles for him. He can do the rest," she says over her shoulder. Then she stops and turns to glare at me. "Lucile Moore. You didn't even say hello to him. You march over there right now and wish him a merry Christmas."

"He didn't say anything to me," I protest. "It's not like he didn't see me."

"Stop being rude," she snaps. "I will not have a repeat of what happened last year."

My pulse quickens and I open my mouth to let her have it, but Cadan speaks before I can get the words out. "Don't worry, Mrs. P. Everything's going to be great." He takes the pill bottles from me and strides into the family room. His voice carries into the kitchen. "Hey, Randy. Claire asked me to bring these to you."

There's a pause, then Randy says, "So she's here, then."

"Yes. She's in the kitchen talking to her mom. She'll be out to say hello soon."

"Go!" Mom says in a hushed tone. "Before trouble starts. You know how he is."

"Why doesn't he get up and come in here?" I grab a bottle of lemonade from the fridge and lean against the counter, refusing to play the game. It's always the same. Tiptoe around Randy and pray you don't say anything to set him off.

Mom gives me a withering look. "Why do you have to be so selfish? It's Christmas. Can't you at least try?"

The familiar sense of rejection and abandonment hits me. Only instead of crying like I've done in the past, I'm numb, resigned to the realization that she won't change. No matter what happens, she'll choose Randy over me every time. Of course she will. He's her soul mate. That's always her defense.

Without a word, I spin on my heel and head to Cadan's side. It's unbelievable how grateful I am that he's here. I slip my arm around his waist, holding on for support. "Merry Christmas, Randy."

"Lucy. I was wondering when you'd get around to gracing me with your presence."

Cadan wraps his arm around my shoulder, pulling me close. I want to lean into him and pull away at the same time.

"You know," Randy continues, "I can't believe your mother keeps spending my hard-earned money on gifts for you when it's clear that's the only thing you show up here for."

Cadan's arm tightens around me, and before I can spar with Randy, Cadan says, "That's uncalled for, Randy. Lucy doesn't ask her mother for anything. Can we put past issues aside for today? Claire is going to be awfully disappointed if we have to leave early."

Randy plants both feet on the floor and leans forward, glaring at me. "Last I heard, the label was suing you for breach of contract. Don't you think for a minute I'm going to bail you out again."

"Bail me out? Again?" I cry and then huff out a laugh. "Is that what you think you did?"

"Yes," Mom says from behind me. "Didn't you ever think it would be awkward for us to pay for Mack's funeral? And you've shown no gratitude for our help."

My mouth drops open. I'm too stunned to speak. Is that what all the hostility is about this time? It's always something unexpected. My stomach rolls with nausea at her audacity to make me feel bad about how I'd dealt with paying for Dad's funeral. I'd been waiting on a payment from the label and his insurance money hadn't kicked in yet.

My fingers ache from squeezing into fists and a headache starts to form above my left eye. "You didn't pay for anything. You loaned me the money for all of three weeks. And if it was such a problem, you should've said no."

"How could I say no?" Mom asks with an incredulous look on her face. "What would people think?"

"Oh my God! Is that all you care about? What other people think?" I stalk to the kitchen, grab my purse, and head for the front door.

Mom follows me. "Where are you going?"

"Home. This holiday is over."

"Right," she says with a sneer. "Walk out. It's what you're good at."

I spin, vibrating with the urge to throw something. I take a moment to collect myself and then stare her dead in the eye. "I guess that's one thing I learned from you."

Her mouth drops open in outrage. "Randy is my soul mate. I don't know why you can't understand that. I figured since you've met Cadan, you might be a little more sympathetic to what I went through."

"Right. Because being with your soul mate is more important than anything else, like family or commitments, or self-respect."

"Do not speak to your mother that way," Randy says as he finally joins us in the hall. "You will treat her with respect or you can get out."

Mom throws her hands up and tears fill her eyes. "I can't take this." Her breathing becomes uneven. "All I wanted was a nice Christmas and for you and Cadan to work things out. That's why I invited him."

I shake my head. "It's not your place to try to fix my relationship, Mom. You have to let me work this out on my own."

Randy lets out a skeptical snort while Mom cries harder.

"I'm going. Clearly this was a bad idea."

She lets out a sob and then disappears down the hall, saying something about how ungrateful and selfish I am.

I pull the door open and step out onto the porch. Before I leave, I turn back around and shoot daggers at Randy with my eyes. "Treat her with respect, huh? Do you call belittling her in front of her friends respectful? Or what about hitting on my friends when she was at work? Or my personal favorite, spying on me when I was in the shower?"

"Why, you little liar," Randy says through clenched teeth.

"He did what?" Cadan demands and takes a step forward, clearly ready to knock the shit out of him. I grab his arm and pull him back.

"Stop, Cadan. It's not worth the shit-storm that's sure to follow. Let's go."

"Don't even think about coming back," Randy yells.

I say nothing as he slams the door, getting exactly what he wanted—my mom all to himself.

CHAPTER 26

Lucy

Cadan walks me to my car and, without saying a word, takes my keys from my hand. And I let him. I'm shaking and too upset to do anything other than climb into the passenger seat and lean back with my eyes closed.

"Do you want to go somewhere and talk, or would you rather I take you home?" Cadan asks.

Every fiber in my being is screaming to be back at Dad's house. "Home."

"You sure?"

I open my eyes and study him. "Yes. Unless you really don't want to."

"Oh, I want to," he says with a smile. "But I don't want you to be uncomfortable. I probably won't be able to get a rental car until Monday. I'll be stuck in Mendo until then."

I wave a hand. "It's fine. If none of the inns have a room available, you can stay in my guest room."

He gives me a skeptical look as if he highly doubts I'm going to let him in the house. Why wouldn't he? I'd run from him earlier in the week. But he'd just stood up for me and was so much like the Cadan I first fell for that I want him in the car. Want to feel safe and comfortable. I'm still angry about what he'd done. Who wouldn't be? But maybe we could move past that and find our way back to friends. Especially since I'm going to be forced to record the new album.

Cadan leaves me to my own thoughts as he navigates through the pouring rain. It really is bad out. Seth had every reason to be concerned. The thought of him reminds me he's supposed to meet me at the house later. I glance at Cadan. It's Christmas, and he's taking care of me. I can't imagine kicking him out as soon as we get back. I pull out my phone and tap in a message to Seth.

Have to cancel tonight, but don't worry. I'm fine. I pause. I don't want to go into detail about what went down or the fact that I'm with Cadan through a text. It's too complicated. *I'll call you later tonight.*

I hit Send and tuck the phone back into my purse.

"Jax?" Cadan asks.

It would be easier to let him think that, but I shake my head, not willing to lie. I'm not willing to do to him what he's done to me. "I canceled my plans for later."

"The guy from the bar?" His tone is clipped, and his jerky driving makes it obvious he's having trouble staying calm.

I close my eyes again and heave a sigh. "Does it matter?"

No response. Then minutes later he says, "Yes. To me it does."

I turn in my seat to look at him. He glances at me with pain in his eyes. I don't know whether to laugh or cry. "Sucks, doesn't it?"

His hands tighten around the wheel. "I know I hurt you, Luce. And I also know it's going to take a lot to earn your trust back, if that's even possible. But dammit, I'm going to. That's a promise you can count on."

All of the swagger and cockiness he'd adopted in the last two years is gone. This Cadan, the one driving me home in the pouring-down rain, the one who'd stood up to my mother and Randy, is the one I fell for. The one I'd loved beyond what our combined voices could achieve. It's comforting and terrifying at the same time. I don't trust him, but my heart wants to.

As we make the turn onto Highway 128, Cadan turns the radio on and switches the satellite radio to one of the pop-rock stations. "Rebel Beat" by the Goo Goo Dolls fills the car. The catchy tune pulls me out of my funk, and I start to sing along. Smiling, Cadan joins in.

The tension from the day evaporates with our connection, and I feel almost weightless with joy. I know it's only temporary, but that doesn't stop me from embracing all the magic sparking between us. Our voices meld perfectly, and I long for the days we'd hole up over a weekend to write and sing just for ourselves.

When the song ends, "In Repair" by John Mayer comes on. This time Cadan lets me take the lead and only contributes to the chorus. It's sad and hopeful at the same time, not unlike this moment we seem to be sharing.

"That was beautiful," he says when the notes fade away.

"All of his songs are."

"No, I meant the way you sang it." His eyes soften with tenderness. "It's good to be here with you like this… though not the best circumstances with your mom, I admit."

I wave a hand, indicating the drama doesn't matter. It should. And the fact he'd manipulated his way into a Christmas invitation is annoying as hell, but if he hadn't been there, it would have been infinitely worse. "Just promise you won't try to get to me through my mother again. Please."

"If you promise to not completely shut me out again."

I give him my you've-got-to-be-kidding-me look.

"I know. I deserved it." His eyes are locked on the road, and he sounds more serious than I think I've ever heard him. Sincerity practically streams off him. "It won't happen again. I swear my life on it, Lucy."

"What exactly is it that won't happen again, Cadan?" I ask, my voice barely audible over the music.

"All of it. I won't ever step out on you again. I got caught up in the lifestyle and lost my sense of self. I lost respect for everyone, including myself. I won't make any decisions about our careers without discussing it with you first. Honest, Luce. I really thought I was doing what was best for you. I didn't mean for things to go down the way they did."

They are the words I'd longed to hear six months ago. A year ago even. Now they aren't enough. I take my time to collect my thoughts. Seth's image flashes in my mind. Sure, he's a self-proclaimed womanizer, though his actions portray something else. Yes, I'd run into the one-night-stand chick at the bar, and everyone—Jax, Mike, and even Seth himself—had warned me to not get involved with him. None of that scared me though because of his honesty. Seth clearly cared about other people. His relationship with Jax was evidence enough.

Cadan, on the other hand, has gone around me and behind my back on several occasions. He was still doing it by conspiring with my mother. "I'm sorry," I say. "I can't trust you."

He lets out a long breath. "Okay, I deserve that, too. But will you give me a chance to prove myself to you?"

I honestly don't know what to say. I'm going to have to record the new songs any day now. The choice is already out of my hands. I won't risk Dad's house or the loss of my creative work over something Cadan did to me. I'll record them and tour for as long as the label requires. It sure would be a lot easier if Cadan and I could get along, maybe even be friends again. I'm not sure I can survive another romantic relationship with him. At the same time, I'm not sure I can resist one either. Not if I'm with him day in and day out.

Even now in the shadows of the car, his tall rocker body catches my eye, and I have trouble focusing on why I need to keep my distance. I know what's under his designer jeans and long-sleeved Henley shirt. Slim from his vegetarian diet and toned from months of a diligent workout, he's damned sexy.

"Lucy?"

"Huh?" I snap out of my daze.

"What do you say?"

He's holding his breath, more nervous now than I've ever seen him.

I swallow the lump clogged in my throat. "I'll try."

His breath comes out in a soft whoosh. "Really?"

"Yeah. No promises though."

He grins in obvious relief. "I'll take it."

Not wanting to talk anymore, I reach over and turn the radio up again. The familiar music washes over me and embraces me like an old friend. It's the perfect end to our conversation. The first song we ever recorded together.

As we'd done literally thousands of times before, we both hum the intro and then start to sing.

The world outside is an illusion
One of straight confusion
You're content to live there
But your heart won't accept that forever
No, no, no
Your heart won't accept that forever

Our voices build, getting stronger with each note. And as Cadan's voice winds through me, melding with everything I am, I don't even try to fight it this time. Instead, I embrace it, letting the magic of our harmony rinse away all the bitterness of the day.

By the time Cadan pulls into my driveway, I'm completely relaxed, and we're reminiscing about the time Cadan wore a kilt during one of our performances.

Laughing, I say, "It was hot until the wind machine blew it up and revealed those heart-print boxers."

He snorts. "You bought those for me. Besides, it's better I was wearing those and not going commando."

"Really?" I stare at him incredulously. "If you'd been going native Scotsman, that news would have boosted iTunes sales to new heights."

He chuckles. "Okay. I'm in for the next performance on one condition."

"What?"

He's eyeing me mischievously, and I can't help but be a little smitten. He's fun and easy to be with when he's like this. And he knows everything about me. His grin turns to one of pure sexual prowess. "You wear that red flared dress that barely covers your ass. The crowd will lose their minds trying to find out what you're wearing under it as you dance across the stage.

"I'm not going commando," I say as haughtily as I can without cracking up.

"No, I don't want anyone to have a heart attack. I think a thong or G-string should be fine."

I can't help the giggle that escapes me. He'd absolutely wear nothing under that kilt if I asked him to. Me? It would take a lot more than a few shots of tequila to get me on board. He knows it, too.

"We'll keep that on the back burner for when we're desperate." He grabs the umbrella sitting in my backseat and opens the door. "Hang tight. I'll come around to get you."

I wait until he's at the passenger door with my oversized umbrella. Cadan pulls me close, his arm around me as we head to my front porch. I have my key in the door when he says, "Do you want me to go?"

"Go where?" I ask surprised.

"To an inn or a hotel." He shrugs. "I could call around and get a cab."

"On Christmas Eve?" I make a face. "No, Cadan. It's all right. Please, just come inside. I'm sure I can scrounge something to make for dinner."

His eyes are full of concern, but I also see a twinge of hope. "You're sure?"

I shake my head and push the door open. "Considering you've been relentless about talking to me this last week, you sure do seem hesitant to take your shot."

He follows me into the house and drops the umbrella in the stand near the door but doesn't take his coat off or move farther into the house.

I pull the coffee beans from the fridge and raise an eyebrow. "Are you going to join me?"

"I want to." He shoves his hands in his jacket pockets.

"Cadan?"

"You're sure? I don't want you to feel like you have to let me stay. I know I was over the line accepting your mom's invitation to Christmas. But you know how she is, and I really wanted to spend some time with you. If it's not okay, please tell me and I'll be on my way."

Biting my lip, I drop the beans on the counter. Then I stride over to him and gently begin to undo the buttons on his jacket. He gazes down at me, his blue eyes full of questions. I focus on my fingers as I work the last button.

"Hold still," I say and move behind him, slipping the jacket from his shoulders. Once it's hanging on the coatrack, I take him by the hand and lead him into the kitchen. He sits in the same chair I did earlier that morning while Seth made me breakfast.

Seth. He was supposed to be here tonight. My body goes tense with desire at just the thought of him. And I'm a little sad I won't be spending Christmas with him. The night would've no doubt been fun and full of mischief. There wouldn't be all this crazy emotion combined with awkwardness. Still, I'm not unhappy Cadan is here. It's just not exactly what I wanted for the holiday.

I move to stand on the other side of the counter and take Cadan's hands in mine. Holding his gaze, I say, "It's Christmas. A time to spend with those you love. I wouldn't let you leave if you tried."

He stares at me for a long moment and then swallows. "You still love me?"

"Yes," I say, emotion trying to strangle me. As much as I wish I didn't, I know I always will. "You're a part of me. That isn't going to change." I let go of his hands and retreat back to the coffeemaker. "Can we not talk about this anymore?"

"Yeah, sure." His tone is smooth and confident, but when I turn to glance at him, he's staring at his phone, frowning.

"What is it?"

He pulls his gaze from the screen and scowls. "Your mom. She sent me eight texts, begging us to come back tomorrow."

I stalk back over to him and grab his phone. It's a long stream of messages telling him we're being immature and that we can't ruin her Christmas like this. That I'm being selfish as usual and she doesn't understand why I can't get along with Randy.

My vision turns red, and before I know what I'm doing, I hit Call and press the phone to my ear, waiting for her to pick up. She will.

"Cadan," Mom says, breathless as if she'd run to get the phone. "Tell me you're coming over tomorrow. If not, I'll never hear the end of it."

"So that's why you're harassing him, then? Randy's upset and taking it out on you?"

Mom gasps. "Lucy. Why are you using Cadan's phone? Something happen to yours?"

"No, Mom. God, who cares about my phone?" I pull the device away from my ear and shake my head, trying for some sort of calm.

"I was just asking. Don't be difficult." Her voice fills the kitchen she's speaking so loud.

I clutch the phone to my ear once more. "I'm being difficult?"

"Yes. You're the one who stalked out for no reason. And now I have to deal with the fallout. Again. Why do you always do this? Your father—"

"Do not call Randy my father ever again!" I yell into the phone. "My father would never hit on my friends and make them so uncomfortable they never wanted to come over to my house. My father would never walk into my room without knocking and then laugh when he caught me half-naked, changing clothes. My father would never proposition me on my graduation day and offer me a new car to keep my silence."

"Lucile Marie Moore. What did you just say? How dare you spew those lies? Randy never... He wouldn't... I can't believe any daughter of mine would ever behave this way."

I grit my teeth, knowing this is how she'd react. I'd tried to talk to her about this once, but she'd shut me down before I could spell it out for her. I'm certain she knows it's true, but she's too cowardly to face it. "My father was my rock, the one person I could count on always. Your husband was never that person." A sob rips from my throat, and my voice cracks as I push out the next words. "My father is the only parent I've ever been able to count on. Don't call me or bother Cadan again. Not until you can accept that I'm telling you the truth."

My heart pounds against my chest while the tears stream down my cheeks. The phone slips from my hand, but I don't even hear it hit the floor. I'm too overcome by my outburst. The words had been pent up inside for the last three years as I'd tried to ignore what had happened. I just can't do it anymore.

I stumble forward, tripping over one of the barstools. Pain shoots through my knee, and instead of getting up, I sit on the floor and hug my knees to my chest.

"Lucy, Holy Christ," Cadan says and sits next to me, wrapping an arm around my shoulders. He kisses my temple and gently guides my head to rest on his chest.

Sobs wrack my body as I lean against him, crying for the broken relationship with my mother, for the hole left in my chest after Dad passed, and because Cadan is here, but I'm acutely aware that he's not the one I want holding me right now.

"Shh," he says and runs a hand over my hair. "It's okay, baby. Everything is going to be okay now."

His words light a fire in me. I suck in a breath and pull away from him. "Really? Why? Because you're here?"

He frowns, looking more troubled than ever. "No, not just because I'm here. Because we can work on everything now. And once we get back into the studio, all this will be behind you and we can focus on what's important."

I clamber to my feet. "On what's important?" I say, outraged. "And what's that? Your career? Not my family issues? Which you helped to escalate, by the way."

He stands and stares down at me. "What's that mean? I didn't do anything except drive you home."

"Ha!" I stomp out of the kitchen and head for the living room. "You've been using Mom to get to me, pushing her buttons. My relationship with her has been more strained than ever because all she can do is tell me how stupid I am for leaving you."

His eyes narrow, all sympathy gone. "I had nothing to do with that. All I wanted was your number to get in touch with you. You're the one who cut me off."

"And you're the one who fucked everyone within a fifty-mile radius!"

He strides toward me, anger streaming off him in waves. Clearly trying to calm himself, he stops a few feet from me and takes a deep breath. "I told you already, that's over. I made a mistake. If this thing between us is going to work, you're going to have to let it go."

"Are you kidding me right now?" I can't believe him. Selfish Cadan is back in full force. He's learned nothing. Yes, I'd brought it up, but I'm not over what he did to me. If we're going to move forward, he has to acknowledge I have a few things to work through. "You're turning this on me? Really?"

He steps back and clutches the back of his head with his hand. "No. Fuck." He turns and moves toward the kitchen but stops and faces me once more. "I never meant to hurt you, Luce."

A sound of someone clearing his throat comes from the hallway and I jump, startled.

"Sorry," Seth says. He's dressed up more than usual in dark jeans and a black button-down shirt. He must have come straight from his parents' house. "I didn't mean to intrude. My knock went unanswered and when I heard yelling I got worried."

"Everything's fine," Cadan says in a clipped tone. Then he narrows his eyes at Seth. "Why are you here?"

Seth ignores him and walks to my side. "Are you all right?"

I nod, unable to form words for a moment. Then I grab him and push him back toward the entry hall. Once out of

Cadan's view, I wrap my arms around him and bury my head into his chest.

"What happened?" His tone is low, and I can tell it's meant to be gentle, but it's laced with an edge.

I shake my head. "Terrible day."

He holds me until Cadan walks in and says, "Lucy? Can we talk?"

I extract myself from Seth's arms and turn around, sending him a flat stare. "I need a minute."

He hesitates, eyeing Seth.

"Cadan," I warn.

He raises his hands in defeat and backs up. "Yeah. Fine. I'll wait in the living room."

When he's gone, I turn to Seth and frown at the judgment I see in his expression. "It's not what you think."

"Oh? What do I think?"

"I…" Dammit, I don't know. "Can we go outside for a minute?"

His jaw tightens as he glances down the hall. When his gaze meets mine again, he nods once.

I stifle a sigh of relief and follow him out the door.

CHAPTER 27

Seth

Lucy's tearstained face once again triggers a primal instinct to stride back inside her house and tear Kinx limb from limb. What the hell had he done to her? And why am I the one being escorted outside?

She walks until she gets to my truck and then stands in front of me, staring at the ground.

"What's going on?" I ask, ignoring the rain already soaking through my shirt. Lucy doesn't seem to notice the weather.

She kicks a rock across the driveway. "You should have waited for my call."

I wait for her to lift her head, to look me in the eye, and when she doesn't, I use two fingers to lift her chin. There's pain in her deep blue eyes. Lots of it. "When I didn't hear from you, I got worried." I gestured to the night. "Anything could've happened on those windy roads." The familiar heartache clutches at me, but I swallow it down. Lucy is not Elsa.

"You didn't get my text?" A lone tear rolls down her cheek and she wipes it away angrily.

I want to wrap her in my arms again, to protect her from whatever's happening, but she crosses her arms over her chest while she waits for me to answer. "No." I pull my phone out and scroll through the messages. Shaking my head, I hand her the phone to check for herself.

"Nothing."

Her frown deepens. "I sent a text letting you know I needed to cancel and that I'd call you later."

I raise my eyebrows and jerk my head toward the house. "Because of him?"

"Yes and no," she says, her voice low.

"What does that mean? Are you saying if he wasn't here you still would've canceled?" My insides clench with dread. This last week has been nothing short of perfect. Our time together, the fact that I'm painting again. That I can even talk about Elsa. It's because of her. And if I lose her to that jackass so soon, I don't think I'll recover.

"No, probably not." She steps closer, and for a moment I think she's going to wrap her arms around me again, but she only places one hand on my chest as she stares up at me. "I had a fight with my mom and walked out. Cadan drove me home. I couldn't just kick him out on Christmas. His car is in Santa Rosa."

I wrap my hand around hers and pull her a little closer. Cupping her cheek with my palm, I wipe away the tears mixing with the rain.

"It's almost impossible for him to find a way back now," she adds.

"No doubt. But I'm more concerned about you and these tears."

"Oh." Her brow crinkles and she closes her eyes as she tries to blink back a fresh onslaught. "Mom and I had another fight on the phone and then Cadan and I got into it after I hung up on her."

"I see," I say, but I don't. Not really. I don't understand what it must be like to be her and to have such tenuous relationships.

"I'm sorry," she says.

"For what?"

"For having to deal with this crap. For walking in and finding him here." She steps back, her voice stronger now. "I think I need to take a break from whatever this is while I deal with Cadan and figure out what I'm going to do about my contract."

My heart clenches so tight actual pain ripples through my chest. "This is how it's always going to be, isn't it?"

"What do you mean how it's always going to be?" Her eyes meet mine, and I can tell by the resignation I find there that she knows exactly what I'm talking about. But she wants me to put it into words. To make the break for her so she doesn't have to.

But I refuse to let go so easily. I should. It's the best thing for me. If I stay in this relationship, my heart is going to be shredded. But I can't. Not yet. I reach out once more and brush her matted hair from her face. "Nothing. Call me when you need a friend."

She frowns and her lower lip trembles as her eyes well up again. "I could use a friend right now."

My resolve melts and I pull her close. This time instead of hugging her, I lean down and brush a soft kiss over her lips. It's all I can do to not stuff her in my truck and take her home. Forcing myself to let her go, I take a step back. "I'm your friend, Lucy. Truly. No matter what you decide to do about Kinx." The words send a bolt of jealousy through me. That ass has this gorgeous, sweet, sexy woman and yet all he can manage to do is hurt her. She deserves better. I'm acutely aware I want to be the one to give it to her. I shake myself.

Stop it, Keenan. She's not yours.

"If there's anything I can do or if you need to talk, I'm around." I grin, trying to shake the mood. "Or if you just need someone to take your mind off of everything, I can think of a few ways…"

That gets a smile out of her. "Yeah, I'm intimately aware of your distraction techniques."

We both chuckle. Silence stretches between us for a few moments. I should get in my truck and drive away. She needs to deal with her ex one way or another. Hanging around isn't helping. Too bad all my instincts are screaming for me to stay.

"I better go in," she says.

"That's my cue." Reluctantly I climb into my truck and stuff the key into the ignition. The engine roars to life, and before I can talk myself out of it, I back out of her driveway, swearing at myself for getting emotionally involved with the most unavailable single girl I know.

She's still standing in the rain watching me leave when I crank the wheel and head back toward town. Emptiness creeps into my gut and spreads. I can't help but feel that by leaving her with him that I've lost her before I ever really had her.

I tighten my grip on the wheel and lay into the gas, needing to get as far away from the pair of them as possible. Otherwise, I'll turn around and go back. And I'm not that guy. For the first time, I start to really understand what Jax has been going through since the big breakup. I touch the Call button on my media center and hit Jax's name.

"Merry Christmas!" she says by way of greeting.

"Hey," I say.

"What's up?" Her bubbly tone shifts to one of concern.

Feeling foolish for calling, I press harder on the pedal and take a corner a little too fast. The truck fishtails. "Oh shit!"

"Seth!"

I get the truck under control and slow to the speed limit. "Sorry. Took a corner too fast."

"Pull over right this minute."

"Jax." I sigh. "I'm on Bluetooth."

"Still. It's awful out. You shouldn't be talking while driving."

Ignoring her admonishment, I ask, "Are you busy with family?"

"No. We've already done dinner, and I'm holed up in my apartment pretending I don't have to get up at the ass crack of dawn to open presents no one wants."

I snort. Jax's mom still thinks her kids are eight. They get pajamas and board games just as they had every year since she was five. "What time is the wakeup call?"

"Seven-fucking-thirty. You're so lucky your family does Christmas Eve and skips the morning torture ritual."

"Yeah." We used to do Christmas morning. That is until I'd just stopped going the year E died. That Christmas I'd stayed in bed and pretended the day didn't exist. For some reason, after that, Mom stopped making a big deal about holidays. She said as long as we were together on a regular basis that's all she cared about. The cold chill of loss hit me again. "Do you mind company?"

"Not if the company is you."

"I'll be there in twenty minutes."

Jax is waiting for me in her doorway when I pull up in front of her house. "What's going on?" she asks when I reach her side.

Still soaked from standing in the rain with Lucy, I shiver.

"Jesus," she whispers. "Come on. Get inside."

She pushes me into the bathroom and hands me a dry towel. "I don't have any clothes that will fit you. Just strip and I'll throw yours in Mom's dryer. You can wrap yourself in a blanket or whatever while they dry."

Too cold and wet to care, I do as I'm told and wrap the bath sheet around my hips. I emerge with my wet clothes and hand them to her.

She runs them downstairs to the dryer she shares with her parents, and when she returns, she rakes her gaze down my body. "Damn. No wonder Lucy keeps going back for more."

"Not tonight," I say almost to myself.

"Well sure. Isn't she at her mom's?"

"No." I run a hand through my damp hair. "She's home... with Cadan."

Jax straightens. "What? No. She can't be. I thought he finally left." Her eyes narrow. "Are you sure?"

I nod and sit on her couch, wrapping a blanket around me. "Yep. Positive. I just came from there."

"Oh, damn." Jax sits next to me, staring straight ahead, curling a lock of her blond hair with her fingers. Then she turns her sympathetic eyes on me. "You've fallen for her, haven't you?"

I close my eyes, not wanting to answer. Of course I have. But I don't want to admit it even to myself, much less Lucy's best friend. "Does it matter? Her mate is back. Nothing I can do."

She doesn't deny it. After a minute, she leans over and hugs me. The way a sister would hug a little brother, even though I'm about a foot taller than she is. "What can I do to help?"

"Don't worry about it. I mostly came over so I didn't have to explain to Lillian why I was home."

She straightens. "You've moved back to your house?"

I nod. "It would appear so."

"It's about time." She jumps to her feet. "Since you're staying over, I think it's time to drink. A lot." In three steps she's in her kitchen with her liquor cabinet open. "What's your poison?"

"Whiskey?" I say hopefully.

"Of course." She fills two lowball glasses half-full and returns to the couch, the bottle dangling from her fingers. "I don't know about you, but I won't be happy until I can't feel my lips."

I raise an eyebrow in her direction. "Rough day?"

"Not as bad as yours, but bad enough. Remind me to fill you in later." She raises her glass to mine. I follow suit, clinking my crystal against hers.

"To friends who stock plenty of whiskey," I say.

She laughs and scans her gaze over my body once more. The blanket has fallen, and I'm once again only wearing the towel. "To hot half-naked friends who drink said whiskey."

I nod, appreciating the ego boost more than I care to admit, and then throw the drink back with one gulp.

"More?" She holds the bottle out.

"Yes. And keep 'em coming."

CHAPTER 28

Lucy

Seth's red taillights glow in the distance. I stand in the rain, ignoring the water streaming down my face as I focus on his truck until he eases around a bend and the taillights disappear. A sense of loss hits me, and I start to shake. It's evident who I want to be with, and it isn't the guy waiting for me inside the house.

I drag my feet across the gravel walkway, wishing I could get in my car and follow Seth home. But I have to deal with my problems. Running away isn't going to help. Once inside, I grab a towel from the downstairs bathroom and then head straight for my room to change. At the top of the stairs, I pause. There's a light glowing from my bedroom.

Oh my God. Cadan's in there. I yank the door open and storm in. "What do you think—" I stop mid-sentence, silenced by his pained expression. He's holding the picture Seth drew of me this morning. Sadness haunts his eyes as he glances up at me.

"He drew this, didn't he?"

I nod.

Running his fingers gently over the paper, he crumples the edge with his other hand as he appears to fight with his emotions. It's all I can do not to rip it out of his grip to smooth the best gift anyone has ever given me. "Please be careful with it."

His fingers uncurl, and with effort he puts it on my nightstand.

"You don't have any reason to be angry, you know," I say. "You and me? We're not together."

He stands and walks over to me. "I know, Lucy. The last thing I need is a reminder."

I take a step back, and even though I'm fully clothed, I press the towel to my body. The way he's gazing at me makes me feel as if I'm completely naked. As if he's seeing more than he should.

"That picture?" He waves a hand toward it. "I don't think I've ever seen you look that content. That peaceful."

"I was asleep."

"I saw that." He closes his eyes and takes a deep breath. "Do you love this guy?"

I stand frozen, unable to move, unable to answer his question.

"You do." Cadan hangs his head, defeated.

"I... I don't know. I mean, that's not a fair question," I stammer out.

He brushes past me and then pauses in the doorway facing the hallway. He doesn't look back when he says, "You should get into dry clothes. We can talk downstairs."

Once he's gone, I shut the door with a soft click. I can't recall ever seeing Cadan appear so sad. The guy who just left was a stranger to me. Usually cocky and full of more confidence than should be legal, he's subdued, maybe even apologetic, as if he really is remorseful. I don't know what to make of this new development.

I head to my bathroom and turn the shower on. Memories of this morning flash through my mind. Seth's hands ghost over my body, making me tingle with remembered desire. It's hard not to compare Seth to Cadan since Cadan is the only other person I've been with. I can't stop myself though. When Cadan and I were together, we had plenty of fire and intensity fueled by our connection. But with Seth there is something else. When we're together, there's a tenderness combined with heat and raw emotion that doesn't have anything to do with mates or magic. We're two people desperate to know one another. By choice, not fate. And it seems more real.

After a hot shower, I emerge and dress in jeans and a sweat-shirt. Wearing thick wool socks, I pad downstairs, dreading the coming conversation. Cadan is sitting stiffly on the couch in front of the fireplace.

"Hey," I say.

He turns and gives me a slight smile. "You look warmer."

"Definitely."

"Have a seat." He gets up and disappears into the kitchen while I settle in and wait. When he comes back, he hands me one of the two mugs he's carrying. "It's mocha."

I tuck my feet under me, grateful I have something to concentrate on.

Cadan sits at the opposite end of the couch. After a few moments, he clears his throat. "I'm going to tell Cassie we're not recording the new songs."

I snap my head up and stare at him. "But what about the publishing contract?"

He shrugs. "We can write new songs for it. I'm sure we can work something out. I bet we can even get a shortened tour if you want. We'll have to do a few television appearances, but not much more. Jeff's been digging through the contract, and it's pretty flexible on the promotional stuff."

"Really?" I turn to face him, my brows pinched in confusion. "Last time I talked to him he said the contract was ironclad."

"He was mistaken." Cadan puts his mug down and gazes into my eyes. "I want you to be happy, Luce. Like that pic-ture. I want you to sleep soundly and not look like you're in a perpetual state of frustration or anger. After I saw the picture, I realized just how unhappy I've made you."

"You didn't make me unhappy per se…" I don't really know what else to say.

He snorts out a sardonic laugh. "Right. Well, I disagree. When we first met you smiled a heck of a lot more than you do now. I'm pretty sure I'm a large part of that."

"Cadan." I sigh. "I just lost my dad. Mom and I have been fighting. Our relationship has been unsettled at best, but you're not the reason I'm struggling. I'm just going through a rough patch right now."

He scoots forward and places his hand on my thigh. "I know, babe. And that's why I want you to have whatever it is you need. As much as it kills me to say it, this tattoo guy seems to be better for you than I am."

I straighten. "Are you really trying to hand me off to someone else?"

"No." He says it with finality. "Definitely not. I want you with me. Always. But not if it's not the best thing for you. One day we'll be together. But not now I don't think."

"One day, huh?" The pressure in my chest loosens a bit. It makes it easier to think we might have a chance to find our way together someday, even if I don't feel it now. And I don't. My heart lies elsewhere.

"Yeah." His arms come around me and he holds me against him, stroking my hair. I let him, comforted by the fact that he finally seems to be thinking of me for once in his life. He lets go and stands. "I think I'll go to bed. Merry Christmas Eve, Luce. I'll see you in the morning."

A moment later, the stairs creak under his footsteps and then the guest room door shuts with a soft click. Sitting on the couch with my legs tucked under me, I contemplate calling Seth. But I want to talk to Jax first about Cadan and this new turn of events. Pulling out my phone, I hit Jax's name and wait. It goes straight to voice mail. Damn.

An hour and three more tries later, I give up and go to bed. As warm and cozy as I am, sleep eludes me. Not even the soft strum of the rain on the windows can lull me into oblivion. After staring at the ceiling and watching the clock tick until well past three a.m., I finally fall into a fitful sleep where I dream of Seth. He's with me, but not really. We're standing together, but he doesn't seem to know I'm there, as if one of us is a ghost, but I don't know which one. Frustrated, I do everything I can think of to get him to notice me. I yell, wave my arms, and even go so far as to wrap my arms around him and kiss him, but he stands there, impassive and unaware.

Finally he turns his head in my direction, but he doesn't see me. No. He sees someone else walking out of the coastal fog. She's tall and slender, her long hair blowing in the breeze.

Seth's eyes light up with wonder, and he lets out a surprised gasp as he strides toward her. She grins and holds out her hand. Almost running now, he reaches for her, but just as his arms wrap around her, she disappears once again.

A guttural cry of loss tears from Seth, and it's so heart wrenching it feels as if someone has stabbed me in the chest. I run to his side, wanting to comfort him, to ease his suffering, but still he doesn't hear or see me. He sinks to his knees, anguish-ridden with grief.

I wake with a start. "Elsa." Her name slips from my lips in a whisper, and I sit straight up in bed, wide awake, my heart racing. My eyes adjust quickly in the predawn light as I take in the familiar surroundings of my bedroom. The dream seemed so real I still feel the moisture on my skin.

Leaning back against my mountains of pillows, I rub my eyes and start when the sound of the front door opening catches my attention. Low voices reverberate from downstairs. I glance at the clock. Six a.m. Jumping out of bed, I stuff my feet into my slippers, wrap myself in my robe, and descend to the first floor to investigate.

Cadan and Will, our blue-haired bass player, are sitting at my bar drinking coffee. "Hey." I rub my eyes. "What's going on?"

"Will came to pick me up," Cadan says into his coffee. "We'll be on our way in a few minutes."

"What?" I sink down onto a barstool. "But it's Christmas and it's so early."

Cadan gives me a sad look. "I don't mean to leave you alone today, but really, I think it's for the best." He gets up and nods to Will. "If you're ready, I think now's a good time."

Will tosses him a set of keys. "Whatever, man. You're driving. I haven't even gone to bed yet."

I grab Will's arm. "You drove here from Sac?" It's where the band is hanging out while waiting to see what Cadan and I decide.

He yawns and nods. "Don't worry. I didn't get up until four." He gives me a quick hug and whispers, "I'm sorry about what went down. You didn't deserve that."

I squeeze him in acknowledgement. It feels good to have someone admit I'm not totally crazy. "It's good to see you, even if only for a few minutes."

"You, too, Luce." He releases me and disappears out the front door. Cadan gazes at me, taking me in as if he's trying to memorize this moment. Then without a word, he follows Will outside.

I sit back down, trying to reconcile the sadness of watching him go with the desire to dance around my kitchen in sheer elation. Without another thought, I run upstairs, throw on some clothes, and race to my car.

Twenty minutes later, I pull up to Jax's house and stop behind a familiar red truck. I frown and glance at the clock. Six forty-nine. What is Seth doing at her house so early on Christmas morning?

More curious than anything else, I grab Jax's present and jog up the stairs to her front door. I knock and hop back and forth, trying to stave off the cold. After a few moments, I knock again and blow on my now-frozen fingers while I wait.

Impatient, I press against one of her side windows and peer in. I gasp, then shock turns me to stone. I blink, certain I'm hallucinating. It isn't possible. But the scene doesn't shift. Right there on the couch is Jax, sprawled across Seth. She's wearing tiny sleep shorts and a camisole top. He's wearing nothing. Her shirt is riding up, helped along by his hand splayed across her lower back.

I jump back, a sob forming in my throat. Dropping Jax's present, I spin and bolt.

CHAPTER 29

Seth

An elbow slams into my gut and I groan. "What the—"

"Jesus, Seth. Cover yourself." Jax throws the towel at me and runs to the window. "Oh, dammit!" She pulls the door open and yells, "Lucy!"

"What's going on?" I ask, clutching the towel around my waist.

"It's Lucy." Jax scowls and waves a hand toward the street. "She must have seen us sleeping and got the wrong idea. 'Cause look."

I peer out the door. The woman I've been dreaming about all night has a horrified expression on her face as she frantically tries to unlock her car door. She drops her keys, and when she bends to pick them up, she knocks her head on the mirror. "Ouch. Fuck," she cries.

"Lucy," I call, stepping out onto the porch. The cold morning air nearly freezes my balls off, but she's so upset, I can't force myself to go back inside.

She pauses but doesn't look up before pulling her door open and climbing into her car.

Shit!

Barefoot and all but stark naked, there's no way I can catch her before she peels away from the curb. "Son of a... fuck." I slam the door shut and immediately search for my phone on the coffee table. Her line rings and rings and rings and finally her voice mail answers.

"Lucy. Jesus, babe. It's not what you think. I slept on Jax's couch. My clothes were drying and I passed out before they were done." A knot forms in my stomach. "We were drinking and... Shit, that sounds bad. But really, Lucy. Nothing happened. Jax must've fallen asleep on me. I swear to God all we did was sleep. I'd really like to see you. Give me a call. I'll come over. Or you can come to my place if you're free. Call me back."

Jax stares at me for a minute, her brows pinched, then makes a disgusted smacking noise with her mouth. "I have got to brush my teeth. I'll be right back."

I sit on the couch, running my hands through my hair while I wait for Jax to finish in the bathroom. By the time she finally emerges, I'm pacing. "I need my clothes."

She quirks an eyebrow. "You're not going to go over there, are you?"

"Of course I am. I can't let her think something went on here." I frown. "Why aren't you more upset? You have to know what she was thinking."

"I am upset. But we didn't do anything, so this will blow over." She crosses the room and fishes her phone off her desk and curses under her breath. "Dead."

I wait for her while she digs around for the cord and eventually plugs it in. When she turns around, she actually takes a step back even though I'm across the room from her. "Damn, Seth. You look like you're going to murder someone."

"My clothes, Jax. I need to go." The look on Lucy's face, the obvious pain—I can't let her go on thinking Jax and I... just no.

"No, you don't. Isn't Cadan still there? She doesn't need you barging in on her. I'll talk to her. Trust me."

"Jax," I growl.

She crosses her arms over her chest and juts her chin out stubbornly. "Wait for her to calm down."

"Fuck me." I stuff my feet into my shoes and grab the blanket off the couch. Wrapped in purple chenille, I'm halfway down the stairs before Jax catches up.

"Wait!" she calls.

Too late. I pull open the side door to her parents' kitchen and come to a screeching stop. Holy shit. Jax's dad's bare ass is on full display as he pounds into her mom, right there on the counter. They're too engrossed to notice me, and I spin, heading straight back out the door. But before I can escape, Jax barrels in.

"Seth, no. What will my parents—Mom? Dad? Omigod!" She stares at them in horror. "It's Christmas morning. What are you doing?"

Despite my desperation to get my damn clothes and chase after Lucy, I can't help the laughter that rumbles from my chest. "Pretty good present if you ask me."

"Jax!" Her mom gasps and buries her face into her husband's shoulder. "Could you give us a moment?"

Her dad doesn't speak, but his entire body flushes red in embarrassment. Jax runs back out the door.

"Sorry," I force out through the laughter and escape into the next room, unwilling to abandon my clothes now that I've been spotted. After a quick stop in the laundry room, I hurry out the back door and take the stairs two at a time back up to Jax's apartment.

She's fuming when I get inside. "What the hell was that?"

"Uh, some holiday cheer?" I offer with a snicker.

"No, you ass." She grabs a pillow and throws it at my head. "I meant you barging in on my parents. Now they're going to think I have something going on with you."

Having easily dodged her assault, I pass her on my way to her bathroom. "I needed my clothes, and you weren't cooperating. But don't worry, your parents aren't likely to mention this incident ever again." I slam the door shut. It takes me less than a minute to pull my clothes on.

On my way out, I give Jax a quick hug. "Thanks for the couch. I have to talk to Lucy."

"I'm coming with you."

"What about Christmas with your parents?" I ask.

"Oh, hell no. They'll be lucky if they see me before New Year's at this point."

"All right. If you're sure." Maybe Jax can reason with her.

"I'm sure."

Jax spends the entire time in the truck using my phone to call Lucy. But it always goes straight to voice mail.

"She's turned her phone off," I say.

"I know. I just want to catch her if she turns it back on." Now that it's settled in how upset Lucy is, Jax is more anxious to set her straight than I am. "I can't believe she thought we'd been together like that."

I give her an incredulous look. "Seriously? I slept with her the first night we met. And my reputation isn't a shining beacon of respectability."

"Mine is," she says with conviction.

"True, but you were looking for someone to take home the night of your birthday."

Her face turns a bright shade of red, and she focuses on the ocean view as we head south on the highway.

"One-night stands are no big deal," I say.

She lets out a huff. "Easy for you to say. You never seem to have a shortage of options."

I chuckle. "I think if you'd had less tequila, you would've noticed a few solid possibilities."

"Maybe." She presses a button on my phone again and sighs. "Still voice mail."

"We'll be there in a minute."

The second I pull up, Jax is out of the truck and pounding on the door. "Lucy! Open up."

There isn't any ambient noise from inside the house, but Lucy's car is in the driveway. She pretty much has to be here. "Luce!"

I leave Jax at the front door and head around to the sliding glass doors in the back. There's a small gap in the curtains, but the room is dark. And no Lucy. Feeling entirely too much like a stalker, I rejoin Jax at the front door. "Anything?" I ask.

"Nope," she says to me and then pounds on the door. "Lucy, come on. We're worried about you. Open up. Please?"

We stare at each other, both of us at a loss for what to do. Jax throws her hands up and takes a seat on the front step. "We'll just wait her out. She can't stay in there forever."

I pace and finally end up sitting in my truck. We've been here for over a half hour. At what point does this become harassment? Unease settles in my gut. "Jax, let's go."

"No. She'll crack sooner or later."

"I don't want her to crack. I want her to talk to me, not feel like she has to call the cops to get rid of us. She can call when she's ready." I tap out a text to Lucy, asking her to get in touch with me, and then fire the truck up. Jax is still sitting on the front porch. "I'm going. You coming?"

She glances over her shoulder and lets out a huff of frustration. "Yeah. But I'm not happy about it." Taking her time, she slowly retreats back to the truck. After climbing in, she slams the door and crosses her arms over her chest. Like a petulant child, she glares at the house. "Merry fucking Christmas, Lucy."

I ease out of the driveway. "Give her a break. She's upset."

She lets out a huff of irritation. "But I'm her best friend. She can't honestly believe I'd sleep with *you*."

"Ouch." Damn. Way to punch a guy when he's down.

"That's not what I meant and you know it." Her scowl deepens.

We're silent as I drive her home. Once parked outside her house, she doesn't move to get out. "Are you going to your parents'?" she asks.

"Later for dinner."

She nods. "We have dinner planned as well. But I might skip it after this morning's events." She makes a face.

"It's Christmas. You have to go." I smile. "Just avoid the kitchen. That should help."

"Disgusting! Nothing will help." She climbs out of my truck. "Call me if you hear from Lucy."

"You, too. And thanks for the couch."

"Anytime."

I drive home in a stupor, worse off than I was the night before when I'd gone to Jax's house. What is Lucy thinking? Why isn't she with Kinx? After spending the morning in her driveway, I highly doubt he's still there. Had he gotten a car and taken her somewhere? Had she left town with him? Would she even say good-bye?

The questions and doubts swirl in my mind until my head starts to pound.

The lights are on at my house. Damn. Lillian is still here. She's not going to leave me alone until I tell her where I've been. My only hope is that she's locked in the second bathroom, primping for what's his name. Her mate who never seems to be around.

I quietly let myself into the kitchen, relieved to find it empty. The whiskey bottle beckons. It's before nine a.m. on Christmas day. "Screw it." I wash two aspirin down with a pull of the harsh liquor. It burns straight to my gut. I take another swig and the tension in my shoulders eases slightly.

"Hey." Lillian leans against the threshold of the doorway leading into the living room. "Rough night?"

"Awful. And even worse morning." I brush past her, heading for my bedroom.

"Seth?"

"Yeah," I say without stopping.

"Are you living here full time now?"

That makes me pause and I turn to look at her. I'm not sure how to answer. For the past few weeks I had been either here, at the shop, or at Lucy's. I hadn't been back to Mom and Dad's at all. "I guess so."

She nods. "Good. Don't get so drunk you miss Christmas dinner."

I hold the bottle up, eyeing the contents. If I take it with me, I'll likely finish it out of sheer frustration. Walking back down the stairs, I tip the bottle to my lips once more, then hand it to her. "You take it."

Her hand wraps around mine and she squeezes.

I want to pull away, but if I do the bottle will smash to the floor.

Lillian steps forward and wraps her other arm around me, squeezing hard. "Whatever happened, little brother, you're stronger than this." She pulls the booze from my hand. "Spend the day wallowing, or head up to your studio, or go work out, but don't let this get you again." She kisses me on the cheek and silently slips from the room.

My breathing turns choked and I press my hand to the wall. Jesus. Was I really going there again? Whiskey for breakfast? Yeah. I was.

I'm not an alcoholic. I don't crave booze on a daily basis. But since I lost Elsa, I have been known to be destructive when I don't want to deal with something. And whiskey is one of my go-to vices. Shit. She's right. My head is already spinning. If I keep it up, I'll be passed out by noon. I should've eaten something at least.

After grabbing a box of left over pizza and two Cokes, I climb the stairs to my sanctuary. My studio. The room instantly calms me. Then it hits me. No matter what happens with Lucy, she'll always be in my heart. Her presence in my life has given me what Elsa's death stole from me. The desire to create just for me.

CHAPTER 30

Lucy

Jax and Seth are outside, but I can't bring myself to go downstairs to talk to them. Lying in my bed staring at the ceiling, I know I'm being unreasonable, refusing to even talk to them. It's as if I'm floating above myself, watching myself push away everyone who loves me.

I can't help it, though. Seeing Jax and Seth sleeping together had flipped a switch in me. My trust in everyone is shot. I don't know what happened between them. And it *shouldn't* matter this much. Seth and I barely know each other. We haven't made any promises to be together. I have no claim on him. I'd even sent him away because my soul mate was here.

But my heart is broken at the thought of him with my best friend. And the fact that Jax might use Seth for her one-night stand after I'd spent the week with him is unimaginable. Yet, I'd been the one to keep pushing her to go to him. She trusts him. Loves him even… as a friend. It's just too much to process. And I trust no one.

When I hear the roar of Seth's truck start again, I get up and move to the window. He's calling to Jax to get in the truck, but she's refusing. She looks so upset, I want to run down and pull her in the house. But there's that nagging doubt. What if it's true and she's only upset that I found out?

Before they leave, I crawl back into bed and pull my pillow over my head. It's time to spend the day with only myself. No boys. No awful parents. Just me.

I lie in the bed for hours, going over and over what I'd seen this morning. It's a reel that plays on a continuous loop and makes me sick to my stomach. The thought of even talking to Seth or Jax has me running to the bathroom. After I empty the contents of my stomach twice, I curl up in the bed and cry myself to sleep.

I wake much later to the inky blackness of the wee hours of the morning. I'm groggy and hollow. Wrung out from grief. With my eyes burning from the gritty sandpaper sensation that comes from a fitful sleep, I glance at the picture of Dad on my nightstand and make an instant decision. I need to move forward. To get on with my life. Hiding here, using Jax and Seth as emotional shields, isn't solving anything. I've got a contract to fulfill.

And despite everything, at least Cadan and I understand each other. I know who and what he is, and he knows me. With some firm rules, I'll be able to make this work.

Without hesitation, I grab my phone, power it on, ignore the two dozen alert notifications, and then punch in the number I want to call.

It rings three, four, five times. On the sixth ring he answers. "Lucy? Are you okay?"

I glance at the clock. Two twenty-two a.m. I would apologize, but familiar voices filter over the line. He's hanging with the band.

"Cadan," I say, "I've made a decision."

"Hey, guys, shut up!" he calls, clearly holding the phone away so he's not shouting in my ear. His volume returns to normal, but there's a new lilt of hopefulness. "About us?"

"About coming back to the band."

"Oh." The background noise coming from his end fades to silence.

"Are you outside now?" I stall.

"Yes. Everyone else is inside. Where are you?"

"In bed."

"Always a good choice." I can hear the smile in his voice. It eases me into a familiar comfort, making what I need to say next simple.

"I'm ready to record Dad's songs. When's the soonest we can start?"

Silence.

"Cadan? You there?"

He clears his throat. "Yeah. Sorry. You just shocked me. Are you sure?"

"I'm sure."

"What happened? I mean, why did you change your mind?"

"I…" Telling him I'm ready to put the past behind me and move on is still too personal. I need this to feel whole again. To let go of all the pain. And I don't want to answer questions about what this might mean for our relationship in the future. As far as I'm concerned, we'll just be business partners.

"Never mind. It doesn't matter. Do you want me to come get you?"

"No," I say. "I'm going to pack, and I'll come to Sacramento in the morning. I need the name of your hotel."

He gives it to me. Then he hesitates as if thinking something over.

"What's wrong?"

"Nothing," he says quickly. "I just want to make sure this is what you really want. We can record something else if you're more comfortable." His tone is achingly sincere.

"It is. I'm ready to let go."

"Ah, babe." He sighs sympathetically. "Your dad will always be with you."

"I know. And these songs will honor him." I run a hand over my soft comforter. "See you early afternoon tomorrow."

"Goodnight, Luce. Merry Christmas."

"Night." I hit End on the phone and lean back against the pillows. The decision is made. The pit in my stomach doesn't go away. It only widens and my heart breaks a little more. A voice deep inside says I should run as far from everything and everyone as I can. But I tried that and it didn't work. All I managed to do was get hurt again. At least with Cadan I'll have my career.

I pull up to the Grand Marquis Hotel in downtown Sacramento and climb out. Straight away a bellman rushes over.

"Hello, Ms. Moore. We've been expecting you. Your party is waiting inside in the bar area. We'll take care of everything from here."

"Thank you." I hand him the keys and, with more than a little trepidation, head into the hotel. The bar is just off the lobby, and I spot them right away. Cadan and the band are lounging around a table drinking beer and watching a snowboarding competition on ESPN. It's different than what I'm used to. Usually they're all still passed out with half a dozen girls hanging around their rooms.

"Lucy!" Jessie, our drummer, calls and jumps up from his chair. In five long strides, he's by my side, wrapping me in a bear hug. "Thank God you're back. I need someone other than these ugly a-holes to look at." He lifts me up until my feet are dangling off the ground.

Laughing, I hit his arm. "Put me down so I can get a good look at you."

He does as he's told and steps back, holding his arms out. Then he does a slow three-sixty, showing off his lean runner's physique. "See anything you like?"

"Hey, now," Cadan says, coming to a stop at his side. "Stop hitting on my girl."

I ignore Cadan's possessive demand and raise an eyebrow at Jessie. "You look… normal."

He chuckles. "As opposed to?"

I grin. "Wrung out and hungover."

"Oh that." He gives Cadan a stern look. "This bozo said we were partying too hard and put the kibosh on the after-show invites. It's no fun to sit around drinking without the ladies. So our social lives have taken a little bit of a hit."

"Really?" I turn to Cadan. "You banned visitors?"

"No." He puts an arm around my shoulders and pulls me in. "Just random groupies. Friends are welcome. But it was getting out of hand and… the music was suffering."

Jessie scoffs. "Not nearly as much as this guy." He punches Cadan in the arm. "We thought we were going to have to get a bulk supply of Prozac there for a while. Talk about a downer. One minute he's working on a new song and the next he's—"

"Shut up, you fucker," Cadan says as he pushes Jessie back. "Lucy doesn't need to hear all this right now." He grabs my hand and tugs me out of the bar.

"Hey," I say. "I didn't get to say hi to the rest of the guys."

"You'll see them tonight. First we have a meeting with Cassie."

I stop and face him. "Already?"

"Yeah. She was in town meeting with another band, and when I told her you'd called she cleared her afternoon in order to welcome you back."

"Oh." I straighten my shirt and run a nervous hand over my hair. I'm not exactly prepared for a business meeting.

"Relax. She just wants to hammer out the schedule so we're all on the same page." He guides me to the elevator, and we ride to the thirty-ninth floor. It's the highest before the penthouse suite.

The plush carpet is glorious under our feet as we make our way to the end of the hallway. "Pretty nice place," I say.

Cadan nods and raps once on the door.

The door swings open, and Cassie's smile turns to a huge grin when she focuses on me. Her onyx eyes sparkle with true pleasure. "Lucy! Dang, is it good to see you." She pulls me into the room and then gives me a tight hug, wrinkling her silk pantsuit. "I hope your break was restful."

I glance at Cadan over her shoulder. *Break?* I'd quit.

He holds his hands up as if to say he doesn't have a clue what she's talking about.

"I know your dad's passing was really tough for you. It's no wonder you needed some time." Cassie pulls back and stares me in the eye. "You let me know if you need anything, okay? A day off to be normal for a while. Someone to cook for you. A personal shopper if you don't want to go out. Whatever you need. We've got you covered."

"Uh…"

"Just don't worry about a thing. We're here to make life as easy as possible. The top priority is the new album. Whatever it takes to make it happen, that's what we'll do."

"Okay," I say, more confused than ever. I'd never gotten this treatment before.

"Everyone's real excited about the new album, Luce," Cadan says by way of explanation.

"Yes, we are!" Cassie waves a hand around the room. "Have a seat. I'll be right back." She disappears into the adjoining bedroom while we settle into chairs at a table near the window. There's a view of the Sacramento River. It's better than a parking lot, but still not very scenic.

Cadan reaches out and wraps his hand around mine, giving it a squeeze, and leans in. "I'm really happy you decided to give us another try."

My insides tingle with nervousness. And not the good kind. I hadn't said I wanted to get back together with him. I pull my hand from his. "Let's just take this one day at a time, all right?"

"Sure," he says and leans back. "A lot has happened."

"For both of us," I say almost under my breath. I'm trying hard not to still be upset about his cheating, but being back here in a hotel room, it's all surfacing again. The image of Seth relaxing on my couch, laughing at something I'd said, flashes through my mind and that sense of loss deepens. Had I ever been that content around Cadan?

I search his tight expression. No. Not ever. What we have is fraught with tension. It can be exciting, but more often than not, it's exhausting. Pulling out my phone, I hover over the twenty unopened texts. I'm certain some of them are from Seth. But I can't read them now. Not here in Cassie's hotel room. Maybe I can't read them ever. I made the decision to come back here. I should delete them and let everything about Seth go. I don't, though. Instead, I slip the phone back into my purse as Cassie breezes back into the room, her sleek black hair flying behind her.

"So exciting," she says with a huge smile. "Want something to drink? Water? Coffee? Soft drink?"

"Coffee," I say, just so I can have something else to focus on during this conversation.

"I'll get it." Cadan jumps up and pours coffee from a silver carafe already on the table. Cassie is prepared as always. He adds plenty of cream and one spoonful of sugar, just the way I like it. "Here you go."

I wrap both hands around the mug. "Thanks."

"Okay then." Cassie hands us both a packet of papers. "I've worked out a schedule I want to go over so we can get everything rolling as soon as possible."

I scan the sheet and my mouth drops open. "You want us to perform tomorrow night in San Francisco?"

She frowns. "Is that a problem?"

"Not at all," Cadan says.

I scowl at him. "I thought you were done making my decisions for me?"

He jerks as if I've slapped him. Then he leans back in his chair. "Sorry, Luce. I didn't mean to answer for you." Then he turns to Cassie. "It's not a problem for me if it's not a problem for Lucy."

His condescension irritates the crap out of me, but I put it on the back burner and focus.

"Is it okay, Lucy? Or do you have a prior commitment? I was under the impression you were back and available, but if not, I'll need to redo some things here." She twists her pen and starts scribbling on her copy of the schedule.

"No. I'm back and my schedule is clear. It's only that I haven't practiced with the band in almost four months. The new songs… they're rusty. We can't perform them."

"Don't worry about that. You can sing songs off the last album, and if you feel up to it, maybe one of the new songs."

I open my mouth to protest, but she continues, "Really. Only if you want to. No pressure."

"We can practice this afternoon and tomorrow before the show." Cadan studies me with guarded eyes. "Then only if you feel up to it. We'll leave the decision in your hands."

His statement floors me. Cadan has always been the one to jump in and take charge, making the decisions for both of us before I even have a chance to process what's happening. This is a new Cadan. A welcome, better version. Maybe there's hope for him yet. "Okay. We'll leave it open."

"Excellent." Cassie spends the next twenty minutes going over travel schedules, bookings, recording-session dates, and media events. My eyes are glazing over by the time she gets to the end of her list. "Any questions?"

"Yeah." I close the folder, knowing our manager will keep us informed of daily events. "Just one. I drove my car here. What will happen to it if we leave in the morning?"

"I'll have it delivered to your house. Not to worry about a thing." She makes a note in her book. "Excellent. Then that's it. The new contracts are being drawn up now. You'll have them by tomorrow."

"New contracts?" I ask.

"It's all the standard legal stuff. Your agent has been negotiating fiercely." Her phone rings and she holds her hand up. "Gotta take this." She crosses the room, leaving us to ourselves.

"New contracts?" I ask Cadan. "I thought we were already locked in?"

He smiles. "We are. But these are renegotiated to be more flexible and with more money. They were so desperate to have you back they've been working to sweeten the deal. Don't worry, Lucy. This is a good thing."

I frown in Cassie's direction. "That doesn't sound like something the label would do."

He shrugs. "Jeff's been earning his money, I guess."

"I guess so."

CHAPTER 31

Lucy

The afternoon practice session falls into an easy rhythm that's so familiar it seems as if no time has passed at all. Cassie's right. We can do one of the new songs. I'm not sure what's changed, but when the band strikes up the slow and haunting music, I throw my emotions into the song, really giving it everything I have. It's raw and more than a little gut-wrenching, but by the time the last notes fade away, I feel purged of something. Maybe a small bit of grief. Or maybe some of my recent pain.

Either way, by the time we get back to the hotel, my nerves have settled and I'm actually looking forward to the perfor- mance the next night.

"Are you up for a late dinner?" Cadan asks as we walk into the lobby.

"Sure. Just let me wash up. Where should I meet you?"

"I'll come by your room in about a half hour."

I nod and take off, leaving him in the bar with the rest of the band.

Once in my room, I take my time washing my face and redoing my makeup. Performing is hard, sweat-inducing work. I've just finished painting my lips with a new lipstick when the hotel phone rings. I frown, wondering why anyone wouldn't just call my cell.

"Hello?"

"Jesus fucking Christ!" Jax yells. "I can't believe you took off without even telling me. Or Seth. Do you have any idea what you did to him?"

Righteous outrage has me seeing red. She should understand how hurtful it was finding them together like that. "Are you kidding? This is what I get after *you* spent the night with him? God, Jax. You knew I was falling for him."

She scoffs. "We didn't do anything. And if you'd taken one of our phone calls, you'd know that."

I haven't had the courage to listen to my messages yet. But I had read the text messages. Most of them were pleas to call one of them. Or to ask where I was. I should have called Jax to let her know. No matter what they'd done or hadn't done, it wasn't fair to just leave town and let her worry. "Nothing happened? But I saw you two sleeping together on the couch, and Seth was naked. How is that nothing?"

"Lucy," she says with a long sigh. "He came over after seeing you, and his clothes were drenched. I don't have anything that fits him, so he wrapped up in a towel and a blanket. We spent the night talking on the couch and we fell asleep. That's it. He was talking about you all night long. If you'd answered your damn phone or come to the door when we came over, you'd have known this. And maybe you wouldn't have run off to Destructionville."

"Well, what was I supposed to think?" I demand, but the bottom falls out of my stomach. What she said sounded so much more plausible than the two of them sleeping together. "Shit," I say under my breath.

"Yeah," she agrees and then lowers her voice. "I'm sorry, Luce. I know how it looked. I can only imagine what went through your mind. But you can't just run away."

"I didn't," I insist.

"Yes, you did. You're back with Cadan already. After what he did to you? Have you lost your mind?"

"No... Yes." I press two fingers to my temple and sink onto the bed. "Jax?"

"What?" She's still angry, and I can hardly blame her. I'd shut her out and made a huge snap judgment after leaning on her for three months.

"I don't think I came back because of what I saw yesterday morning."

There's a pause on her end, then she clears her throat. "You mean you went back for Cadan?"

"Yes and no. Let me try to explain this."

"I'm all ears."

"Okay, here goes." I lean back against the pillows and take a deep breath. "When I saw you and Seth… Well, I sort of snapped. I mean everyone I ever loved has let me down. My mom, Cadan, even my dad when he shipped me off to my mom's. You're the only one who has always been there for me. And then Seth."

"We're still here, Luce. We can't force you to trust us, though."

"I know. I really do. And this isn't about that. The thing is, I have no hold over Seth. We spent a week together. It's not like we had a commitment or anything. But the pain I felt just then, it was more than I could bear. I had to do something. Go somewhere. Do something with my life besides hide out in Mendocino, waiting for something that isn't coming."

I take a moment to gather myself, then continue. "Cadan and I are soul mates. That means something. But again, that's not why I came back. I'm not here to start back up with him. I'm here to sing. I know what he is and what he isn't. And the man he is today isn't one I can be with romantically. Not with the way he trampled my heart."

"Then why—"

Clearing my throat, I cut her off. "The one thing I can't deny is that singing with him fills my soul and makes me feel like I'm doing something important. That's why I came back. For me. To finish out my contract and to give myself something I want. Not because I'm hurt, but because I need to move forward and stop standing still. Being with Seth helped awaken that part of me that died three months ago. The part of me that is strong, that makes me my own person."

"Wow," Jax says. "And you think you can be your own person with Cadan there?"

"I'm damn sure going to try. I can't make my own album until I fulfill my contract. That's ultimately what I want to do. So I'm here to do what I have to. Whatever happens, happens. I just have to do this."

"I see. Can't say I think it's a good idea."

I laugh. She's probably right. "I'd say the same thing if the situation were reversed."

"Humph."

"Jax?"

"Yeah?"

"We have a show tomorrow night in San Francisco. I'd love it if you could come. I really want to see you before I leave for SoCal."

"By myself? I'd love to, but damn, it's a long drive."

I hesitate, then force the words out. "You could bring Seth." My tone is strained and anxious.

"Seriously? You think that's a good idea, having Seth and Cadan within miles of each other?"

I sigh. "Not especially, but I really want to apologize in person." And see him one last time before I move on. Seth has given me something no one else could. I want to tell him about it. "Cadan will either be onstage or backstage. I could meet you and Seth after. Without him."

"Oh."

I pluck at the blanket on the bed, waiting for her to say something. Anything.

"You should call him."

My heart rate picks up speed. Crap. "I was hoping to speak to him in person."

"He won't come unless you ask him to. He's not into chasing anyone. And he already feels stalkerish for following you home yesterday. Just call him. If he says yes, we'll be there."

My stomach flips over at the thought. I'm terrified of what he'll say, but I have to try. "Okay. I will."

"Good. And remember to apologize." Her tone suggests she's teasing, but I know for certain she's dead serious. I'd hurt them both by shutting them out. That hadn't been my intention. I'd just been in a bad place.

"I will. And, Jax?"

"Yeah?"

"I'm sorry. I love you."

"You're forgiven. And I love you too. Do your best to be sure I have a ride to see you tomorrow night."

"I will." I set the receiver on the base of the phone and stare into space for a moment. I contemplate breaking out one of the vodka bottles from the minibar, but then decide against it. Instead, I crack open a Diet Coke and fish my cell phone out of my purse.

"Time to listen to these messages." Of the sixteen messages on my phone, two are from Seth. Four from Jax. They both denied anything happened and asked me to call them. And the rest are from my mother. Half are berating me for running out on Christmas. The other half are to tell me how glad she is I came to my senses and am back with Cadan. At least two explain to me in great detail how not to mess it up again. By the time I delete them all, I'm hot with silent rage. How dare she?

I have no doubt she's been calling Cadan just as much. He probably told her I'd come back in an effort to get rid of her. Why she can't just focus on her own life and leave mine alone, I can't understand.

"Let it go," I say to myself as I change into fresh clothes. "Time to woman up."

Sitting back on the bed, I call. It immediately goes to voice mail. I clear my throat. "Seth. Hi... It's Lucy. I was hoping to catch you, but maybe you're working. Umm... I called to apologize for leaving without saying anything and for, uh, not calling you back. Yesterday was a tough day." I clear my throat again. "I'm singing tomorrow night in San Francisco. If you're not busy, maybe you and Jax can come. Eight at Blue Jays. I know it's a long drive, but please consider it. I really want to see you… to talk to you in person. Okay, then. Hope to see you."

I hit End, feeling emptier than ever. If he doesn't show up, I know I'm going to regret how I handled things for the rest of my life. I text Jax to let her know I called, but he didn't answer.

She texts back. *I'll work on him.*

Cadan comes by as promised, and we head to the hotel bar for burgers. I'm even more quiet than usual. When he asks me about it, I claim exhaustion. It's not long before I'm back up in my room. Alone.

The rest of the night crawls by as I watch reruns of *Friends* on TV. I once again fall into a fitful sleep. I'm awake by six a.m., and by eight, I'm showered, fed, and ready to go. I know it's too early, but I have to get out of this room. I take off and find myself heading toward Cadan's room. For some reason, I have to know if he's alone.

His room is on the same floor as mine, at the end of the hall. I pause outside to steel myself. I could be walking in on anything. With a boatload of trepidation tempered with determination, I knock.

The door opens almost immediately. Cadan is shirtless, dressed in jeans, his hair wet. He has a new tattoo on his chest, but I'm too flustered to focus on it. "Morning, Luce. Come on in."

I raise a questioning eyebrow, trying not to be affected by his stellar body. The boy has abs a Calvin Klein model would kill for.

He grins. "I was just getting ready to order breakfast. Want anything?"

"Coffee, I guess. I just ate."

"Early riser. You got it." He makes the call and then comes to stand in front of me. He towers over me, my face level with his chest. I can't help but focus on the tattoo over his heart.

I let out a little gasp and lift my hand, gently tracing the dragon. The scales remind me a lot of the one Seth has on his arm. Then I trail my fingers over the letters. L and C. "When did you have this done?"

"Last week."

I take a step back. "While you were on the coast?"

He nods, his eyes serious.

"Who... ah, I mean, where did you have it done?"

"Your friend did it... or most of it, anyway."

"Seth?" My voice raises a few octaves. "Are you kidding me?"

"No. He's really good." He places both of his hands on my shoulders, then slowly runs them down my arms. "What is it? What did I do?"

"Nothing. I mean..." What *had* he done? Hired Seth to tattoo a soul mate mark that included our initials? It just seems so cruel. And why hadn't Seth said anything about it? "It's just weird, that's all."

"Why? Because you were seeing him? I didn't know that at the time. Honestly, Lucy, I did this for me. And you. But mostly for me. I wanted you close to my heart, always. Now you are."

I don't know what to say. Cadan is different than he was when I left him in Denver three months ago. The tattoo touches me. It's not as if girls wouldn't still be hanging all over him at shows and willing to sleep with him, but this is a clear declaration of commitment to me. Tattoos like that tell the world you're taken.

"It's beautiful," I say.

"Your friend is talented," he says. Then he disappears into the bathroom to finish his morning ritual while I sit at the desk, trying to reconcile the feelings swirling inside me. Cadan really does appear to be trying to clean up his act and is doing things that are both thoughtful and sweet. And while I appreciate it, I'm acutely aware that my heart lies elsewhere. Sure. I love Cadan. I always will, but what I feel for Seth is more tangible. It's a different kind of connection. Meaningful on a basic human level, not a mystical one like what I have with Cadan.

I take a deep breath and check my phone for the fiftieth time to see if Seth has answered. He hasn't. Nothing from Jax yet either. Damn. My heart sinks a little. I don't really want to admit just how much I want to see him.

A knock sounds at the door. I cross the room, expecting room service, but instead there's a courier holding a thick manila envelope. "Package for Mr. Kinx."

"I'll sign for it," I say and scribble my name on his form.

"Have a good day, ma'am."

Ma'am? What the hell? Do I look like I'm forty? I cross the room and go to lay the envelope on the desk, but it slides off and falls to the carpet, landing upside down. Near the flap it's marked CONTRACTS. I pick it up and inspect the note taped to it.

Contracts for Cadan Kinx and Lucy Moore. *Please look these over at your earliest convenience and get them back to us as soon as possible. Cassie.*

I sit and tear into the packet. There are two sets of contracts. One marked Cadan and the other Lucy. Cadan's has a note from Cassie.

As requested, the contracts were delivered to your room. Please pass Lucy's on to her as soon as possible. C

I frown. Why couldn't mine be delivered to me? Was it an excuse to come see me? Because he didn't need one if he wanted to talk to me.

Settling back into the chair, I dig into the contracts. They're pretty standard, though Jeff has managed to get us better terms than when we originally signed. Both the new and old are present with an addendum. The old one is rendered complete. With the addition of the new contract, they aren't requiring us to finish the old tour. Everything is focused on the new one. Good. All bases covered there.

Then I come to the publishing contract. There is only one. The old one isn't included. Maybe they forgot. So I start to read. By the time I get two paragraphs in, my stomach clenches and nausea rolls through me. By the third paragraph, I'm on my feet and striding across the room. I don't knock. I just throw the door open to the bathroom and barge right in, the contract fisted in my hand.

"What's up?" Cadan asks around the toothbrush lodged in his mouth.

"This." I slap the contract on the counter.

He scans it, and the blood drains from his face. He spits the toothbrush out. "It's not what you think."

"Really? Am I mistaken that there was never a contract for the new songs? That this new one specifically says that any songs I wrote during the lapsed time between my old contract and the new contract are to be considered represented by the label? That if I sign this, I may not sell them to any other label? You're saying I don't understand what that means? Because this implies none of my new songs are currently under contract. I can walk if I want to."

"No. That's not..." He holds his hands up in a surrender motion. "I told them I signed for you. Since the contract wasn't valid, they didn't include it. And yes, you're correct. You don't have to sign the new publishing contract. That's entirely up to you."

I step back, holding the contracts to my chest.

"I swear," he says.

"And just like that they voided it? All this time Jeff's been struggling to get me out of my contract and now they've suddenly caved when you confessed to signing for me?"

He nods. "But that was also after you decided to come back. So it isn't like they were losing anything. And trust me, they were not happy with me. If it wasn't for you, I think they would've dropped me." He steps forward and grabs my hand. "I'm really trying to do the right thing here, Luce. Give me a chance to prove myself?"

The mistrust and anger are still actively gripping me, but I relent anyway. "Okay. But you're going to have to give me some time to catch up. This new you... it's a little overwhelming."

He cracks a smile and leans in, kissing me on the forehead. "I'm still getting used to it myself, babe."

The label goes all out and hires an SUV limo for the ride to San Francisco. The guys are in good spirits, hyped up for the show. Their energy is intoxicating, and before long, I find myself singing along with their rendition of "Sweet Child of Mine." When the high note comes, I give it my all, stretching it out in my best Axl Rose impersonation.

"Holy shit, Luce, That was fucking amazing," Jess exclaims, giving me a high five.

I grin as Cadan and the rest of the band chimes in with appreciation.

By the time we get to Blue Jays, I'm more than ready for the show to start. I'm pacing my dressing room and going over the set list when a knock sounds at my door. My heart does a little flip. It could be Seth. I'd put his name along with Jax's on the guest list.

"Lucy?" Cassie's voice filters through the door.

Disappointment sets in. Damn, I have it bad. "Hi," I say as I open the door.

"Oh, you look fantastic." She sweeps into the room, her arms full of paperwork. There's also a pen tucked behind her ear.

"Thank you." I tug at the leather skirt and smile when I think of the last time I wore these boots.

"I've got some schedule changes and itineraries for you." She sits down on the secondhand plaid couch, wrinkling her nose. "For such a nice club, you'd think they could update their dressing rooms."

I shrug. "Can you blame them? Most bands are pretty hard on furniture."

"True. Anyway, tomorrow we have you booked to visit two radio shows and then a spot on the morning show. So we'll need you down in the lobby of the hotel no later than five forty-five."

I groan. "That's really early, especially after a show."

"I know. No one ever said the life of a rock star was all spas and relaxation."

"You've got a point."

"Okay, I have to fill in the guys." She makes a face. "I'll probably have to drag their asses out of bed in order to make it on time."

"Probably." I grin. "Good luck with that."

"Promise me you'll help. I don't think I can take walking in on a naked Jess again."

That gets a snort of laughter out of me. One morning she'd found him passed out with no clothes on. That was bad enough, but he'd also had pudding smeared all over his man bits. Chocolate pudding. It wasn't pretty. "Yeah, I'll help."

"Thank God." She throws her arms around me and gives me a quick hug. "It's so good to have someone on my side again. To be honest, I wasn't sure we were going to get you back. It hasn't been the same without you."

"Well, we did have that contract," I say, trying to keep my voice light. I don't want an altercation, but I also don't want to ignore the fact they'd pretty much forced my hand.

She frowns. "The one for the rest of the tour? I thought Cadan told you the label suspended that because of your dad."

"Suspended?"

"Sure. We only had a few months left, and with your dad passing, we weren't going to force it. I really thought we'd lost you for good. But here you are. And I couldn't be more thrilled. The new song is going to make chart history. You just wait and see."

"So I was free? My publishing contract was fulfilled as well?"

"Yeah." Her brows pinch as she studies me. "Why?"

Red-hot anger flares to life, instantly replaced by a cold, unfeeling acceptance. I'd been lied to. "It's nothing." My voice comes out even, with not a trace that anything is wrong. "Nothing at all."

CHAPTER 32
Seth

The closer we get to the city, the more I'm tempted to turn the truck around and drive back home. "I don't know how I let you talk me into this," I say to Jax.

"Yes, you do. You want to see her sing again, and so do I. Besides, she called and asked you to come. I think that's what got you on the road. Not me."

She's right. I do want to see Lucy one more time. But I don't know if I'll be able to survive seeing her with Kinx. Jesus Christ. What am I doing?

"It's too late now anyway," Jax says. "We're almost there. And I'm not letting you chickenshit out. Got it?"

I make a face but keep driving. If she wasn't in the car, I would turn around. This seems like a colossally big mistake.

Once in the city, it takes a while to find parking. And even then we end up more than six blocks away. "Damn. Are they all here for the show?"

"Looks like it." Jax slides her arm through mine. "Everyone's headed in the same direction."

The line is impressively long, wrapping around the block. Jax glides past everyone to speak with the doorman. "We're on the list," she says and gives him our names.

He frowns. "Sorry. No one by either name is listed."

She spends ten minutes trying to get him to double-check, but no amount of insisting helps and we end up at the back of the line.

"Thanks for nothing." Jax scowls at the doorman an hour later when we finally make it through the line. "Lucy has been waiting for us."

"Sure she has." He rolls his eyes and goes back to checking IDs.

"Asshole," she says under her breath.

"It's fine. We'll talk to her after." I position Jax in front of me and place my hands on her shoulders, letting her lead us through the crowd. The place is so packed I'm certain the club is breaking some fire codes.

"Wow," Jax says. "Giant crowd and they only announced this show last night. Crazy."

The line at the bar is too insane to even contemplate. It's just as well. I'm driving Jax back to Mendo tonight anyway. Better to stay as alert as possible. Though after I see Lucy, I'm certain I'm going to need that drink.

And then it happens. The lights go down over the venue, and after a short introduction, there she is, her short skirt showing off those gorgeous legs. My body comes alive as I focus on those boots. *The* boots. The ones that will forever be burned in my brain. Damn her. A knife to the heart would've been kinder.

"She looks amazing," Jax says into my ear.

I nod, unable to speak. What I wouldn't give to go back to Christmas Eve morning and make good on my threat to keep her locked away in her bedroom all day. Hell, all week.

Kinx joins her on the stage and every female in the place loses her fucking mind. There's a lot of jumping, screaming, and even some crying. It's nuts. I had no idea they were this popular.

He plays to the crowd, announcing their reunion and promising the best damn show, which is going to be full of surprises. My chest constricts, and I feel as though my heart is withering under my breastbone.

The band starts up, and all the lights go down except for the spotlights illuminating Lucy and Kinx. Lucy is more beautiful than ever, her dark hair framing her face seductively. She's sexy as hell, and it's torturous knowing she won't be mine. But when she starts to sing and Kinx joins in, it's as if a beacon of hope lights up inside me. The sensation is so overwhelming it almost brings tears to my eyes. I want her so badly, more than I wanted Elsa maybe. The pain bolts through my veins, but it's tempered with the strange hopefulness that seems to be invading my heart and mind.

"It's amazing, isn't it?" Jax says. "The magic they bring to everyone. I…" She clutches her chest and lets the tears roll freely.

I nod once and keep my eyes locked on Lucy. I want to study this moment, to remember her in her element. To experience her talent as I had the first night we met. Only this time she isn't focused on me. She's there for the entire crowd. Touching as many people as she can. Everyone *except* me. Even when her gaze flickers past us, she doesn't linger or give any indication she knows we're here.

The song ends, and they move right into the next one. My emotions run the gamut of joy, contentment, and despair, but through it all, hope is at the forefront. If this is the way most people feel while experiencing them sing, I can see why they're so fucking popular.

Curiously though, while Kinx keeps trying to engage her onstage, she does her best to keep her distance. She sings in all the right places, makes eye contact when needing to stay on cue, but any time he moves toward her, she repositions herself to keep her personal space. That tiny knowledge keeps me sane right up until they get to the last song.

The music winds down and Lucy takes the microphone. "Hi, folks. Thanks for coming out tonight. You've been a fantastic crowd. San Francisco always is."

The crowd goes batshit, and she smiles through it all, waiting for them to dial it back a notch.

"You may have heard we have a new song to reveal. However, I hope you'll forgive me if I change things up a bit. There's another song that's more appropriate to my life right now. I think it's fitting that I sing it tonight. What do you say? Are you with me?"

The crowd responds with enthusiasm, just as I'm sure she knew they would.

She smiles. "You're the best." Turning around, she nods to the band, and the keyboardist starts the entry to "Let Her Go" by Passenger.

Kinx frowns at her, clearly unhappy. There's nothing he can do to change things now, though, and he starts in on the lyrics, his eyes burning in a hole in my head all the way from the stage. Lucy joins in when he starts singing about letting her go. Their eyes lock, and the whole room can feel the tension and struggle between them. He doesn't want to be singing this, but she's giving it her all.

Finally, she turns, and her smoldering gaze lands on me as she sings the last line.

"I can't do this," I say to Jax, unable to breathe. "I can't stand here while she says good-bye to me." Before she can answer, I take off out of the club, desperate for fresh air. The cold December night air assaults me, but I barely feel it at all. My one goal is to get to the truck. Six blocks away.

Once I finally find my ride, I unlock it and climb in, realizing there's no way in hell Jax should be walking through the streets of San Francisco by herself at this hour. I take out my phone and instruct her to text me whenever she's ready to leave and I'll pick her up at the front door. It takes a while before she texts back, and when she does, she tells me to get her in one hour.

That hour turns out to be the worst hour of my life. Lucy's inside that club, and I'm not going to be able to say my own good-bye. She's had her say, and I got nothing. Electric anger pulses through my blood. Damn Kinx and their soul-mate connection. Damn him to hell. He has what I want. Desperately. Maybe I'm not what she needs, but I'm damn sure Kinx is a disaster waiting to happen.

It turns out to be two hours later by the time Jax emerges from the club. She's serious and reserved, but that may be from my mood. I say nothing, opting to ignore the turmoil churning inside me.

"Don't you even want to know what happened?" Jax demands.

"No."

"No? That's it?"

"Right. I want to remember the way she was onstage. Not some lame brush-off excuse. I don't need one. Look, I got it. She's with him now. It makes sense. He's her soul mate."

Jax narrows her eyes and gives me a disgusted look. "You're an idiot."

"Maybe." The urge to demand that she tell me what Lucy had to say is overwhelming. But deep in my gut I know whatever she says will only make it worse. Lucy is gone. I need to let it go, and the sooner I do that, the better.

Jax huffs out a sigh of frustration, taps something into her phone, and then pulls my blanket around her shoulders and closes her eyes.

Good. At least she won't nag me for the rest of the drive back.

The road is virtually empty and we make good time, cutting the three-hour drive down to two and a half. When I finally pull up to Jax's house just before four a.m., she speaks for the first time since we left the city. "Will you keep painting?"

I shrug. "Eventually."

She rubs her sleepy eyes and gives me a worried look. "You're not going to give it up again, are you?"

I shake my head. "No. But there's something I have to take care of first before I spend any more time in there."

Confusion is written all over her face, but then her expression morphs into understanding. She knows. And oddly the knowledge puts me at peace.

She reaches over and squeezes my hand. "You know where to find me if you need me."

I nod and turn to stare out the window. If I look at her, I might lose my shit. So much for peace. With one simple statement, I'm back to being the poor bastard who hasn't let go of the past. "'Night, Jax. I'll call you."

"You better." She scrambles out of the truck and up to her apartment.

I wait until she's safely inside, then go home, to the one I shared with Elsa. It's time to come to terms with the cards I've been dealt.

Sitting on the beach, I gaze out at the ocean, seeing nothing but a wall of fog with the surf rolling in from under it. The day is one of my favorites. The sun is shining bright on the shore, holding the mist over the sea.

I've been sitting in the same spot for over an hour, trying to work up the courage to do what I came here to do. It's not the first time I've come here for this purpose. But I've never been able to go through with it. I feel close to Elsa here. Almost as if she's sitting right beside me, sketching the ocean and the fog. Once it's done, will I come back here? I don't know. This place is painful, right to my very core, yet I crave that pain, crave the weight that settles over me every time I sit on these rocks.

Today is different, though. The pain is there just beneath my breastbone as usual, but it's tinged with sadness and acceptance. Before it had always been laced with anger and despair, a feeling I'd come to associate with the last time I'd seen her.

I know today is the day. It has to be. I've turned a corner and I won't go back.

CHAPTER 33

Lucy

After three days of renegotiations and uncovering the truth of what has really been going on with my contracts, I headed back to Mendocino. Desperate to talk to Seth, I tried his shop and his house, then called Jax. She didn't know where he was, but she'd had a good idea of where to look.

Now I'm standing in a small parking lot about thirty miles south of Mendocino, scanning the beach for Seth. The fog hovering over the ocean is a dramatic contrast to the sunny day, but it's still pretty cold, and the beach is empty. I know he's here. I'm parked right next to his truck.

Wrapping my scarf tighter around my neck, I take off down the path to the beach. After what seems like forever, my lips are frozen, and I can't seem to feel my toes anymore. I'm about to give up and go back to wait in my car when I catch a flash of green on top of an outcropping of rocks that meets the shoreline.

I squint and keep moving. Soon enough he comes into focus. Seth is at the edge, his head bowed as the waves crash below him. I pick up my pace, more anxious than ever to talk to him. To just look into his eyes and see the warmth that's always there. But then he lifts a vessel and starts to pour the contents into the wind.

I freeze. Oh my God. He's scattering ashes. The intrusion is utterly unforgiveable. I never would have come here if I'd known this was what he was doing. Slowly, I sidestep across the beach until I'm next to the cliffs, as far from the shore as possible, trying to stay out of his sight line. I don't want him to know I'm here. I don't want to interrupt this very private moment.

The wind picks up, and I huddle into my jacket, moving as quickly as I can, but I'm not fast enough.

"Lucy?" His voice carries on the wind.

I stop and slowly turn around.

Seth is scrambling off the rocks and staring at me in wonder.

I lift a tentative hand and wave.

When he finally catches up to me, he places his frozen hands on my cheeks and crushes his lips to mine. I open my mouth in shock and he deepens the kiss, devouring me with intensity and what appears to be desperation.

My fists curl in the fabric of his jacket as I hang on, meeting his frantic pace with one of my own. All too soon, he pulls back, leaving me completely breathless.

His hands are still cupping my face as he gazes down at me. "You're really here."

I take a breath and nod. "I am."

Then his gorgeous eyes turn worried. "Why?"

"It's a long story." The way he looks at me makes it hard to think. Through the worry is also joy. He's happy and scared at the same time. I want to cling to him and tell him I'm never leaving again. But that would be a lie.

"I've got time," he says.

"So do I." I grin, loving the way his eyes light up at my statement.

"How much?"

"Enough."

The light in his eyes dims.

I stand on my toes and say, "I'm not going anywhere until spring, and then it's only temporary."

"Really?"

"Really." I push up on my tiptoes and give him a slow kiss, wanting to taste every inch of him right here on the beach. And I would have if it weren't less than forty degrees.

He pulls away, our lips still touching. "Let's get out of here and go somewhere warm."

"Are you sure? I didn't mean to intrude." I glance at the rocks he'd been standing on. "Honestly, Jax said you come here sometimes, and all I wanted to do was talk to you."

"I want to do a lot more than talk," he says, teasing me, but I can see emotion in his eyes.

"Seth?"

He takes my hand, holding it in both of his, and jerks his head, indicating we should start moving back toward the cars. "I made the decision to finally say good-bye today."

"To Elsa." It has to be. I saw him scattering ashes.

"Yes. This was one of her favorite places. I've been trying to find the nerve to do this for the past year."

"What was different about today?" I ask gently.

He turns and scans my face then gives me a small smile. "You."

"You saw me?" I ask, horrified.

"No. That's not it. I realized after you came into my life that I was holding on to her because I didn't *want* to move on. Didn't think I deserved to."

"And now you do?" I hold my breath, praying he doesn't say he made a mistake.

"Honestly?"

I nod.

"Yes… and no." He takes a step back and rubs his palm over the back of his neck. "It's time. I've been punishing myself for far too long." Staring at his feet, he takes another step back.

I grab his hand and hold it between both of mine. "Why?"

He flinches as if I'd slapped him.

"Seth?"

Then he jerks his head up, sadness shining in his beautiful eyes as his brow creases with barely controlled emotion. "It was my fault she was driving that night. I went out drinking, and she had to come get me."

"Oh, Seth." I sigh. "You can't blame yourself for an accident."

He stiffens. "She asked me not to go. But I went anyway. If it hadn't been—"

I raise my hand and graze my thumb over his cheek. "She loved you and wanted to see you safe. You would have done the same if the situation were reversed. It's what we do for those we love. You have to let it go. It isn't your fault she lost control of the car, no matter how much you want to blame yourself. It was a senseless accident."

"I know. I've been telling myself that for the last year. It's hard to change what's in here, though." He points to his chest, and I feel like mine is going to split open from the ache I have for him. "I didn't want to say good-bye, but I have to," he continues. "There's no getting around it."

"Why?" I ask gently.

"I think my heart belongs to someone else now."

I stop, utterly shocked. "What... I mean, you didn't know I was coming back."

"No, I didn't." He tugs me back toward him. "But that isn't the point. I realized I wasn't living. I was a shell of myself, and part of the reason is because I couldn't move forward. I know I have to. And the only way to do that was to let her go."

I slide my arms around his waist and gaze up at him. "Are you okay?"

"Yeah. I think so. It helps more than you know that you *are* here."

I press my head against his chest. "I'm glad I'm here then."

He holds me until I start to shiver. "Let's go."

When we get to the cars, I say, "Will you follow me back to my house?"

"There was no way I wasn't going to... unless Kinx is there."

I laugh. "No. Definitely not."

"Good. I don't like that guy."

We make it back to my house in record time. We're barely inside the door before Seth has his hands on me again. He grips my hips from behind and lowers his mouth to my neck, trailing hot, sensual kisses along my skin until my knees start to go weak.

"Seth?"

"Hmm?"

"Can we talk for a minute?"

He clutches me tighter for a moment and then takes a step back, his brows pinched with unease. "Lay it on me. How long do we have until you have to go back to Kinx and the band?"

"Forever," I say.

"What?"

"You heard me. I'm not singing with Cadan anymore. And there's nothing in my contract that says I have to."

"Wait a minute." He presses his hand to the small of my back and leads me into my living room. "I think we need to sit down for this. How in the world did that happen?"

I curl up next to him and pull a blanket over our legs. "Turns out Cadan and my lawyer were working together. I wasn't under contract at all. I had been, but once my dad passed, they waived the remaining dates on our tour. And there never was a publishing contract for my songs. Cadan didn't sign my name, only his. He lied to me to get me back and paid the lawyer to make it seem legit. And the song he recorded? He finally told them he didn't write it. And since the truth has come out, they pulled it from distribution. All the royalties are being transferred to me."

"Whoa." Seth's eyes go wide with shock, then anger. "Is he really that much of a selfish asshole?"

"Yes," I say without hesitation. "I thought he was making positive changes, but turns out he was playing me to get what he wanted. When I found out the truth, I had a long talk with my rep at the label about what I wanted, and she agreed to sign me separately from Cadan. I still get to record my songs, but I don't have to do a world tour and I don't have to be on the road with my ex."

"So you're staying here, then?"

I smile. "Yes."

"And no touring? That's a shame. You're a fantastic performer."

"We'll still tour a little bit, but it will be more like a few weeks on, a few weeks off, so I'm not living in a hotel for a year and a half. I want to perform. I just don't want to kill myself to do it."

"So…" He brushes a lock of hair from my eyes. "This means we're neighbors? Permanently?"

"Looks like it."

"Thank God." Seth rises and reaches down, easily picking me up in his arms.

I giggle. "What are you doing?"

"Taking my girl to bed. Does that work for you?"

"I'm your girl?" My breath catches and tears sting my eyes.

"If you want to be." There's a tremble in his voice. He's just as nervous about my answer as I am.

"I've never been someone's girl."

He frowns. "What does that mean?"

"The only other person I dated was Cadan. And while we were mates, he's never treated me as his girl. I always felt more like I was an asset to be exploited rather than his actual girlfriend."

"That guy deserves an ass-kicking." Seth heads into the hall-way and starts up the stairs. A moment later he gently lays me on my bed. "So, you didn't answer. Do you want to be my girl?"

"Hell yes. Besides, my heart already belongs to you. You might as well have the rest of me."

He stills as he takes in my words. "Do you mean that?"

I nod solemnly. He makes me into a better version of myself, unlike others in my life who are only interested in what's good for them. "Yeah. I really do."

Hovering over me, he closes his eyes, presumably taking in the moment.

"Seth?"

"Yeah, love?"

"Make love to me."

His eyes turn emerald from the desire sparking down at me. "Gladly." He kisses my temple, my eyes, and my jawline, and moves lower, nestling his mouth between my breasts. Lifting his head, he presses his lips to mine once more. "That's what it is, you know," he says against my lips.

"What?"

"Making love. Every single time I touch you."

A lump forms in my throat, and I'm certain if I try to speak, I'll start to cry.

"I love you, Lucy Moore."

I can't help the tear that spills down my temple. Raw emotion takes over. I swallow the lump in my throat and force out what I have to say. "I didn't come back because things didn't work out with Cadan."

"You didn't?" His body goes tight, as if he's bracing for bad news.

"No." I reach up and brush my fingers over his worried brow. "I could've started working on my album right away. I could've toured some. Or just stayed in a hotel and worked on my songs, all at the label's expense. It was tempting. I have producing rights, which means most of it will be under my control."

"That sounds amazing."

"It is. But I'm not quite ready. I came back because of you. Because I had to see you."

The worry lines disappear, but now he's searching my gaze as if he's looking for something. But he doesn't have to try too hard, because what he's looking for comes flying out of my mouth, "I came back because although Cadan might be my soul mate, I have a much deeper connection to you. I'm in love with you."

His eyes close, and when he opens them, they're filled with joy. He gathers me in his arms and pulls me tight against him. "You're never getting rid of me now."

"That's a hardship I'm willing to live with," I say and work the top button of his shirt open.

"What do you think you're doing?"

"Seducing you." I press my hips against him, feeling the hard outline of his arousal. A tingle of satisfaction ripples through me, and I unbutton two more buttons. "Looks like it's working."

"You have no idea."

"Show me," I say with heat and scrape my nails lightly down his chest.

He visibly shivers, and then a second later, he pins me beneath him. His penetrating gaze holds me captive. "I'm not going to let go, you know."

A slow smile blossoms over my face. "I'm counting on it."

Mate or not, I know Seth is the person I'm supposed to be with. And when he claims my lips again, we give ourselves to each other so completely, a new magic blossoms. One that is born from what we carry in our hearts. Each other.

About the Author

Deanna is a native Californian, transplanted to the slower paced lifestyle of southeastern Louisiana. When she isn't writing, she is often goofing off with her husband in New Orleans, playing with her two Shih Tzu dogs, making glass beads, or out hocking her wares at various bead shows across the country. For more information visit her website at www.deannachase.com.

Book Two of the Destiny series will be released in Fall 2014.